APPOINTMENT IN TEHRAN

Author's Other Works

Fiction

A Question of Time: The Snake Eater Chronicles, Book 1

Non-Fiction

No Moon as Witness: Missions of the SOE and OSS in WWII

Masters of Mayhem: Lawrence of Arabia and the British Military Mission to the Hejaz—The Seeds of British Special Operations

Special Forces Berlin: Clandestine Cold War Operations of the US Army's Elite, 1956–1990

The Horns of the Beast: The Swakop River Campaign and World War I in South-West Africa, 1914–15

APPOINTMENT IN TEHRAN

THE SNAKE EATER CHRONICLES 2

JAMES STEJSKAL

CASEMATE
Philadelphia & Oxford

Published in the United States of America and Great Britain in 2021 by
CASEMATE PUBLISHERS
1950 Lawrence Road, Havertown, PA 19083, USA
and
The Old Music Hall, 106–108 Cowley Road, Oxford OX4 1JE, UK

Copyright 2021 © James Stejskal

Hardcover Edition: ISBN 978-1-61200-966-7
Digital Edition: ISBN 978-1-61200-967-4

A CIP record for this book is available from the British Library

Printed and bound in the United States of America by Sheridan

Typeset by Lapiz

For a complete list of Casemate titles, please contact:

CASEMATE PUBLISHERS (US)
Telephone (610) 853-9131
Fax (610) 853-9146
Email: casemate@casematepublishers.com
www.casematepublishers.com

CASEMATE PUBLISHERS (UK)
Telephone (01865) 241249
Email: casemate-uk@casematepublishers.co.uk
www.casematepublishers.co.uk

Note:
This book is a work of fiction. Names, character, places, and incidents either are the
product of the author's imagination or, if real, are used fictitiously.

For Wanda

Tehran 1979

On November 4, 1979, Iranian revolutionaries overran the United States Embassy in Tehran and took over fifty American diplomats hostage. Europeans had been touched by international terrorism since the late 1960s, but for most Americans, the Iran Hostage Crisis was a watershed; the first time America felt it directly—and on a large scale.

The Cold War was also in full swing and the United States had only begun to fight international terrorism, only begun to understand the tactics of terror that are now all too familiar. The learning curve, both political and military, has been steep and often deadly.

This is a story retold. This story is about valor and vanity, ingenuity and incapacity, teamwork and parochialism. In short, it's about real life. The bravery and valor depicted in this story are real; the names of the people described are not. Other personalities are purely fictional despite their resemblance to actual people. Sometimes imperfect, often questioning their abilities, they typify every American serviceman and woman who has for so long stood ready to do what was necessary to protect their loved ones overseas or on the home front.

"Like all great travellers, I have seen more than I remember, and remember more than I have seen."

—Benjamin Disraeli

1

In his apartment several blocks from the university campus, Abdul Mezad knelt on a carpet facing the Holy Cities of Mecca and Medina and prayed. He was one of the few people in the city who knew what was about to happen. Although the Shah had been overthrown and the revolutionary republic proclaimed months earlier, there was still an infuriating presence in the city: the den of spies—the American Embassy—that housed the very same snakes who had installed the Shah onto his Peacock Throne. It had been a quarter-century, but many Iranians still felt the insult deeply—that the Americans could overthrow their elected government and install a puppet Shah, Mohammad Reza Pahlavi. It was a brazen act by insolent foreigners who knew nothing about the true nature of Iran and its people. The infidel cared only for Iran's oil.

After his prayers, Abdul walked in the drizzling rain through the stirring city. The early morning commuters passing him would have assumed he was a student, dressed in faded jeans and a loose sweater topped off with an olive-drab fatigue jacket he had bought cheaply in a market long ago. But anyone who looked at him closely might have reconsidered, not that Abdul cared. The intensity of a zealot on a *Jihad* burned in his eyes, his vision reduced to tunnel vision, focused only on his destination and little else. He had a mission, and if he was to be a martyr this day, so be it.

It was cool, as November mornings in Tehran often were. To the north, the Alborz mountains were shrouded in a blanket of gray cloud. The day had started out quietly enough for a city that had been tense for months as internecine squabbles, demonstrations, and street fights broke out across the country between the moderates, the communists, and Islamists vying for influence. The hard-liners of the Council of the Islamic Revolution had only tenuous control. That would soon change.

The shops were still shuttered. Despite the dampness in the air, the smell of *barbari* baking in the wood- and coal-burning ovens wafted through the neighborhood. Abdul ignored his hunger; there would be time enough for food later. Walking with determination, he covered the few kilometers to his place of appointment rapidly. He turned into Taleqani Street and, in front of him, he saw his goal. Abdul strode on, over the glistening, damp concrete and stopped outside the embassy gates where crowds had started to gather. He glared at the Americans inside the fence who looked back at him with a stare that conveyed their sense that this day would be unlike any they had experienced before. The Marine Security Guards gathered in small groups near the gates, the front entrance, and even on the roof as the embassy staff hurried to their desks inside the Chancery. They were worried; they were too few to contain the threatening crowd that gathered beyond the fence.

As the city slowly awakened, the crowd outside grew to hundreds, then thousands of young people outside the 27-acre embassy compound. As the rain tapered off, the throngs grew, made up mostly of students who had not attended school since the uprisings had begun the previous January. Most believed they were there for just a peaceful protest, but the rain had dampened their spirits. Wistfully, some thought of going home, out of the damp, to enjoy a cup of tea and some savory cakes. They wanted the Americans out of their new Islamic republic, but had not come with violence in mind. They were not aware of the real plan, the plan a small group, the "Brethren," had in mind. Today, they would finally swing the balance of power over to Ruhollah Khomeini.

Abdul was aware of the plan. He was one of the "Brethren," a true insider. They were the core element, even closer knit than the "Islamic Brothers." They were the vanguard of the revolution. While the placards and shouts outside the compound only demanded that the Americans leave Iran, the Brethren had other ideas. They wanted to consolidate the Imam's power and eliminate rival militias. By seizing the embassy, they would not only break the links between the supporters of the provisional government, who wanted a "democratic Iran," and the Americans, they would also destroy the power of the leftists who remained a threat to the Islamic revolution.

While hundreds of young men and women kept the Marines busy on the perimeter of the facility, others climbed over the barrier fence and engaged in a tug of war over the halyards of the flag pole. These distractions occupied the Marine guards. Unseen in the crowd, a small group of men pulled bolt cutters from bags and severed the chains that secured the perimeter gates. With that last physical and psychological barrier breached, the masses outside were easily pushed to storm the compound.

***

After a few hours, Abdul found another of the Brethren, Ervin Rajavi, his friend and confidant, in the ambassador's office suite looking out the window at the thousands of students roaming the property below him.

The embassy Chancery had succumbed to the tidal wave of humanity that stormed inside the now meaningless perimeter fence. Bedlam followed. Not only did they occupy the grounds, the students penetrated every secure building on the compound. The ninety members of the staff inside the compound, sixty of whom were American, were herded into the basement for safekeeping.

Abdul Mezad was ecstatic—he hadn't expected the den of spies to give up so quickly and certainly not without a shot. They had been prepared to accept martyrs, but the Americans held their fire.

Were they scared of us? Or did they just want to avoid a massacre?

As Abdul regarded his ostensible leader, he knew Rajavi was wavering in his commitment.

Rajavi turned to Abdul as he walked in but said nothing.

Abdul spoke: "What now?"

"We read our declaration and leave," Rajavi said.

"But we have an opportunity here. We have their people and all their secrets. We can hold them hostage to embarrass and punish the Great Satan."

"No, we read our declaration and leave. That was our plan."

"I'm sorry my brother. The plan has changed," Abdul said.

"On whose authority?"

"Imam Khomeini himself."

2

Three Americans sat in the Iranian foreign minister's opulently decorated waiting room. The tall windows that looked out over Tehran were flanked by ornate geometric designs executed in polished gold, silver, and copper plate that glittered with reflected light from the crystal chandeliers. Huge rugs covered the floor, most prominently a blue and white silk Isfahan that would cover half of a basketball court. The room still reeked of the Shah's riches.

Despite that, they were not comfortable. One, deep in thought, hung his head while another was constantly wringing his hands. The third stared at the ceiling, his mouth open like he was amazed at the sight. They were all anxiously waiting, both for their scheduled meeting but also so they could return to their offices at the American embassy across town. Shortly after they arrived, the US Chargé d'Affairs, Francis Long, had been handed a telephone by the minister's secretary. The call was from the deputy political officer who was still in the embassy Chancery building. Long was informed in a matter-of-fact tone that the demonstrations had intensified and the walls of the compound had been breached. That the call managed to reach them at all was an indication of how uncoordinated the day's events actually were across the city.

The Iranians were also concerned. Foreign Minister Ibrahim Yazdi had hoped for some sort of reconciliation with the United States but the occupation of the embassy now seemed to ensure that idea would be derailed once and for all. Worse still, Yazdi knew that the "students" fomenting the disturbance were opposed to him. They said he was too moderate; some even went as far as to say he was an apostate. If he was to remain in his position, or even stay alive, he would have to play his cards very close to his chest.

Finally the minister's aide beckoned for the Americans to approach. He pulled open the tall wooden doors and bowed slightly, an affectation of subservience he did not feel for Westerners. Chargé Long nodded as he passed by, followed by his two companions.

Yazdi walked around his desk and grasped Long's hand. He knew the American was under stress and, as he actually liked the man, he expressed his concern physically and verbally to him.

"Thank you for coming. I know this must be a difficult day for you and your people."

"It is very concerning, Minister, and since this is the second time it's happened this year, I need the government's assurances that they will send assistance to disperse the demonstrators as soon as possible. I don't want anyone hurt on either side. The repercussions would damage our countries' relations even further."

"Mister Long, please remember that I warned you several months ago that allowing the Shah to enter the United States even for medical treatment would be a very dangerous move. Although I know it is not the case, many people in Iran believe this to mean your government intends to reinstate the Shah to power. That said, I am sure your people will be safe and we will do our best to ensure that remains the case, but I cannot promise that security forces will be sent to the embassy. You must understand my position here."

Long understood exactly what Yazdi meant. His job and even his life might be endangered if he were to show too much deference to the Americans.

"I was hoping that you would be able to persuade the council to send help."

"I suspect their larger interest lies in letting the students continue their protest. There are many forces at play here and your country provides a convenient foil for the *mullahs* as well as the extremists. I will keep you informed, but for now, I would tell you to advise your people not to resist and they will be all right."

"It's probably too late for that anyway. I've been told the embassy has been broken into and completely occupied. Your government's refusal to help is a breach of diplomatic conventions."

"I understand your concerns, and I sympathize with you but the ruling council is not very attuned to or even interested in diplomacy or conventions. There is little I can do."

"In that case, I believe our business in concluded. We will return to the embassy to be with our people."

"Unfortunately, Mister Long, I cannot permit you to put yourself in danger. You will stay here as my guests for as long as necessary. My people have set up a place for you to remain during these events. There is no other way and you'll be safe here."

***

Afterwards, Chargé Long spoke with his deputies in the third-floor room that had become their temporary home.

"We need to account for everyone. I told the embassy to send a Flash message to State listing everyone's whereabouts, who is at the embassy and who might be at home or out in the city. And, thanks to Yazdi, as long as we have access to a telephone here, we can continue to communicate with Washington. They'll need everything we can give them before we lose contact."

"Any idea of how long we'll have to remain here?"

"Not a clue, but I suspect it will be a while. I hope none of you snore."

It would be a long wait.

7

3

It was a cold, crisp day as Master Sergeant Kim Becker and Staff Sergeant Paul Stavros walked up to the 500-meter firing range. Both were in full assault uniform, Walther semi-auto pistols in belt holsters and Walther MPK submachine guns slung over their shoulders. In their dark olive-green coveralls with blue-gray SMG magazine pouches attached to their gear, they looked more like *Fallschirmjäger*—German paratroopers—than US Army soldiers. Except maybe for their long hair. They called it "relaxed grooming standards." As team sergeant, Becker was fine with that. It was better that he and his men be confused for the local *Polizei* than be identified as Americans. They held back and together silently watched the two men on the firing line in front of them, not wishing to disturb their intense concentration. They knew better than to distract a man with a gun, especially one that could swat a gnat at 100 meters in the dead of night. One of the two was peering through a 20-power M49 spotter scope; the other lay unmoving on the ground, a long black rifle extending out in front of him.

The outdoor range facility was old; it predated World War II and there still was an air of Prussian Army formality about the place. But the *Bundeswehr* was prohibited by the Four Power Treaty from being stationed in West Berlin and because of that the range was used by the civilian Berlin Police and the American occupation forces for training. Today it was closed to everyone but a small team of Americans. The rifle marksmanship stands were narrow, only 10 meters, wide enough for only three shooters side by side but they were long. On this day, however, there was just the one shooter on Stand Four. A small rise allowed the man to lie on the ground and see the target stands down range. There were thick brick walls about 5 meters high on either side of the lane that guaranteed privacy, but more importantly prevented stray bullets from escaping anywhere but up. In the early morning, steam rose as the dew on the grass evaporated into the warming air.

The man behind the Heckler & Koch PSG1 rifle controlled his breathing as he had been taught to do a number of years before. He peered through the Hensoldt ZF 6x42 scope at the target down range and tightened his index finger on the sensitive trigger. Just so much pressure at first, then slowly increasing the pull while regulating his breathing. His mind was focused not on his body functions or the reticle in the scope, but on the target down range. Just at the pause between his exhale and inhale, the trigger released the sear and the firing pin sprang forward to impact the primer of the Lake City 7.62mm M118 Match cartridge. Propelled by the burning gases, the 168 grain Sierra MatchKing bullet left the barrel at a supersonic 2,550 feet per second and cracked through the cardboard target seven-tenths of a second later. It was his fifth shot. He waited.

Down range, the target slipped down into the pit so the sniper's shots could be graded. A voice came over the radio speaker.

"I have four rounds in the center of the ten ring, the group is a little less than two and a half inches in diameter. You're missing one round. Still, not bad for a cold barrel."

"Check the oblique target behind," said Fred Lindt, the spotter.

"Stand by… Okay, all five are there. One round must have gone through the same hole. You're good."

"Of course he's good," said Lindt back into the mike.

Of course I am, Logan Finch smiled to himself.

Becker finally spoke up. "Okay, good shooting Logan, but let's wrap things up quickly. Training is cancelled. We've been recalled to the building."

As they packed up their gear, Finch and Lindt exchanged glances, not sure whether to be disgusted or worried. Recalls generally meant one of two things, either some bullshit training exercise or the real thing—just possibly an alert for a live mission.

***

Five of Support Detachment Berlin's six Special Forces "A" Teams were assembled on the second floor of their headquarters building. They were waiting expectantly as it was unusual to have more than one formation in a single day. The teams had been recalled to the building from their training at the range or off the streets by the Motorola pagers they carried. It had taken about an hour for the men to gather. The only team absent was Team 3, which was training with SEAL Team 2 in Greece.

Becker stood in front of Team 5, engaged in banter with Bill Simpson, Team 6's senior sergeant. Stavros tried to listen in but all he caught was what he guessed to be a Serbian expletive from Simpson and Becker's counter in French.

Whatever...

Otherwise it was quiet, quieter than the usual raucous morning formation. Everyone was expecting something important but not even the bravest dared to hazard a guess.

Finally, Colonel Jelinek and Sergeant Major Jeffrey Bergmann came up the stairs. Without a word of command, the unit came to attention. Bergmann slowly surveyed the assembly before him—one of the best trained and most unusual units in the US Army—and then with his usual gruffness addressed the men.

"Team Sergeants, are all your people here?"

Receiving an affirmative from each, he continued.

"Stand at ease, gentlemen."

Colonel Jelinek stepped in front of the sergeant major. Everyone knew something was up; he rarely addressed a formation. Jelinek was a big man. At six foot three and around 240 pounds he stood several inches taller than Bergmann. He was also very fit for a man over fifty. He had his sternest expression on, not than he often showed any other. He rarely laughed, but when he did, the sound carried through the building. And you didn't want to be on the end of one of his counseling sessions. Luckily, he left most of those to the sergeant major, at least for the enlisted men. For the officers, it was a different story.

A young refugee from Czechoslovakia during World War II, Jelinek had fought with the French resistance against the Germans. His accented English hinted at his eastern European origins.

"Gentlemen, as you already know the US Embassy in Tehran was overrun yesterday and occupied by a group that some have called 'radical Islamic students.' As far as the description of the hostage takers as 'students' goes, I reserve my call of 'bull shit' for the moment. The most important thing is that around sixty Americans are being held hostage. A planning group has been set up and I will be departing for Washington tonight. As for you, Special Operations Task Force Europe has put us on alert as of 0900 Zulu. I want to see team leaders and sergeants in my office now."

Bergmann waited until the colonel disappeared down the stairs before he spoke.

"In case it needs to be said, all TDYs and leaves are cancelled. We're on a twelve-hour string. Get your gear together and prepare to upload the alert package. Go to it!"

4

Jonny Panagasos sat at the small table in a tiny kitchen that served as both his breakfast nook and formal dining room. He sipped a coffee and picked at his breakfast while he listened to the local news. It had been a day since his radio blared out the details of the embassy takeover and now it carried updates praising the students and the Islamic revolution and increasingly harsher words about the "Great Satan." Jonny's fluency in Persian gave him an edge over most of the Americans in the embassy, who could barely order dinner, let alone converse with an Iranian in their language.

People on the street thought he was Iranian. He wasn't: he was Greek-American, with dark brown curly hair and a heavy beard. Although not tall at five foot seven inches, he was a former collegiate-level athlete and in fit condition. His habit of dressing like a local, along with his dark olive complexion and deep brown eyes, only added to the confusion because he was American as anything.

Many American diplomats were made uncomfortable by the religious shift in the regime and the prescient ones had curtailed their tours. Jonny didn't have that option; his project had been too important to drop.

He was just glad for the small bit of luck he had yesterday, when he had delayed his departure for work. If he had not taken the extra time to write up some notes from his asset meeting of the previous evening, he too would be stuck in the embassy with all the other Americans.

Normally, he worked in an office separated from the other case officers. They ostensibly were part of the Counternarcotics Bureau but Jonny rarely went into the Station proper. He was a singleton. His officious title of Special Assistant to the Chief of Mission made for a great acronym, but he didn't use it. He preferred to say he was the ambassador's aide. It sounded better, more relaxed, and it gave him a lot of latitude in what he did and with whom he spoke.

The notes he had taken were written in a cryptic shorthand that only he could understand but when he heard the initial reports of unrest, he had burnt them and flushed the ashes down the toilet. As an Agency case officer, he knew he had to destroy anything that could be potentially damaging to the United States, his operations, or his own life. Now he pondered his next move. He couldn't be taken hostage—his knowledge of Project Perses was too dangerous to be compromised.

Jonny knew Perses was doomed. With the embassy occupied and a hostile regime consolidating its hold on power, he would not be able to accomplish his mission, but he needed to salvage what he could.

He decided to get away from the apartment, which was registered to the US Mission. If anyone looked through the admin officer's records at the embassy they would know where all the American residences could be found. He needed to go to ground and disappear until he could figure out what to do next. He got up and looked out the front window through the ornate lace curtains. It was bright outside. The rain had stopped and rays of sunshine cascaded down through scattered clouds. He would wait until the early evening when it was becoming dark.

Jonny walked into his small bedroom—everything about his apartment was small—and opened the closet. He pushed on a piece of wood trim around the ceiling panel above his hanging clothing.

It clicked and popped open, revealing a brass catch that he pulled into a vertical position. With the lock disengaged, he pushed on the panel and it swung silently upwards, opening the way into his private cache.

Peering into the darkened space, he could just see the straps of his cloth rucksack. It held the things he knew he would need in the coming days. He had planned for this occasion not knowing when or even if it would come, but as any good Boy Scout knows, it is better to be prepared. And Jonny was prepared, as he had been even before the red, white, and blue ribbon with the silver eagle dangling below it was pinned to his uniform during his junior high school year. Eagle and Explorer Scout, Princeton wrestler, *Magna Cum Laude* in international relations from the Woodrow Wilson School—all of these led to his recruitment by the Agency years before. But those weren't the only qualifications he brought to the table. Despite his all-round, nice young man appearance, Jonny had spent his teens practicing the skills he read about in Ian Fleming's training manuals—breaking and entering was one of them. He remembered working the train yards looking at the seals of the railway freight cars, trying to find interesting cargo. A success on one raid was finding a car filled with beer kegs, one of which followed him home. The next time he found a beer company tag on a door, however, was a near disaster. Opening the door revealed a wall of grain that promptly emptied out onto his head. Luckily, the railway "dicks" never caught up with him. But those details were never admitted to and, with no arrest record to stop him, he was recruited into the Agency. After two overseas tours with the Special Activities Staff, he had been entrusted with a sensitive project unlike any other. Unfortunately, he could see now that it wasn't going to go anywhere.

It's ruined but I need to figure out how to make sure things don't go further south.

At least he didn't need to worry about liaison. He was a unilateral officer, completely unknown to the local intel service. The Iranians were thoroughly penetrated by fundamentalists anyway. As it was, he had only the most tenuous of connections with the Station; he was an anomaly and completely separate from the three other declared officers. That gave him some comfort and security to operate.

He pulled the rucksack out of its hiding place and began to sort through the contents. A few things he tossed back into the hide site. He would not need them, but he wasn't going to leave them in the open to be found either. The rest he wrapped in the clothing he would need and repacked the bag. It wasn't heavy or too large; he wouldn't look like a refugee when he walked out onto the street. He had to be the grey man; the man no one would pay any attention to or notice. When he wanted to, or needed to, he could look like a manual laborer or he could look like a university professor. Every case officer needs several chameleon outfits they can slip into and out of with ease. Knowing which one worked at any given time was the key. Today he would blend into the scenery and project someone else's persona.

Just another guy carrying his load.

A long, slow day passed. Jonny spent it reviewing his maps and making sure all his papers were either well hidden or destroyed. He would not return to this apartment anytime soon, if ever.

Before dusk fell he put on his leather jacket, shrugged the rucksack onto one shoulder and left his little apartment, the crepe rubber soles of his boots making no noise on the sidewalk. He began to walk north, away from the center of the city toward the one spot in the city where he could totally break his connection with the embassy: his safe house. He would work from there until things sorted themselves out. *Hopefully, the station's records had all been shredded.*

Once outside, he had to establish his status—whether he was being watched or not. He walked on in a stair-step pattern, crossing streets in logical ways that offered him quick opportunities to do a look back without exposing his interest. He saw no repeats, no correlations, no signs of interest.

Just another worker carrying his load, head down, earning a day's living.

By the time he got to the post office, he knew he was black, free of surveillance. He walked inside looking for Mashad, the one worker he had gotten to know over the previous year. Mashad was behind the middle counter taking care of a customer. Jonny picked up a form and began to fill it out laboriously, taking his time until he saw that the transaction was just about complete. He took the form and walked to the window as the woman turned to leave. Smiling broadly, although she probably could not see through his beard, he gave her room to pass and spoke to Mashad in Persian, the only language the postal worker knew him to speak.

"I need to make an overseas phone call to this number," he said as he slipped the paper though the small opening.

Mashad looked at the country code and calculated the cost.

"For three minutes, that will be six hundred rial."

Jonny pushed the notes through the opening in the window and added an extra hundred rial.

"In case I go over time," he said.

"Booth Three. Pick up when it rings."

Jonny went into the booth and waited. Through the glass door, he watched the lobby of the post office for anything or anyone out of place. Nothing, no repeats, no inconsistencies. About two minutes later the phone rang and he picked it up. When he heard a voice answer, he asked for a man by name.

"He's not here, may I take a message?" asked the voice in Paris.

"Yes, please," Jonny said.

Speaking slowly, Jonny left a short note using the agreed brevity codes and hung up. He stepped out of the booth and went back to Mashad's window.

"It was only two minutes," Mashad said, pushing money back to Jonny through the window.

Jonny trapped the notes in the tray and pushed them back to the clerk, smiling.

"Thanks, my friend. Take care."

Mashad smiled; since the change in government, his pay wasn't guaranteed.

Jonny left the post office and continued on his way. It would be several hours before he reached the safe house and could relax. On the street, many things bombarded his senses and he tried to block them all out. He had to concentrate on his surveillance detection route, he could think about next steps soon enough. His focus narrowed to the streets in front of and behind him, the people and the cocoon around him. He could feel his concentration intensifying. There was just one thought that kept coming back to him—the Perses device.

5

The director's black limousine rolled into the cavernous parking garage under the headquarters building along the Potomac River. It stopped in front of a glass enclosed alcove that led to a single elevator. A uniformed guard held the door open as a tall, broad-shouldered man in a very expensive suit climbed out of the car and went inside. The elevator was waiting for him, as were the two men standing next to it. One wore a suit that appeared equally as expensive as the director's, the second was an ex-Marine whose tweed sport coat and open shirt reflected an air of disdain. Neither man liked the director, a former general and political appointee who had come into the Agency and decided to drastically reform the outfit he now led. Both pointedly refused to call him "Director," "General," or even "Sir." They could get away with that in the supposedly egalitarian world of the Agency but the director hated not being recognized as their superior. Instead, the toadies the director had brought with him as aides had to fill the gap and constantly reinforce his ego.

"John, Charles, good to see you. Let's go on up, you can fill me in on what got me out of bed so early this morning."

John, the DDO in the nice suit, handed the big man a folder and said, "Take a look at this, first."

Charles, the Near East Division chief, stepped in with the director and John and hit the button for the seventh floor. They remained silent as the director looked at the two pages in the folder. When the doors opened, he closed the folder and spoke.

"Let's go to my conference room."

The move had been anticipated. The doors were open and pots of coffee and a plate of pastries were already arranged on the small table. Unlike the first-floor employee cafe, the seventh floor was catered to by professional chefs; the spread on the table included smoked salmon and fresh fruit, while hot Yemeni *mokha* coffee in a French press complemented the rarefied atmosphere as well as the director's self-indulgent personality perfectly. After being served a cup of coffee by his aide, he was ready to address his subordinates.

"We had one incident at the embassy earlier this year and the students left after a few hours. Why do you think this one is any different?" the director asked.

"This one is much more serious," Charles replied. "First, we don't think these are students. And second, the chancery and all the secure buildings have been breached and occupied. Tehran Station's last message said the embassy was about to surrender to the mob and that they were in the process of shredding the classified documents and destroying the consular seals, the crypto gear, and all the codes. Foggy Bottom is in contact with the Chargé, Francis Long, who is at the Foreign Ministry across town with two other State officers. Long told State that the Iranian government won't move to help. There have been threats to shoot the Americans as spies but we don't think it will come to that. I believe it will turn into a hostage situation. Not a good scenario in either case."

"And why didn't you know this was going to happen?" said the director.

The director's criticism hit the DDO's main sore spot and it was evident in his answer.

"Because we don't have the assets we need. Headquarters told us to eliminate many of our overseas assets and Tehran Station was especially hard hit."

The DDO's comment was directed at the director's decision to cut the Agency's operations directorate by over eight hundred positions and he knew it. The director bristled even more when he heard his orders referred to in the hallways as the "Halloween Massacre."

"What I did was necessary because this Agency was bloated with too many case officers sitting around or chasing ghosts. Nine times out of ten what they collect is useless drivel. Human intelligence is fallible, we need better technical means of finding out what our enemy is up to."

The DDO just shook his head. "Bullshit. Moreover, when the enemy doesn't use tech, you're blind to what he's thinking or doing."

An uneasy standoff followed with the two giant egos staring at each other, waiting for the other's next move. The retired four-star general and the Senior Intelligence Service-6 officer faced off on the carpet, the director with his coffee cup and saucer, the DDO with a Danish in hand. Except for the fact both men were wearing expensive suits in a carpeted office, they could have been over-the-hill gunslingers on a dusty street in the old West.

"What information do you have on our officers?" the director finally asked.

"Three Station officers are accounted for in the Chancery. The fourth is outside the embassy. He called into an accommodation number in Paris and reported that he is at a safe house in the city," said Charles, the division chief.

"Who is he?"

"Jonny Panagasos, he's the project officer for Perses."

"Perses?"

John, the DDO, took over.

"Perses is the plan to interdict the Soviet invasion of Afghanistan. The finding was signed by the president a year and a half ago and you were briefed on it when you came on board."

Perses, the Titan god of destruction.

The director searched his memory in vain. Even after almost a year on the job, there were just too many things he needed to remember and couldn't.

"How far along is the project?"

"It was ready to go. The Russians have been massing forces to the north of the Termaz river. We assess they will launch across into Afghanistan around the New Year and Perses was aimed at disrupting their river crossing. It's all part of the larger Operation *Cyclone.*"

"How was this Perses thing supposed to go down?" he asked incredulously.

"We had a group of friendly guerrillas, *Mujahideen*, ready to attack the site."

The general's superior strategic intellect kicked into gear and he gave the only analogy he could think of to deride a project of which he knew little.

"A few guerrillas armed with Enfields and Martini-Henrys against the Soviet Army? That sounds almost as stupid as the Bay of Pigs fiasco! How many divisions were the guerrillas going to take on?"

"They were only going to knock out the bridge and they had an ace in the hole to do that."

"Just what in hell kind of ace might that be?"

"A tactical nuke."

"You're kidding me, right? Is it in Afghanistan now?"

"No, it's in Iran."

"Jesus, where?"

"It's in a safe site on the outskirts of Tehran. Panagasos is the only station officer in country who knows where it is exactly."

21

"Get it and him out of there. I don't care how you do it, just do it." He stood to leave.

"What about the embassy and our folks?"

The director was walking out the door but stopped and turned back to face his two subordinates. Looking at them both he said, "That's the State Department's problem. The only thing you need to worry about is the nuke. If the Iranians find that thing before we get to it, we'll all be toast."

6

Kim Becker came into the team room, shut the door firmly, and walked to his desk without saying a word. The team members continued their work of unpacking, adjusting, and repacking their alert gear silently, waiting expectantly for their leader to tell them what was happening.

With Becker, they were nine. The team had been without a commander for over two years. Good Special Forces-qualified captains who could speak German or an eastern European language were hard to find. Which was fine for Becker. He had only a bunch of non-coms to worry about, no officers. There was Nick Kaiser, the slightly manic intelligence sergeant who was a ghost in the woods or on the street. Fred Lindt, the light weapons specialist and mechanical wizard. Paul Stavros, who handled heavy weapons and did a consummate job forging documents. Logan Finch, a medic who could do an appendectomy as well as he shot a sniper rifle. Stefan Mann, the junior medic who moonlighted in German hospital emergency rooms. Then there was Neil Fitzpatrick, the demolitions sergeant who occasionally ate his morning Cheerios with gin, but only when he ran out of milk. The last two on the team were "Poncho" Ponchelli and Jake Novak, the communications sergeants who could send Morse code at twenty-five words per minute as well as decrypt incoming messages while they copied them out of the ether. Team 5 was, to understate things, a very eclectic crew of soldiers who had mastered the intricacies of working alone on the streets as well as they operated in the forest. There were five more "A" Teams in the unit with similar profiles.

Becker turned and sat on the edge of his desk, looking over everyone's heads at the map of Berlin on the wall. Finally he spoke.

"The 509th Airborne in Vicenza was put on alert for Iran yesterday." He paused. "But the Pentagon must have wised up because they were just as quickly taken off alert status. It took them twenty-four hours to make a decision, but now it's us along with the boys from the Stockade at Fort Bragg who are on call. Whatever comes next is not going to happen quickly. We have no information, no intel on the embassy, no idea who the bad guys are nor what is going on with negotiations, or, most importantly, how we're even supposed to get there. The colonel doesn't think this alert is going anywhere, so training is back on and life goes on as usual, with a couple of exceptions. He still wants us to be ready. No one knows how it will turn out, so, three teams will stay in Berlin at full complement at all times, rotating status every month. Our turn in the barrel starts now, along with Teams 2 and 4. Training is to concentrate on clandestine urban ops and hostage recovery—getting in and out without any fireworks. That's our bailiwick, so start thinking how it will apply in Tehran."

"We still need to gather as much info as possible, just in case," said Kaiser.

"Agreed. While I start reworking our training schedule, why don't you figure out how we can do that," said Becker.

"How about we do some city training on elicitation and open source research? We can hit all the universities, libraries, map stores, and maybe even the Iranians themselves to collect information."

"Do we want to tip off the Iranians to our interest?" asked Novak.

"I said elicit. That means you get information without telling the people you get it from why you want it. Besides, if we go in as Germans, or anything but Americans, we shouldn't spook them. I'll coordinate with the other teams so we're not duplicating efforts and we can start canvassing the city. At the same time, we need to work with the S-2 to get out some interagency requests for imagery and maps," said Kaiser.

"Good idea, Nick. You take the lead on that," Becker said.

"What fun, I can see us now, we few against Xerxes' army," Lindt quipped.

"Don't get your hopes up. We'll probably sit here waiting for nothing. Anyway, I really don't want to replay the battle of Thermopylae," Stavros said.

Remember, forty selected men can shake the world, Becker thought to himself.

"What's a bailiwick?" said Finch.

Becker tossed his desktop dictionary to Finch and started to think about tactics but stopped himself. He knew everyone had to be up to snuff on basics first.

"Fred, talk with the other weapons sergeants and come up with an intensive marksmanship program. We've been pre-occupied with other stuff, we need to get back up to speed with our shooting."

Lindt's experience with weapons was not easily matched. Among other things, he had spent a year with the Special Air Service on an exchange program. He even talked like a Brit now and again.

"You mean CQB—close quarter battle. Oddly enough, I have a five- and a ten-day program ready to go. Eleven-Bravo hip pocket training, so to speak. We just need ammunition."

"How much?" asked Becker.

"Lots, at least five hundred rounds to start. More later."

"Five hundred per what?"

"Per man, per day. Like I said, lots," said Lindt.

"I'll talk with the sergeant major. We should have a pretty good justification."

"I'd say so," Kaiser commented, "national security is generally a pretty good reason."

7

Trattoria Candela was a small, cozy restaurant with maybe eight tables. Stavros had picked it because it was quiet. They could talk and hopefully not be disturbed by too many people. The waiters didn't speak much English and it was too far from any American or West German government office for the *Stasi* to have bothered with listening devices. He suspected it would be a night of reveals and heart tugs since Sarah had told him she had received her orders.

There were not many German restaurants in Berlin. *Berliners* did not want to eat German food when they went out. There were Balkan and Chinese, of course, and Italian by the boatload. It seemed like every German liked to eat Italian food. Even the Greeks opened Italian restaurants when they came north.

Stavros steered Sarah to a table in the back corner and sat her down so that he could keep the front entrance and the other tables under watch. It was a habit he had picked up from the older guys on his team.

He and Sarah had been together over a year. He had been attracted to her from the first time they met and quickly realized it wasn't casual. She was different from any other woman he'd met before. He couldn't really explain why so he never mentioned it to her. He knew she would ask, "How so?"

Beyond good looks she was intelligent: over and above her ability to speak at least five languages (he'd seen young kids in Africa who could speak three or four), she had an incisive and inquisitive mind. Moreover, she cared about what was happening around her, not just what was happening *to* her—she cared about others. He also admired her for joining the army and being willing to risk everything for her adopted country. He could go on and on but basically he knew she was special and therefore not to be treated lightly.

Tonight the meal was *spaghetti aglio e olio* with lots of garlic as he liked it. Sarah picked through a *rucola e parmigiano* salad while they shared a bottle of Barbera. The waiters left them alone, sensing perhaps that they had serious things to talk about.

"I've been assigned to Fort Meade. I have to leave in a week for training."

"Did they say how long your training would be?" Stavros said.

"No, but it's a permanent change of station."

"You won't spend much time at Meade."

"No? Why?"

"That's where they check you in and enter your personnel records into a separate system. After that you'll being heading off to training in Virginia."

Sarah picked a piece of bresaola out of her dish, rolled it up, and stuck it in her mouth as she listened. A sip of the wine gave her a moment to reflect.

"Where in Virginia?" she asked.

"A place called the 'Farm' where the Agency does its training."

"I'm not doing it with the army?"

"No, and you're better off for it. The Agency's training is much better."

"How do you know?"

"What? Where you're going or that the training is better?"

"Both, maybe. Why do you even care?"

"That's a silly question, but the answer is that I like you. And second, Sergeant Major Bergmann told me. After your adventures with Becker, he made sure your application got to all the right people. He's pretty good at getting things like that done."

Stavros was alluding to Sarah's recent forays into East Berlin to help extract two Agency assets.

"Ha! My commander told me he got me the training. I should have known he was lying. I think he just wanted me to show him gratitude."

"What kind of gratitude?"

"I didn't give him a chance to find out. He's an eel, kinda slimy."

"You've just painted me a good picture. I'll remember that when I see him."

"Just don't kill him or anything."

"No worries. I don't need that on my record."

"Do you think I'll do okay?"

"You'll be fine. You've got the skills they want, education, languages, life experience, and a level head. It's not physical, it's more mental. It's not Ranger school. They'll give you a little field training, but not enough to scare anyone off. They want people who can think fast on their feet."

"So it's not as hard as your training," Sarah said, a statement, not a question.

"Physically, no. Mentally, I think it's different but just as hard, maybe harder. But, I've only talked to some of the guys who went through it."

"Guys? No women?"

"There aren't many women case officers that I know of. The Agency has been male dominated and mostly Ivy League since it started. I think they're starting to come around some. Once you get through training, you're in the front door, but you're gonna need a thick skin to deal with the men," Stavros warned.

"If I can handle my CO and the first sergeant, I think I can handle them."

"So, the first is one too?"

"He's an ass with all the women."

"You'll do okay. I think the army is worse. Women can't even try out for combat arms slots."

"You're all sexist bastards," Sarah smiled, baiting him. "So, what was hardest about your training? How did you even get the idea to try out?"

"It's my dad's fault. He was army and his experiences got me interested. I was planning to go to college but I couldn't figure out what to major in, so I quit and volunteered. I wanted to shake the pillars of the earth. I was a bit naive about what it was really all about."

"But you must have liked it because you're still here. So what was hardest? Tell me," she asked.

"The hardest part? Taking the first step. That first step out of your cot for a run at five in the morning. The first step down the long trail and the 30-foot rope climb when you know it's just the first of many obstacles on the course. The first step after lifting the yoke with two five-gallon cans of water onto your shoulders knowing it's going to be there for a while. Each day, the first step was always the hardest, especially knowing there would be many more just like it along the way. It was both physical and mental."

"How mental?"

"They didn't play games, but you had to get out of bed on your own, you had to show up on time. They didn't come and look for you if you were late. They never yelled or screamed, they just told you what you had to do and said, 'If you want to quit just say so.' Things started out difficult and got harder each day. Some guys took them up on quitting. Some just couldn't meet the standards. A few got injured."

"How many made it through?"

"We ended up with thirteen. Out of over a hundred."

"That sorted the wheat from the chaff."

"Mostly. If you don't really want it, you'll find a reason to quit. Think about that when you're at school. Think about how you'll feel when you're finished and you'll do fine."

"I'm not too worried. The guy that interviewed me thought I would do fine," Sarah said.

"They sent someone to interview you?"

"Some guy from Frankfurt. I think he was a psychologist because he asked me all kinds of strange questions."

"If they accepted you, you must be sane. That's good news."

"I'm not so sure. I like you, that must mean I'm not totally right in the head."

"What? Why?"

"I don't know. You take me out, we talk, but it's always about other stuff: news, museums, vacations you'll take when you get the time. It's never about us."

The front door opened sending a gust of cold air through the restaurant. Stavros watched a woman enter and join a friend at another table, while the table candle flickered for moment in the wind.

"Did you hear me?" Sarah's words were softly spoken.

"I'm sorry, the door distracted me. I'm not sure what to say..."

"I know," she reached out and took Stavros' hand. "But try."

She leaned in and looked up at him. A trace of moisture rimmed her eyelids. Stavros took a deep breath. *The first step is always the hardest.*

"I'm not very good at this. All I know is that I like you very much."

"That's a start, but I imagine your other girls didn't hang around long."

"They never had much to talk about. Besides, I'm an introvert."

"You, shy? A big, strong Green Beret?"

"I never told you what I am!"

"You didn't have to. Sergeant Major Bergmann told me after the East Berlin thing."

"He *told* you?"

"Not a big deal. Anyway, try some more."

"Did all your other boyfriends talk more than me?"

"I never had any. They talked too much."

"I'm confused, I thought that was what you wanted?"

"You don't understand. They only talked about themselves. It was always how great they were, never what they were feeling."

"I hope I don't do that?"

"You don't, that's why I like you. Now, will you let go of my hand? You're crushing it."

Stavros released her hand. "I'm sorry, I guess I don't want to let you go."

"That's a definite start." She reached over and brushed his cheek lightly. "Keep that up and you won't have to worry about it."

A waiter brought the bill to the table discreetly enclosed in a small wooden box, along with two small liquors, sambuca with three coffee beans floating on top, a traditional thank you from the restaurant owner. The waiter fired them with his lighter and let them burn for a couple of seconds, then covered the glasses with a coaster to extinguish the flames before setting them on the table.

"Fire and ice," Stavros said, picking out the coffee beans with a spoon. Sarah demurred as he picked up his glass and tossed it back in one swallow.

"You like that stuff?"

"Italian jet fuel, good for the digestion," he said as he picked up Sarah's glass and drank it as well. "Waste not."

He paid the bill, tacking on a generous tip for being ignored so well. He helped Sarah on with her coat and pulled on his leather jacket, then pushed through the door to the outside.

The street lamps hardly lit the area. They looked like they were from a much earlier era, with heavy filigreed decoration and old cut-glass lenses. They might have been reclaimed from the wreckage of Berlin after the war because they weren't as bright as the new ones on the Ku'damm. The air was crisp and the night was cool, not yet as cold as it would be when the winds swept in from the eastern steppes. Soon it would be winter.

"I'm going to miss you," she said.

"Me too, but we're going to be pretty busy soon, so will that help any?"

"Something to do with Iran?"

Stavros hesitated, knowing there was a line not to be crossed, but he went across it anyway.

"We're not supposed to tell anyone anything, but we will be doing a lot of intense training and practice soon."

"I thought so. The radio traffic we're picking up on Teufelsberg is heavy with speculation. I think the Russians are watching everything we Americans do very closely."

"I'm sure they are. We have to be careful with how we train. They might tell the Iranians just to sabotage our plans."

"Did you volunteer for this thing?"

"No, but they didn't have to ask either. Every one of us wants to go. Bad."

"I don't want to lose you either. Are you always going to be doing this to me?"

"Probably, it's in my nature. But you're going to the States, don't you think you'll find some James Bond type back there?"

"I told you, I like you. Besides, I don't like James Bond types. They're all players and I have something better with you. I feel safe with you."

They stopped under one of the streetlights, standing close together, wrapped up in each other's arms, Stavros almost a head taller. Sarah looked up at Stavros. He was easy to look at, even good-looking, but there was something else about him—he listened, which she found to be one of his best traits.

He makes me feel not just physically, but mentally safe in this world. Now, if only he would share some more of himself.

He pulled Sarah closer to him. "You have to write me and let me know where I can find you. When this is finished, I'll be there," he said.

Sarah breathed deep and suppressed a tear as they walked home. She wondered if falling for such a soldier was a good idea, then she decided that losing him with him was equally unpalatable. She'd make it work.

At the same time, Stavros was trying to figure out how he had lucked into such a woman but he was also worried. He knew the alpha males at the Farm would hunt Sarah and he just might have to kill them all. But he also knew that separation had a way of ruining relationships and his lifestyle, his need for challenge and adventure could just as easily destroy what they had together.

Just how many "Get out of jail free" cards will she let me play before she walks?

He didn't want to know the answer to that question. He had no idea where the relationship was headed but he wanted to find out.

8

Teams 2, 4, and 5, held in Berlin while the colonel and sergeant major shuttled back and forth between Berlin, the US European Command Headquarters in the southern German town of Stuttgart, and the Pentagon in northern Virginia for coordination and planning meetings, were suffering from a lack of information. They knew the plan was being put together, only to be changed and cancelled, then restarted on the whims of the president, his advisors, the Joint Chiefs of Staff, and occasionally by reality. It was a process much like making sausage, but with more chefs. The only good thing was the teams in Berlin weren't going through the constant changes the main force back in the States had to endure. In this case, ignorance was bliss.

Days passed, then weeks, as the teams trained hard. Becker's men revisited the skills of close quarter battle. Lindt ran the program and supervised each facet.

"How much time do I have?"

"Colonel said we can have two weeks, all the ammo you need and the ranges are yours."

Wearing a black baseball cap with his trademark *Kampfschwimmer* insignia, Lindt would call the routine and every shooter would follow it while he marked the time with his Heuer stopwatch. Hard training was good for morale, especially if there was a purpose. Someone hung a quote on the wall—one from an old soldier who served with Merrill's Marauders but contrary to his admonitions, things did improve, skills did progress. It was probably because the sergeants ran the training, not the officers.

The students were a mixed bag, some having been through the CQB train-up before, while others had only recently joined the unit. Everyone would start at the base level, which was déjà vu for some, but a good review nevertheless. It wasn't the kind of training normally given to every Special Forces soldier. Yes, they all knew how to use many types of weapons in almost any situation, but generally their training was geared for fighting enemy soldiers, not terrorists in the midst of a bunch of innocent civilians. That required precision shooting and meant training at a higher level, a lot of it. There were only four places in the US military to get this kind of training: two were in isolated areas of Fort Bragg, one was in Panama, and the other was in Berlin.

It began slowly. Slow aimed pistol fire at a single 10-inch bullseye target at 25 meters, then 10 meters. Then rapid aimed fire, eight rounds, magazine change, eight more rounds in a 10-inch bullseye. It was familiarization, until you knew how to handle the weapon safely in your sleep.

Then things got interesting. Lindt would give the commands.

"From the standing ready position, two rounds—double tap—on your target, and then recover to the ready. Understood? Fire!"

Five pistols went off nearly simultaneously as Lindt watched.

"What the…? I said shoot *your* target, why are your rounds on his target? And where are your rounds? Are you sure you pulled the trigger?"

Lindt was relentless in his critique. Even if you got all your rounds on target, he wasn't satisfied.

Then they graduated to multiple targets, then shooting numbered targets in the proper order, then moving targets. First came rapid-fire shooting at a man-sized silhouette, then tightening down to 4-inch saucer-sized groups.

Focus. And deft weapon handling, shooting from the ready position and then, when that was mastered, starting from the holster and shooting without hitting your foot, the ground, or your partner.

Same drill with the submachine gun. Then, to induce problems, one of the magazines would be spiked with a dummy round.

"Misfire!" Clear it and continue, there are no breaks on the battlefield or in the alley. The bullseye target became paper people. Men with guns, women with purses, women with guns, children. Bad guy behind two innocents, obscured target, discriminate, and shoot. Take out the bad guy, don't shoot the good guys, even if you can only see a tiny bit of the bad guy to shoot.

Then came the scenarios. From the open range, they graduated to a single room, then added hallways and multiple rooms. The light got bad and then there was no light. Shooting with PVS-5 night vision googles and finding out the hard way that you can't see after the first flash of your pistol renders them useless.

"Send a message to Night Vision Labs and have them fix that. Fast." (They won't.)

Shoot, reload, and start over. It was fun at first, coming back up to speed, then it became work, then it became an obsession. Focus. Shoot faster, shoot tighter, move quicker, more securely, leave no openings, and shoot to kill. You were good when all the rounds went into the tiny target with no flyers.

Don't shoot to wound, don't shoot to disarm.

Shoot to kill.

First with full military jacketed bullets, then with deadlier hollow-points—*Blitz Aktion Trauma,* the Germans called them. No misfires or accidents permitted. Friendly fire isn't, especially with hollow points.

"Are hollow points legal?" someone asked.

"I don't remember any terrorists signing the Hague Convention. Besides, they are criminals, they don't count," said the barracks lawyer.

Fitzpatrick did well, graduating the final exercise with top honors. He got a free beer. Peter Holden from Team 2 got second. Stavros was in the running for a gold star at least until the last moment. Lindt gave him the instructions for the test.

"Seven hostiles, five friendlies, two rooms. I don't know who is where, so you'll have to make sure you clear everything. Points based on hits, kills are ten, wounds are five, misses zero. Only one possibility for each bad guy, ten, five, or zero points. Then you have minus ten for each missed terrorist, minus ten or five for each good guy you nail depending on where you hit them. Got it?"

"Got it."

"Oh, and you have a total of thirty seconds to do it."

"Got it."

Stavros stood on the edge of the door frame at the ready. When Lindt pulled the door open, he launched.

He saw the field and engaged, near to far, most dangerous to least. His focus went from left to right. His pistol automatically aimed where he looked and he fired twice at each of his targets. Once he had to take an extra moment to take out a bad guy mostly hidden behind a friendly. Four targets down, three to go. Reload and a shuffle to the second door. He cleared the section he could see beyond before he entered to clear the rest of the room.

He pulled the trigger and... nothing. He looked at the pistol and tried to jack the slide back but it stuck halfway. He jerked on it again. It was frozen. He had no back-up. End of game.

"Jam, I'm down and out," he yelled as he took a knee.

"Too bad, old man. What happened?"

Stavros dropped the magazine and finally was able to pull the slide back. An expended cartridge dropped out. He looked closer. The frame was cracked. Unlike an M-1911A1, the thirty-year old

P-38 pistols could only take so much abuse. And after thousands of rounds of hot ammo had been fired, their structural limits were well exceeded. He held the pistol up to Lindt.

"It's toast," he said.

"Where's your back-up?"

"You said no back-ups."

"True, but if you're not cheating, you're not trying," he said. "Sorry, Paul, no alibis."

"I was robbed."

The unit acquired new 9mm Walther P-5 pistols. Reliability improved dramatically, although everyone began to carry two pistols along with a submachine gun. And maybe a sawed-off 870P shotgun for good measure.

***

The next week Becker announced a shift in gears—urban tradecraft training.

"The 'Pros from Dover' have arrived. They're here to help us."

"Who the hell are they?"

"The call themselves 'Team Ten,' but they're Agency annuitants."

"What's an annuitant?" said Finch.

This time Becker didn't bother tossing him the dictionary. "It's a fancy name for a retired guy who makes money off the government. They're going to teach us how they do things. I guess our methods are outdated because we use the OSS training manuals from World War II."

"What does the Agency use?"

"OSS training manuals. Although, when I went through their long course, I never saw a manual. It was all experience talking, so I think it will be a lot of 'this is how I did it' kind of training."

He was right. A bunch of old guys showed up and most were OSS veterans. Three very unassuming men with gray hair and drab clothing to be exact. Inside the building they stood out because they were old. Among the much younger guys of the unit they looked like fathers who had shown up for Dad's Day at their kids' school.

Hugh Summer—that was the name he gave anyway—was the lead instructor. He set the scenario for the training which, despite the crisis in Iran, signified that the Cold War had not been put on the back burner.

"We will assume that the war with the Soviet Union is about to begin" he said, "and it's time to go underground to fight an unconventional war in the city. Set up your clandestine network, recruit helpers, communicate secretly, put surveillance on the enemy officers, and be ready to kill them."

Of course, Becker and Team 5 had done much of the groundwork before. So had the other teams. But now, there was a game to be played. All the tradecraft subjects were talked about in the classroom and then practiced outside.

Where better to practice with the "Pros" than Berlin, where you are surrounded by enemy spies every day?

***

Every day, a new problem.

"Stavros, today your mission is item number three on my list. Go case a site."

"What kind of site, what's it for? A meeting site? A signal site? A dead drop?"

"I'm not going to tell you that. What I will say is that I want you to case an art gallery located at Fasanenstraße 107. Inside and out in detail. Just don't get arrested, they have good security."

Wonderful, case a site for an unknown purpose. That means you need to know everything. Not just some things, you need to find out everything about the place.

Stavros was out the door and headed downtown. As usual, he turned on his inner antennae as soon as he stepped outside and began to watch for anomalies. The first guy he picked up within minutes. An older gentleman, no one he had seen before, but the guy stayed on him for several blocks as Stavros stair-stepped through the neighborhood. Then he disappeared.

I either lost him or he quit. Or he's been swapped out.

He didn't pick up anything again and soon he was near the gallery. He put his training to use.

Follow your internal checklist while being innocuous.

Casing was best done over a period of time, several days at different hours to get a feel for the environment. Who lived in the neighborhood and who moved through it? What kind of people visited the gallery? Build up a comprehensive data base. He didn't have that luxury, he had to have the information by the end of the day. He went from far to near, finding ways in and out of the area. What other shops were nearby, which alleys accessed the rear, what doors accessed the inside? All the while, he was thinking about security. What were reaction times for the police, the fire department, calling a taxi? Power and telephone lines, alarms?

What are you missing, what have you forgotten?

Then he went for broke.

Entering the shop, he heard the chime of an entry alert. No one out front but management knows he is there.

One, two cameras, maybe more behind the mirrors. Mostly modern art on the walls, some impressionist.

He looked at the labels. No prices, therefore expensive. He knew a couple of the names: Toulouse-Lautrec, Emil Nolde. All high class, as was the woman who quietly drifted in from the back of the gallery. Tall and thin, yet shapely, late forties, with the pale skin and icy hauteur of a confident woman who had no need for the overcooked bronze of a tanning salon that was the refuge of so many. She was naturally dark haired, wearing a simple black dress without ornamentation—she was the ornament, the personification of *haute couture* that *Berliner* women admired and men loved.

She probably has a Mercedes 450 SL convertible parked out back.

There was an expensive smile on her face.

"May I help you?"

She sounded sincere, although she probably wasn't. Stavros knew he looked like a ruffian and a foreigner to boot. Long hair, vaguely Mediterranean looks, leather jacket, rough wool slacks, and his shoes weren't polished. She probably had him cataloged from the moment she saw him on the television monitor in the back.

He considered saying he was casing the joint, but then a song began to run through his head, something about being cut by a woman and never seeing the blade.

That guy nailed it.

"Actually, I saw your gallery window and wanted to see the artists you have. Do you have anything by Annot?"

Thank God for Sarah's interest in art museums.

The woman's expression changed, softened. Her head inclined to the right, a questioning look on her face.

What manner of miscreant are you?

"No, I'm sorry, not at this moment. Does she... does the artist Annot interest you?"

"I collect a bit from the Succession Movement and I noticed that you have a Liebermann. So I thought, I hoped perhaps you might have one of hers."

He turned about the gallery and looked some more, one hand on his chin, pensively, as he had seen some art snobs do.

"I will have to come back when I have more time. You do have a lovely gallery."

Stavros slipped out the front door leaving the woman to wonder.

Hugh Summer, you bastard. You're pushing us out of our comfort zone.

Across the street, he saw the man he'd seen earlier, watching from the doorway of a shop.

Stavros returned to his team room and wrote up his casing report from memory and using a good map of the area. Three pages of information, organized by subject, including limitations and advantages of the site. He included an assessment of the woman, but not the registration of her Mercedes. He couldn't pinpoint her car in a neighborhood overrun with expensive machines.

Hugh sat down and read the report as he did for everyone he had sent out that day.

"Good report," he said. "You've covered most all the points, but you were obviously rushed. I'm curious though, you didn't mention encountering surveillance."

"I thought he'd mention me."

"He did. Not all of us are inside this building, as you might have realized."

"I picked him up during the first part of my outbound route and then he disappeared. Then I saw him downtown across from the gallery when I left."

"That's right. Obviously, we had an advantage knowing your route and target, but that wasn't our objective. It was to observe your demeanor, which he said was pretty good. You probably wouldn't have gotten noticed by the police. He went into the gallery after you left and said the woman was staring at you as you walked away. He thinks she wants you for her collection."

Stavros shuddered. "I don't think that would end well."

***

Hugh Summer spoke to them again from his podium at the front of the classroom. "Tomorrow, you're going to put the things you've learned over the past days into action. You'll be working as five-man teams to surveil a suspect, a rabbit. There will be four teams downtown chasing four different rabbits. We're going to be observing you, so if you happen to see any of us, we're not there."

"Was that some sort of existential statement?" Becker turned to Hans Landau in the back of the room.

"It's from the lyrics of some song I once heard somewhere."

Landau was chewing on a hardboiled egg that he had just stuffed into his mouth, shell and all. Between that and the *Hochdeutsch* accent that added color to his English, he was difficult to understand.

Summer paused at the front and glared at the two men disturbing the equilibrium of his class. "You two have something to share with us?"

"Nothing that would assist in the furtherance of your instruction," Becker said. "Please continue."

He was daring the instructor to say something else, but Summer refused to take the bait. He knew a hard case when he saw one.

"Some of you might be wondering why we're teaching surveillance right now when you have other more important things to worry about, yes?"

Heads nodded. Some of the men would rather practice shooting people than follow them like a puppy.

"It's simple. You must know how to surveil before you can counter it. Some of you might be needing these skills very soon. That's all I can say right now. Got it?"

Summer had recaptured everyone's interest.

"All right then," he continued, "each of these envelopes contains a photo of the rabbit you'll be following and a start point to find him." Summer passed the envelopes out to the team leaders.

"You need to be at the start point before 0900 to catch your rabbit. I'll leave you to the details."

***

Becker's surveillance team was a mixed bag, three from his team, plus two from Team 2, Sergeant First Class Hans Landau and Staff Sergeant Jan Pavlovich. Becker knew his people well: Stavros and Kaiser were solid. The other two he knew from their reps. Pavlovich was a good soldier, a young guy like Stavros, but Landau had time in Vietnam with a Ranger Long Range Reconnaissance Patrol Company. Landau didn't look like a soldier, he was long and wiry, with dishwater-brown hair that was all over the place. He was more Becker's vision of a European professional football player—the game Americans called "soccer" much to their German friends' chagrin. His native language skills were a plus, except when he told native *Berliners* they didn't know how to speak proper German, which for the most part they didn't. Landau was born and raised in Cologne, where they spoke a proper *Hochdeutsch*. To say he was abrasive missed the point; he just had a tendency to speak the truth inconveniently. He also had an innate ability to blend in. Although most of the American guys in the unit were able to adequately camouflage their origins, a few were just too big and/or bumbling. The European members of the unit didn't need to camouflage anything, they just acted like themselves. And so it was with Landau. He could be as disturbingly obnoxious as he liked because he was, after all, German. Becker looked at Landau that way perhaps because his own Alsatian logic prevented him from accepting that his blood might have been tainted by some long-forgotten Teutonic foray into his homeland.

Landau's humor was a bit dark as well. He, like most soldiers who had actually experienced combat, didn't generally brag about himself or tell stories, but when he did they were memorable. Becker had heard him relate only one and that was in a conversation with Pavlovich. Pavlovich, an eager young soldier who wanted to glean as much knowledge as he could from the "veterans," habitually asked them about this and that mission. What he got was generally BS or comedy. It usually started with Pavlovich setting himself up for the fall.

"You were in the Rangers in Vietnam?"

"Yes," Landau said. This early in the morning, monosyllabic replies were his norm.

"How was it?"

"Not bad, we survived. We were the team that got shit on though."

"Everyone says that they got shit on. By the headquarters pukes and all that."

"No, we actually got shit on."

"How? I heard of one guy that got pissed on by a Viet Cong when he was hiding in the bush. You mean like that?"

"No, the whole team got shit on."

"This I gotta hear."

Landau sighed, looked at Pavlovich like a grandfather accommodating a pestering grandchild, and told the story. And in good soldier story tradition, it didn't start out with "this is no shit" or "there I was"—it was the truth.

"Well, okay," Landau said. He drawled his English a bit as he'd learned it mostly in the army and the lingua franca of the army is "Southern" because the greatest percentage of draftees and recruits seemed to come from the southern states, mostly Texas, Alabama, and Georgia.

"I was in 'G' Company, 75th Rangers at Chu Lai. It was almost time for another monsoon season to start. This meant less flying time for us and more chances for them to move people and supplies at will. While inclement weather might have slowed down the regular infantry, the Line Doggies, it didn't stop us. No, it didn't. My team, Team Vermont, was inserted a few days earlier into an always hot area nicknamed "Happy Valley" although it wasn't a very happy place. It was part of a major transportation route used by the NVA to infiltrate into the 23rd "American" Division's area of operations. We knew the enemy presence was heavy so we always used a lot of caution to remain undetected. We had reported a lot of movement all around the immediate vicinity during the previous daylight hours and it didn't change significantly when darkness fell over the region. All night long we could see flashlights moving around us and we figured we had about a company's worth of bad guys around us. We knew we'd been lucky so far and thought it was time to fold our cards and go home. We were only six guys, remember. Our team leader asked to be pulled out. The Command Center agreed and we got ready to bug out. We quickly and quietly slipped on our rucksacks and waited for the command to detonate our claymores."

"Claymores? When did you put those out?"

"It was SOP. We did it every night. Each man put out one claymore which provided pretty good all-round coverage. Normally, we'd recover them if the night was quiet, but this time, we knew we'd make contact as soon as we moved. So we'd fire them simultaneously and bust ass out of there. Now, the sound of one claymore is loud enough to get somebody's attention—six at once could probably be picked up by sensors way over on the Ho Chi Minh Trail. Something else you have to remember, there was a significant difference in how the Line Doggies deployed their mines and how we did it. They would run the cord out to its max length, which let the enemy turn the things around toward our guys. We used a very short wire so that any VC trying to turn it around would be seen and heard. Anyway, we fired the mines and ran once we had re-gathered our wits and despite the momentary deafness. We ran for the pre-arranged helo LZ.

"So, we got picked up and flown back to base camp where every Ranger not in the field met us on the beach landing pad with two beers, one for themselves and one for us. Of course, they were already smashed, but that's another story. Beers were passed around and our rucksacks were taken and we all—including the chopper pilots—drifted toward the club. Pretty soon everyone is saying, 'What the hell is that smell?' Even the drunk guys yelled, 'It smells like shit.' Then some of the guys who had slapped our backs realized they had shit on their hands. Everyone had to go outside and get hosed down. Next day we figured out someone on the team had taken a dump in our night position. Unfortunately, he did it close to one of the claymores and when it went off, the whole mess came back on us. From then on Team Vermont was known as the team that literally got shit on."

Becker rolled his eyes. Pavlovich just wasn't sure if he'd ever hear a real "John Wayne" story or not.

***

The next morning, Becker's merry band of American soldiers, only two of whom had actually been born American, assembled discreetly near their start point. They were going completely non-technical for the exercise as Summer forbade the use of radios, flags, bullhorns or any other kind of signaling device to conduct their approved "ABC" surveillance formation. They would have to work well together and stay in visual contact to maintain the tail. Only the first man, the A-man, had to keep the rabbit in sight, the other four just needed to keep tabs on the lead and each other. The only guidance Summer gave was "don't get burned." Close or harassing surveillance was too easy.

"Better to lose the rabbit and catch him later. Don't advertise your intent," he told them.

"Easier said than done," said Pavlovich.

"What makes you so smart?" Kaiser asked.

"New York City." Apparently that was enough because Kaiser didn't ask anything else.

It was 0830 on the Kurfürstendamm, Berlin's main shopping drag. It was the place to be seen and to see those who wished to be seen. Each of the team came alone from different directions to the site. They communicated by gestures and head movements, nothing overtly noticeable. First, the team had to hang around on the crowded sidewalks and try not get burned until they saw their rabbit sometime after nine in the morning. They were told only that he was to show up at the *Maison de France*, which sat on a street corner. Then they had to follow him—they knew it was a "him" from his photo.

"We'll cover each of the streets leading away from the place. If he walks toward you, let him pass and then pick up the number two position after the first one of us gets to you. Everyone else falls in trail."

From the beginning the rabbit tried to make life difficult for his would-be surveillants. He showed up at the front door to the *Maison* from somewhere down the street and stood outside reading the posters on upcoming events. Everyone got the opportunity to see what Rabbit really looked like in person. It also gave Rabbit the opportunity to mark anyone who stood out.

There were six guys in a circle, a big circle on four different street corners, watching each other. One was Rabbit, sitting in the middle of a pack of coyotes who were just waiting for him to move.

When he did move, it was not far. He turned and crossed the street and continued down the block along the Ku'damm. Not far at all. Rabbit popped into a cafe, not a big cafe, but big enough that someone needed to be eyes on. At that point, Pavlovich was Number One and plunged into the cafe after him. When he entered, he saw Rabbit sitting in the back with a menu. Pavlovich grabbed a stool at the front counter and ordered a coffee, paying for it with a ten-mark bill before it even arrived. Rabbit got a coffee and some sort of pastry, taking his time to enjoy both while the team milled about outside. They repositioned themselves along the street and waited. Pavlovich got up as soon as he saw Rabbit stir and walked out onto the main street. He nodded to Becker and continued in the same direction Rabbit had been going.

Rabbit was not overly provocative at this point and when he hit the sidewalk, he continued in the same direction as Pavlovich, who was about 50 meters in front of him. Rabbit was about to begin the fun. He turned down Fasanenstraße with Becker now tailing him and the rest strung out behind. Stavros realized where he was; he had a feeling and closed up to Becker. Stavros's feeling paid off, but somehow he knew it was no coincidence. Rabbit went into a shop and Becker paused. Stavros approached him.

"That's the art gallery I cased yesterday. There's a back door onto the alley and I will bet you he's going to use it."

"Go," was all Becker said. He subtly signaled for everyone to close in and he directed his team onto different corners. They had two people to watch for, Rabbit in the gallery and Stavros who disappeared into the alley.

Stavros positioned himself at the far end of the alley where he could observe the gallery's exit and try to remain out of sight. After a five-minute wait, he was rewarded with the door opening and Rabbit stepping into the alley. Rabbit shook hands with someone unseen behind the door and then turned toward Stavros's position and walked on and past him and into the next street.

Pavlovich picked up Stavros following Rabbit as he turned onto Lietzenburger and he followed once he was able to alert Becker. The team was extended out, but by the time they got to the next intersection, only one, Landau, was unaccounted for. Becker figured he was on the Ku'damm and had to hope he would make it back before long.

Rabbit followed a relatively straight path for the next several blocks and the four were able to regroup on the run and trade positions several times until Rabbit walked into a hotel pension. Someone had to commit; Kaiser opted to go in. Rabbit was at the desk picking up a key and deep in conversation with the receptionist. Kaiser thumbed through the tourist brochures and post cards, hoping to get a glimpse at the number on the key fob while he waited.

"May I help you?"

Kaiser was startled back into reality. "Have you any double rooms?"

"Yes, they're 250 marks per night."

Kaiser played for time. He was already stretching his repertoire for tourist talk.

"Would you have three double rooms starting next Monday for three days?"

The second receptionist looked through the log for a moment.

"I have only two and some singles. Sorry, that's all."

Kaiser didn't have any maneuver room.

"Too bad. I really need three doubles." He turned and looked at Rabbit who stared back at him without expression.

At least I saw the key.

Kaiser nodded at Rabbit and left the building. He had time to spot his team which once again included Landau, before he distanced himself from the entrance. Someone else would have to pick up as Number One.

Rabbit came out of the hotel and headed for the underground station. He went straight for the turnstile with ticket in hand and kept going deeper into the earth. The team followed, dispersed as much as possible; they pulled out the U-Bahn tickets each man had for just this contingency and trailed along. They ended up on the platform of a north-bound train and waited. Midday traffic in downtown Berlin was heavy and provided good cover. Landau was closest to Rabbit, with the rest scattered throughout the crowd.

With the call "Stand Back" piped through the station's announcement system, the train arrived behind a bubble of musty warm air it pushed through its tunnel. Rabbit climbed into the closest car with Landau at the opposite end. Becker, Kaiser, and Stavros went for adjacent cars, while Pavlovich waited until the last possible moment before hopping on board.

The train took off, its wheels clacking on the rails. Rabbit stood impassively close to the door. One stop, two stops went by. The third stop came. He stepped out of the car and stopped in his tracks. Everyone waited except for Kaiser, who decided he would commit. Kaiser stepped out just as Rabbit hopped back on the train.

"Damn," Kaiser said and hopped back on as well.

Probably burned myself.

He was sure Rabbit had seen him twice: repetition is not coincidence in this business.

At the next station, Rabbit disembarked and walked with a purpose for the exit with the surveillance team behind him in trail. He didn't leave the station though. At a junction in the exit, he turned and headed back for the opposite platform. He was going back and the team had to follow.

Rabbit climbed onto the south-bound train and again stood close to the door for four stops before exiting right where he had started out from. The team was still with him but somewhat exasperated at having bothered. It was obvious Rabbit was playing with them.

Rabbit had one more trick to play. He walked north, stair-stepping through the neighborhood until he reached Kleiststraße, and then headed east toward KaDeWe, the largest department store in Germany. KaDeWe was the capital of capitalism on the continent, rivaled only by Harrods in London. With five and a half thousand square meters of store and more than fifteen entrances, it was the mother of all surveillance nightmares. But the team didn't know that yet.

Acting as if he was in his home warren, Rabbit led the team through almost every nook on the first floor. He went into a bathroom, came out, went up an escalator and started over. Occasionally one member of the team would pass close to another and they would trade observations.

Landau walked by Becker: "What's this guy doing? He's just wandering around."

Becker, who knew what he was doing, said, "He's leading us through the maze. He's getting to know all of us." Becker knew more than the rest of his team as he'd actually been trained by some of the best rabbits, the Moscow rabbits. Landau shook his head, thinking he had already been burned at least once, maybe thrice.

Around, back, and up. Number One became Number Four. Number Three took over and, by the time they hit the fifth floor, the team was turned totally inside out. They hadn't practiced following a subject in a store and it was difficult to follow a pattern with Rabbit meandering through the wide open display halls. The only thing good about the fifth floor was that it was the food hall with each department delivering its signature smells from savory to pungent. Rabbit led them in a circle through the wild game section, followed by the fish, the cheese, then the bread section before he finally stopped at the center bar and ordered himself an *Urquell*. It was the "EndEx" signal and time for all to come together.

***

While waiting the requisite eight minutes for the pilsner to be poured, the tormenting "Double 'O' Rabbit" regarded his bloodhounds, reassured them with a smile, and then became Sam.

"I can tell you that I only identified three of you before we quit. And I was doing a lot of things meant to burn you, things you should never do if you want to look innocent."

Everyone quietly drank their beer, not wanting to be embarrassed.

"You," Rabbit pointed at Kaiser, "did good coming into the hotel. I think you saw my room number on the key?"

"312," said Kaiser.

"That was good, but two things: first, I noticed that you wear your watch with its face on the inside of your wrist. That is quite common with military people but also surveillants. Second, you messed up

53

getting off the train and then hopping back on so quickly. I wouldn't have given you a second thought except for that."

"You," now pointing at Pavlovich, "stayed too close to me in here. I saw you on three floors; that's too many coincidences. And this morning you paid for your coffee early and left after only a couple of minutes. Classic surveillance mistake; this isn't Italy, Germans are slow with their coffee. Next time, don't leave before me and pay then. I might not have noticed you when I saw you again in the store. Last, but not least, you," he was pointing at Stavros, "kinda looked suspicious when I saw you hanging out at the end of the alleyway. That was one. Then I saw you again in the lingerie section. Guys, especially Germans unless they're gay, generally don't spend much time looking at lingerie. That was two and confirmation."

Turning to Landau and Becker, the two oldest on the team, he added, "You two, I didn't see at all."

Landau, who had to have his usual medication, tossed back a shot of *Jägermeister*, an evil concoction of something that tasted like fuel oil, black pepper, and alcohol. He was perhaps the only guy in the unit that actually liked the stuff.

"I think we did well today, after one day of classroom and practice time and having never worked together before," he said.

"Yeah, you did okay. If you had more practice and some help, you might have done even better," Sam said.

"We *might* have done better," Pavlovich said. "Like we're going to get out there and work on it."

Becker smiled. Landau knew something was coming.

"Tomorrow, 0730 we meet at the Zoo Bahnhof. Same game, different rabbit."

54

9

Colonel Jelinek and Sergeant Major Bergmann sat together in the "Tank," the secure conference room deep inside the Pentagon. Around a table in the small, underventilated room a group of high-ranking men sat, each representing a service or a specialty. Colonel Charlie Beckwith was there as commander of the newly founded Delta Force. The J-2 chief as well as the chief of the Special Operations Division sat fiddling with their US government-issue pens, doodling on the yellow legal pads in front of them.

While they were waiting, Bergmann was looking at the staff officers and noticed a familiar face wearing an air force uniform.

"Sir, isn't that the guy who was wearing a red vest and bow tie at the hotel last night?" Bergmann asked Jelinek.

"Yes, why?"

"I told him to refill our ice bucket. Did you know he was a colonel?"

"Yes."

"I thought he was a waiter. Why didn't you say anything?"

"Because you needed the ice."

***

The door opened and everyone stood. It was the Chairman along with the rest of the Joint Chiefs of Staff. They filed in and took the seats at the head of the table. Twenty-four stars in all, only the National Guard Chief was missing.

Now it would get serious.

"Gentleman," the CJCS began, "When this situation first arose in November, I said we needed a specialized force to have a reasonable chance to free our hostages. You represent that force. Now, I understand you've done some preliminary assessments of our needs and I'd like to hear what they are."

General James Vaught, the task force commander, began. "Sir, we have not yet determined how exactly we'll get the troops into country, although we have several good options that our planners are working through. We must keep in mind that the embassy is in downtown Tehran. It's not like assaulting the airport at Entebbe. Additionally, the restrictions placed on us by the administration mean we are running this camel through the eye of a needle. That said, what we do have is a fairly solid plan for the actual mechanics of the rescue once we're in the city. Colonel Beckwith will brief you on that."

Beckwith wore his customary evil scowl. *He must have PTSD the way he grouses at everyone all the time,* Bergmann thought. *And today he must be pissed at having to brief a bunch of fancy-pants generals.*

Standing next to a basic diagram of the embassy compound on the wall, Beckwith began to outline his plan.

"General, we have put together a package based on what we know about the embassy and the hostages. Right now, my force stands at around ninety shooters. That's what we'll need to get into the compound, clear all 27 acres, and then get the hostages out. I may need more but I'm about tapped out; I only have so many fully qualified men."

"That's a large element to get in and out of country."

"Yes, and I'll need every one of them."

56

"What will you do with the students, the hostage takers?" asked one of the chiefs.

"We'll be prepared to eliminate them," Beckwith said.

"Does that mean kill them?"

"General, if necessary I will personally shoot each one of them in the head and then do it again to make sure."

"I'll take that as a yes."

There was a collective shiver from the staff.

"What about the three hostages in the Ministry of Foreign Affairs? How do you plan to get them out?" asked the Chairman.

"I can't handle the MFA. Every one of my shooters is needed at the embassy and I can't spare any for the ministry."

General Vaught chipped in. "General, Colonel Jelinek, the commander of Special Forces Berlin has some thoughts on that."

"Jelinek, how is your unit involved?"

"Sir, we've been tasked to infiltrate a pilot team into Tehran to collect pre-mission intelligence on the targets and to set up the reception committee."

"Pilot team? Reception committee? What are those exactly?" said the CJCS, an air force general, who wasn't very familiar with unconventional warfare terminology.

"The pilot team is made up of several of my operators who will infiltrate into the city under cover to gather target data on the embassy and the MFA. They will also receive and support the assault forces when they come in, if necessary. But what I wanted to discuss is the Foreign Ministry aspect of the mission."

"Go ahead."

"My unit is prepared to take on the rescue at the Foreign Ministry. I can provide fifty fully trained operators."

"They are ready now?"

"Sir, we've been the EUCOM counterterrorism force since 1975. All we need to do is prepare the detailed operational plans for this mission. Tactically and technically we are ready."

Vaught spoke: "The unit was certified in Europe to the same standards that were used for Delta. They're good to go."

Bergmann held his breath.

The CJCS, head inclined toward the table, hands clasped in front of him, thought for a moment. Bergmann thought he looked like a priest praying to God for guidance.

Air Force pilots do that a lot, they are always closer to God than us ground-pounders.

Having received his instructions from somewhere above, the CJCS raised his eyes to the ceiling and pronounced, "General Vaught, go ahead and tell EUCOM to cut Colonel Jelinek's unit to you for the mission. Make sure they understand this is a JCS directive."

The Joint Chiefs stood as their Chairman finished his final instructions for the morning.

"And Jim, I want a situation report at least every morning and evening, more often if there are significant changes. Let me know when you're ready to brief the next stage. I don't want to be left out of anything. Oh, and one last thing, let me know if anyone gives you resistance. I will straighten them out."

Bergmann exhaled.

10

Sergeant First Class Hans Landau walked out of the arrivals terminal at Berlin's Tegel Airport. The very strange telephone call he had received unsettled and disappointed him. His team had just been released from stand-by alert status to train in southern Germany when the message came. In essence it said: "Get back here as fast as you can."

"I just got here," he had said to no avail.

He had taken a late afternoon flight from Munich and thought he'd have to grab a taxi to get to the unit. Seeing the sergeant major waiting for him on the sidewalk was another surprise he wasn't prepared for. He expected he was in trouble.

"How was training?"

"It was great, Sergeant Major, but I don't understand why I was called back," Landau said. He was not sure what the recall was about but he hoped it wasn't what he feared. It was only two days since he and Don, another guy from Team 2, got banned from the US Armed Forces Recreation Center hotel for spiking the punch of an alcohol-free, evangelical women's group that was having a get-together in the conference room.

As the afternoon went on, the women had become more animated and some even wanted to dance to the music. They appeared to be having a great time but he should have realized it was a bad sign when one of the tipsy women knocked over a serving cart along with the guy pushing it. Apparently the general's wife was not amused. If he and Don hadn't been the guys serving the punch, no one would have been the wiser.

"Let's take a ride." Sergeant Major Bergmann gestured toward a unit sedan, a little Ford Cortina in civilian colors, like all the unit vehicles. Landau climbed in and waited. For once Bergmann wasn't smoking a cigar. That suited Landau just fine, as he disliked the smoke. It reminded him of things he didn't want to be reminded of.

Bergmann maneuvered the car out of the airport and they headed south through the French sector before picking up the high-speed AVUS highway near the Funkturm. Originally built as a race car test track in 1921, the AVUS cut travel time through the heavily congested city by half. Once on the track, Bergmann spoke.

"You're going to take Ewen McKay and Paul Stavros to Frankfurt. I'm putting you in charge. You've been booked on the Duty Train tomorrow night. You're going to this place," Bergmann took a note card out of his pocket and handed it to Landau, "and you will meet with Frank Cavanagh tomorrow. He's the facility chief."

"What's it about, Sergeant Major?"

"It's a job interview. It should be pretty interesting."

"What's the job?"

"What I tell you now doesn't go any further. Don't tell Ewen or Paul until you're briefed down there, understood?"

"Understood."

"The Agency's stable of assets in Iran has been wiped out. Completely gone. They say they have zero information on what's happening inside the country. The JCS decided the military needs to send in its own collectors to get what we need on the embassy in Tehran."

"Can't they send in some Military Intel officers?"

"First, MI dinks don't know squat about what is needed to put an assault force onto target and to rescue the hostages. Second, they couldn't pass themselves off as car salesmen in Columbus, Ohio. JCS wants operators that can represent themselves as foreign businessmen and collect the intel we need. That means us; we are the only outfit that can do that—successfully collect the ground truth information from a denied area. The Agency is on board and has agreed to help with documentation to get us there but they want to see you first and make sure you can properly carry the cover story. You three are my best candidates."

"Why not Rajdik or Becker or Nicolov? They're all foreign-born, native linguists."

"Because two of them are team sergeants and I need them here to lead their teams. The other is a medic and his bedside manner will better serve us elsewhere. One other thing: this portion of the operation is going to happen whether or not we mount the rescue. JCS want the intel and they want it quick so planning can go forward. That means a lot depends on whoever goes. It'll be dangerous but I expect you can handle it."

Landau looked at the sergeant major and thought about saying something suitably motivational, then went back to what he knew best.

"*Unkraut vergeht nicht.*" I'm hard to kill.

"*Das weiß ich schon.*" I know that.

Bergmann took the sedan off the Hüttenweg exit and slowed down to a somewhat more prudent speed through the Grunewald forest, although he was still exercising the car's power plant and suspension. It was a good German driving road except for the bicyclists who always seemed to appear in front of your windshield at the least opportune moments.

***

61

The next day, Ewen McKay and Paul Stavros sat across from Landau in the empty conference room. McKay was the older and looked it; the phrase "rode hard and put away wet" came to mind, as he had a Scotsman's view of how to take on life. He was not as tall as Paul, but his mop of white hair and brilliant blue eyes made him seem taller than he actually was. His personality was just as large.

Stavros was nearly as quiet as Landau. Tall and lean, he had played several sports in high school and university, but never mastered one well enough to letter in them. That, and he was not much interested in team sports. His looks came from his parents, both Greek, with curly, dark brown hair and an olive complexion. His nose might have come from one of the statues of the Parthenon, that is if anyone had retained one from antiquity to compare. He was the introvert to Ewen's extrovert.

"We're going for at least two days, maybe three. We leave tonight so you'll have to get your stuff together as soon as we've finished. Apparently, the guys down there have booked us into a hotel, but we'll figure that out when we get there. The S-3 gave me per diem money for a week. We each get an envelope," he said as he tossed them to his comrades. "And yes, you have to sign for it. I have the TDY orders for all of us. We'll meet at the station at 1830. Now go get your Flag Orders and Duty Train reservations from Admin."

"Mysterious, and you're not telling us everything, are you?" McKay said.

"That's right. It's a prerogative of rank, besides I've been sworn to secrecy by the sergeant major. If you want to talk with him, go right ahead."

"I, for one, am fine with trusting you, fearless leader," said Stavros.

McKay, who knew he would get nowhere with Bergmann, had to agree.

***

After they were ushered into a secure, sound-proof office in the Frankfurt Support Facility, Frank Cavanagh came in and introduced himself.

"Call me Frank. This is my operation and we're going to do some interviews to determine if you're what we need for a sensitive tasking. Sergeant Major Bergmann assured me that you are good candidates, so I'll take that as a starting point."

"What's the mission?" said Landau. He wanted to get the ball rolling with what he knew would be an avalanche of questions from Ewen and Paul.

Cavanagh paused for a moment.

"JCS wants two men to go to Tehran as a pilot team to collect target data on the US Embassy and Ministry of Foreign Affairs. I don't know exactly what the Pentagon wants you to do—they'll brief you on that. Our job is to pick two men with the best profile for the mission. You'll get full cover documentation and as much backstopping as we can put together before you go."

"How will we go in and come out?"

"Commercial air. You'll be businessmen, what kind of businessmen exactly we'll figure out once we take a close look at your backgrounds. So who and what are you?"

Landau began, "I'm Hans Landau. I'm native-born German. I don't have any business experience but a lot of time in the jungle being chased by the North Vietnamese Army. And I speak passable English."

"So I've noticed. And you?"

"I'm Ewen McKay from Dundee, but I was brought up in Glasgow. My father owned a tavern and I did a bit of the management. Not much else before I came to the States and joined the service. I speak Scots and Gaelic."

"And helped drink your Pa out of business," said Landau.

"I never! Ma took me away before that happened, I think."

Cavanagh shook his head.

"All right then, and you," he said, motioning to Stavros.

"I'm Paul Stavros. I was born in Chania on the island of Crete and came to the States with my family when I was three. I went to college for a year before I joined the army. That was six years ago."

"No specific education or work skills?"

"I worked for a construction company during summer vacations in high school and I drove a dump truck. Oh, and I worked in a car wash one summer, too."

"Language?"

"I am quite familiar with English, but we spoke Greek at home. I'm fluent."

"I have to say we're a little short on stuff we can use for your covers."

"But you have to look at us as a blank canvas, man. You can do with us what you will." McKay said, his Lowland accent in full gear.

"Like I was saying," Cavanagh said.

Landau had had experience with the Agency in Vietnam and wasn't about to let the comment pass unchallenged.

"We probably have more street experience overseas than most of your people and all the tradecraft training required. Not to mention we were born outside the US of A and that gives us a big advantage over your Ivy-league boys. Besides, how many of them have the right cover to infiltrate Iran?"

"Okay, I'll give you that. Give us a minute to talk this over. Just wait outside in the hallway."

When the three were gone, Cavanagh turned to his two accomplices, who up to that point had been silent, and gave them a look that indicated it was time for them to contribute something to the discussion.

One of them, an older man of apparent Hispanic heritage, looked at his notes for a moment. "If that's all we have, I think Landau and

McKay are the two for the first run. They're older and look a bit more seasoned. Stavros, I think, is a bit young to be a businessman."

"Agreed," the woman said.

***

When Cavanagh delivered the verdict, Stavros was disappointed. He had been perhaps overly confident about his chances, but then he had always been a bit of a dreamer. Hans, he knew to be the best choice, but he thought he could hold his own with McKay on the streets.

That said, McKay could sell refrigerators to Eskimos and then get them to give him free ice cubes for his whisky. Of course, he'd lose all his money back to them in a poker game.

The Marine colonel who had been monitoring the process set his briefcase on the table and pulled out a Government Printing Office manila folder with some official looking documents that had Department of Defense logos printed at the top.

"Okay, one final bit of paperwork. We need you to sign these before you are fully cleared into this program."

He passed out one copy of each document to Landau, Stavros, and McKay. Stavros read his; it was a simple non-disclosure statement threatening him with UCMJ punishment, tar and feathering, and other harsh things if he ever revealed the fact that he'd been interviewed for Project Gold Leaf.

Stavros was stumped by something on the page: "What is Project Gold Leaf?"

"I'm sorry but you are not cleared for that level of information."

"Then how could I talk to anyone about it?"

Landau interjected, "It's what we just went through, Paul."

McKay stopped reading his paper and said, "Wait, this says if we're arrested in Iran that the DoD will disavow us."

65

"That's right, Sergeant. If you accept this mission, the United States will not admit to your status as US soldiers."

"This means we could be shot as spies, right?" McKay said.

"If they catch us, they'll probably shoot us as spies in any event. I recommend we don't get caught," said Landau.

"What a bunch of crap," said McKay.

"Ein Haufen Fotzen," said Landau as he signed. "Paul, aren't you glad you didn't get picked?"

"What is *ein Haufen Fotzen*?" asked the colonel.

"It's a German term of endearment, sir," Landau said. "By the way, we signed the papers with the special disappearing ink pens the Agency gave us."

"What the…?" The colonel was staring at the signatures closely, waiting for them to fade away.

"Time to go, children." Landau walked out into the hall.

Following close behind, McKay, whose knowledge of colloquial German was lacking, asked, "What is a *Fotzen*?"

"Pussy," said Stavros. "He called them a bunch of pussies."

11

Fritz Klausen a.k.a. Major Anatoli Sergeyvich Aleksandrov walked slowly along the darkened path under a moonless, cloudy sky. He had made several turns through the park after a long counter-surveillance run from Bonn that took him by train to Nürnberg where he picked up a car that had been dropped off for him. The drive to Stuttgart was just as uneventful. He had staggered his way across the countryside at a leisurely pace before picking up the *Autobahn* heading west. From there on, it was a fast drive. But he wasn't the fastest, not by a long shot. The BMWs and Mercedes passed him like he was standing still and, if he made the mistake of getting into the left lane, they flashed their lights until he moved out of the way. In Germany, priority on the road went to the driver who paid the most for his car and drove it the fastest. Just after he passed the city of Heilbronn, he left the A6, took to the countryside again and headed south.

When he arrived in Stuttgart, Klausen had left his car well away from the park. He transitioned to walking the streets two hours before the meet time by following a route he had used before to meet his agent, a man known to the "Center" in Moscow as *Vladyka*. This agent had been reporting tidbits of American military intelligence for almost two years since dropping a note inside a

Russian diplomat's car in Bonn to volunteer his services. *Vladyka* later told Klausen he needed the money, not so much for debts, but for the things he wanted. Klausen knew his motivation was sheer vanity, but he couldn't care less what his agent wanted to spend his money on, as long as he produced intelligence. Klausen was not a good enough agent handler to recognize security lapses and vulnerabilities. For the moment, this moment at least, it just didn't matter to him.

Klausen was near the imposing *Schloß* Rosenstein in the lower park when he saw a shadowy shape enter the far end of the green illuminated by the backlight of the city. It walked the path around the edge of the open space toward a bench that served as their meet point. Klausen didn't budge until the shape stopped. He gazed into the darkness at the far edges of the park and swept along the sides trying as best he could to be sure *Vladyka* hadn't been followed. Only then did he move, walking slowly, the shape in front of him taking on a more recognizable form, the rolled-up paper in his left hand, his blondish hair looking washed-out gray in the night. The first thing he did was go through his well-practiced parole.

"Hello, my friend." *Show empathy.* "How have you been?" *Ensure he has no concerns, allay his fears.* "Is everything all right at work? No problems with anyone? No one shows any suspicion of you?" *Plan ahead.* "If we are interrupted, I want you to walk out of the park in that direction." He pointed the way with a nod of his head. *And the plan for the police.* "Remember our story, you were looking for a prostitute and you have no idea who I am. Maybe I was a beggar or a robber. Got it?"

"Yes."

"You're late," Klausen said, getting straight to business. He was not much for coddling his agents: either they produced and were on time or they got cut from the line-up.

"Sorry, there was an unscheduled meeting. I couldn't break free," *Vladyka*, meaning "lord" in Russian, replied.

68

"Next time you must be on time. Now, do you have something for me? You called for this meeting."

"Yes, yes." *Vladyka* struggled with his wool overcoat and pulled out an envelope. He pulled out a separate piece of paper and pressed both into Klausen's outstretched hand.

"Look at this," *Vladyka* said, lighting his Zippo lighter. It flared in the night, illuminating his fleshy, pale pink face, before Klausen swatted it out of his hand.

"Put that out, you idiot!" Klausen hissed. "Do you want us to be seen?"

"I'm sorry, I was excited to show you. This page, it's an emergency notification message."

"What kind of emergency?"

"A 'Broken Arrow.' That means a lost nuclear weapon."

"Who lost a weapon? Where? What happened?"

"One of ours, lost somewhere in Iran, I don't know how. The country codename in the message gives it away." Despite his regal name, *Vladyka* spoke in the clipped sentences of a nervous man in way over his head.

Klausen felt the excitement of a major coup in his hands.

I have to get this back to the Center.

"I want you to find out where exactly it was lost, what kind of weapon, the circumstances of its loss, and what your government is doing about it. Find out quickly. I will meet you here in three days' time." Klausen knew he had no time to lose.

"And my money?" *Vladyka* asked.

"You'll get your usual for this, deposited in your account, of course, but you will get extra if you can find out those answers," Klausen said. "Go now, go find the answers. But next time, make copies, don't take any more original documents!"

Klausen had been thinking that he would advise Directorate S that it was nearly time to cut this fool loose, but his thoughts turned to other possibilities.

A meeting in three days is pushing it but if Vladyka comes through, it could mean something for me—maybe a promotion.

After *Vladyka* disappeared, the small, undistinguished Russian in the dark gray parka walked away and disappeared into the night. He had miles to go before he could sleep.

12

Major Ralph Spurgin poked around the G-3 Plans office looking through the various folders. There were a couple of other officers and sergeants in the spaces, all of them intent on reading files or slowly hunting and pecking on a typewriter. He felt comfortable looking through the operational plans because they all had a nuclear or chemical defense component that touched on his area of expertise. It was up to him to review those plans. It was all very natural for his job. What he couldn't get close to easily was the current operational traffic and that was where he would find what he was looking for, which was anything on the Broken Arrow incident. He knew he would only get called in to work on that issue if there was a possibility of an accident and contamination. Apparently there wasn't a critical danger. Or maybe there was a danger and it was being kept close hold for some reason.

Spurgin pulled the contingency plan for Iranian operations down from the shelf and looked through the table of contents. There wasn't an annex for nuclear operations.

Maybe...

He walked into the Chief of G-3 Plans' office. Anthony Blackwell, the plans chief, was a grizzled old colonel who knew he would never make general despite his numerous combat tours in Korea

71

and Vietnam; he was just too outspoken. But he knew almost every detail of the plans library by heart.

"Colonel, can I speak to you for a moment?"

"Hi Ralph. Yes, what is it?" Blackwell was sociable despite his blunt assessment of Spurgin as a dead-end major with not much of a career ahead of him.

"The Broken Arrow alert that came in last week. Has there been anything further on that? I'm looking through the Iran plan and there's nothing in there for an NBC emergency. Should I be working something up?"

Colonel Blackwell looked at Spurgin, trying to decide how to pigeon hole him. He went with the bare minimum of false information.

"No, don't worry about it. OGA had a training SADM device in country for a joint operation. Because of the uprising, they have to get it out. It's still a classified piece of equipment. Anyway, it's all under control and there's nothing for us to do."

"What is 'Ohgaa?'"

"It stands for 'Other Government Agency,' *the* Agency."

Spurgin may not have been exceptionally intelligent but he knew he was being lied to. A "Broken Arrow" didn't get issued for a training SADM device; it must be a live weapon.

***

Klausen was glad to see that *Vladyka* was on time for once. He came walking from the same direction as the last meeting, toward the same bench they had used before, the same newspaper in his left hand. Klausen moved out of the shadows after he did a quick scan of the perimeter. It was dark but he was sure he had not been followed. He hoped *Vladyka* had followed the procedures he had taught him.

Klausen went through his mad-minute security and emergency action instructions in case they were interrupted. "Got it?" he said.

"Yes, I remember all that," said Ralph Spurgin. He was eager to get this over with and get his reward. He had some large bills to take care of.

"Did you find anything out about the questions I gave you?"

"As much as I could. I need to find out more but it's all very high level and that makes it difficult."

"What did you find?"

"It's actually pretty crazy. The Agency apparently smuggled a SADM device, 'Special Atomic Demolition Munition' they call it, into Iran for some reason." He passed his handler a small envelope. "It's a small tactical nuke. The basic technical specifications are in there. Now, with the *mullahs* in charge and the embassy taken over, everyone's going crazy. They want to get it back desperately."

"I can imagine. How many people know?"

"Only a few, I only got wind of it because I'm NBC emergency officer and I saw the first warning message. All the communications have been put into restricted traffic now."

"What is this NBC?"

"That stands for Nuclear-Biological-Chemical."

"Where is the weapon?"

"It must be somewhere near Tehran. That's all I have been able to find out."

"So my last question was what are they going to do about it? How will they get it back?"

"I don't know."

"Find out and then signal me for a meeting."

"Okay, if I can."

"No, if you want your reward, you have to find out what I want to know."

"But I thought…"

"You have not told me anything more than last time. Find out! Now go."

Vladyka retreated from the park reluctantly, and with a bad feeling about his finances. If he didn't get the money soon, he would have some explaining to do.

Klausen watched him go. He suspected the American would try harder to find the information if he didn't get his reward too easily. When his agent was gone, he turned and headed out of the park in the opposite direction.

The two men who had been watching turned off their night vision devices. They knew something had been passed by a stranger to the man they knew as Klausen. Identifying the stranger would require work. After a few minutes, the surveillance teams on the outside of the park confirmed that they had picked the other man up and were following him discreetly. From the radio chatter, it sounded like they didn't think their new subject was well trained. They were all over him. They let Klausen go; they had followed him to the meeting in the first place and they knew where he lived.

13

The Soviet 3624th Airbase was a long way from Kabul, and KGB Captain Vladimir Aleksandrovich Pankeshev was quite happy to be in Armenia rather than Afghanistan. There were always moments after a mission that you wanted to be away from ground zero. GRU and KGB *Spetsnaz* forces were in the process of consolidating the situation in the Afghan capital city and the consolidation was turning out to be even messier than the *coup de main* his force had been part of last fall. Standing on the edge of the runway smoking a cigarette, Pankeshev looked up into the darkening sky and thought back to that day when he gave his account of the mission to the archivist from headquarters.

***

"Our operation was code-named 'Storm-333' and Special Purpose Directorate's Alpha Group acted as the advance force. Alpha Group had a simple task: infiltrate Taj-Bek Palace and neutralize President Hafizullah Amin. The Soviet Central Committee had decided that Amin had become erratic and needed to be removed from office. The committee tasked the Ministry of Defense to conduct the mission to get rid of Amin and install a new president.

"D-Day was set for 27 December 1979 at 1930 hours. My twenty-five-man 'Thunder' unit led the assault on the palace. It took forty-three minutes to secure the target." *It was the longest forty-three minutes in my life.*

"When the assault began, we climbed the long, steep road to the fortress palace in our armored BMP. It was the only way in. The hillsides were heavily mined and well covered with heavy machine guns. There were at least two thousand Afghan soldiers guarding the place.

"Several of our BMPs were knocked out by the cannons of the T-55s that were dug in on the hill. Some of the men were fighting their way up the hill. Some weren't so lucky and lay dead on the ground. When we finally reached the wall of the palace, the rear doors of our track clanged open and we poured out, alternating one man right, one man left. It didn't matter which way you went, the fire was coming from all directions. You just had to move at full speed and hope you didn't get hit. Voronin was on top of the vehicle, totally exposed to the enemy, firing a BG-15 '*Mukha*' grenade launcher; lobbing 40mm high-explosive projectiles at the Afghan positions on the hill." *Good man, Voronin.*

"Federov and Vasiliev were first into the building. Afghans were tossing grenades at us as we ran in. Most of them exploded behind us, but not all. We had to destroy the command center first. I saw Sedov leap into the entrance hall. He shot to the right, then to the left, and ran down the hall. Then others rushed in. We took cover behind a wall on the first floor. The area was well illuminated and there was shooting coming and going in all directions. It was pure chaos.

"We advanced on the command center and began to toss in grenades. Our orders were 'Don't take prisoners. Don't leave witnesses.'

"We cleared out the center and started moving again, now toward the stairs. I saw one of us—Petrov—wounded, lying at the base of the wide stairs to the second story.

"'What do we do with the wounded?' was one of the questions asked in the pre-mission briefing. There was dead silence and then someone said, 'You need to finish the mission.' No one said that you shouldn't help a comrade but we understood that our main task was to carry on and complete the job.

"We were all in our first engagement and we now were seeing wounded comrades for the first time. We bandaged Petrov and left him. On the first landing, I saw a soldier lying on his back with a huge hole in his forehead; it was Vasiliev. The seriousness of the operation became clear very quickly. I knew we were on the precipice between life and death. I became more focused and reacted to the smallest movement without giving the enemy a chance to shoot me first.

"As I moved up the stairs, I heard a familiar voice shout, 'Forward, men!' It was Colonel Boykov, leading up front as usual. Boykov bounded up and stopped next to me. He was in his favorite flight jacket, wearing a helmet, brandishing his automatic pistol in one hand, looking like a pirate.

"'Upstairs! We need to get up there!'

"And then he was gone, running up the stairs. He disappeared down one of the corridors. I looked around and rushed upward, following him. I ran low, squatting and dodging, like they taught us in training, firing bursts. At that moment, a fireball exploded 5 meters to my right. It was a grenade which had been hurled down from above. It pissed me off, because I'm sure it was one of the ones we gave the Afghan army and there's nothing worse than getting blown up by your own stuff. I distinctly remember that in the fraction of a second I had as I saw the fragments fly toward me, I instinctively rolled into a ball. Shrapnel stung my face, arms, and leg. The blast threw me against the railing. I lay there for a while before two soldiers ran up the stairs to me.

"'Comrade Captain, are you wounded?' one of them asked.

"'I'm fine! Forward, men!' I said." *What a bunch of crap. I was trying to be optimistic, in reality I was scared shitless. We were fighting inside a hornets' nest and the hornets were mad and very well armed.*

"I ran up the stairs all the way to the second floor and into the corridor I had seen Colonel Boykov disappear down. Ahead, Lebedev was firing his assault rifle into the door of an office. Then he ran up, put a grenade into the room, and got back. I hugged the wall. It exploded with a deafening rumble and suddenly the lights went out on the entire floor. Pitch-black darkness, the power had been knocked out.

"*Damn this place is big*, I thought as I ran along the corridor tossing grenades into the open rooms.

"I saw movement across the corridor. There was a burst of fire and I was hit. Some Afghans were shooting through a half-open door. A bullet pierced my obsolete bulletproof vest and, after it bounced around the titanium plates, hit me under my ribs on the side. It felt like a sledgehammer and knocked me off my feet. I landed on my right side and the light went dim, but I didn't lose consciousness. Instinctively, I let loose a long burst in the general direction of the enemy and heard a piercing howl, like someone kicked a dog.

"I tried to get up and I was surprised when I could. Shooting was going on all around me. There was another explosion and pieces of plaster fell from the ceiling, I pushed forward. Then I saw him, Boykov, the leader of our mission. He would become a Hero of the Soviet Union, but that was later, after he was dead. He was wounded and dazed, lying against the wall, his helmet upside down on the tiled hallway floor. I still remember it spinning as it rocked back and forth. He spoke but I couldn't understand what he said.

"I remember thinking, *We have to hide him, he's a colonel, the Afghans will kill him if they find him.*

"We dragged the colonel into a room and pressed on. A fury came over me after I saw the colonel down. A guard appeared from around a corner somewhere ahead. He began to shoot at me point-blank, a burst of about ten to twelve rounds. All the rounds missed me. He stopped, obviously frightened, and looked at me because I wasn't falling. I remember quite plainly his eyes—such dark, almost black eyes. He was very dark-skinned. I was totally surprised and froze for a moment. Then I remembered what I was doing and lifted my weapon and fired half a magazine. The Afghan fell. Dead.

"We found the president and his family in the living quarters. Some of our partner team, troops of the 'Zenith' group, had gotten there first. Amin was there kneeling on the floor, surrounded by three Afghans: Sayed Gulabzoy, Mohammad Watanjar, and another man I didn't recognize. There in front of us, the three talked for a moment and then Gulabzoy pulled out a little pistol and shot Amin once in the back of the head. He fell over and I watched as his blood flowed across the white tile floor. Our mission was finished."

***

Captain Pankeshev closed his eyes for a moment and was happy to be in Armenia; it was calm and quiet. Thoughts of the operation in Kabul still made him anxious, but he could relax here. Every one of his twenty-five men had been wounded in the operation, some severely. Five men from Zenith and Thunder had died, along with Boykov. Pankeshev mourned all of them but none more than the colonel who had trained and inspired them all. Now he was gone.

You were a good man. Farewell, Hero of the Soviet Union.

He smoked the last of his cigarette, letting the smoke curl slowly up into the sky, and then dropped it from his slightly trembling fingers. He ground what was left of the butt into the dirt, the embers sparkling like shooting stars as they blew across the ground in the dusk. He turned and walked slowly but purposefully back to the hut where he and his men were staying. Tomorrow was another day, another mission, but at least this one would be easier. All they had to do was stand by and maybe help a couple of people out. Whatever

79

the mission was, he planned on bringing sixteen men, almost his entire unit minus the ones who were not yet recovered. With two heavily armed MI-24 *Krokodil* attack helicopters flying cover, any real problem could be easily solved.

***

Three days earlier, Pankeshev had been pulled off the line and told that Chaika wanted to see him. Colonel Mikhail Mikhailovich Chaika commanded all KGB forces in Afghanistan and had good connections to just about anyone of consequence in Moscow. You needed to have good connections if you wanted to survive. Chaika did more than survive—he thrived.

Pankeshev was nervous. He knew Boykov, he had trained with him and even drunk some toasts with him. Chaika was an unknown. Pankeshev didn't worry about most things, but he worried about senior officers he knew nothing about. Chaika had arrived in Kabul from Moscow after the coup and took control of Boykov's command. Supposedly he had a lot of experience. There were rumors that during America's war in Vietnam he had led a raid to steal one of their newest helicopters—a so-called "Super Cobra"—from a "secret" American base inside Cambodia. No one would talk about it much though.

And now he wants to speak with me?

Pankeshev walked into the colonel's office, set off in a well-guarded corner of Bagram Airfield, and saluted.

"Captain Pankeshev reporting, sir."

Chaika looked him up and down critically. Then he stood and walked out from behind the desk. "Welcome captain. Relax, I know my summons may have surprised you, no?"

"Yes, Comrade Colonel."

"*Ne bespokoysya kapitan.*" No worries, captain. "I read the after action reports on the Storm operation and your unit was very well mentioned. I understand you tried to save Colonel Boykov during the assault."

"Not save, protect him, sir. We tried to shelter him during the firefight. Sadly, he didn't make it."

"He was a good man, I'll miss him as I'm sure you do. But, we are here to discuss something else. It is a problem outside Afghanistan and I want you and your men to take care of it."

Pankeshev brightened. "A special mission?"

"Exactly. The Americans seem to have run into a problem in Iran. They have an item inside the country that they want to get out before the Iranians can find it and stop them. I have been directed to recover it and bring it to Russia. Some of our people are already inside looking for it, but I am sending you and your men to our closest staging base to the border with Iran and Turkey, which is where they will probably try to take it. You will wait and be prepared to go into country to help our team get the item out. We may have to take it by force."

"If I may?"

"Yes, Captain."

"Why me?"

"What I heard about your actions in Kabul is one reason. The other is probably closer to home for you. I thought you might want a chance to get back at the Americans because of your father. I knew him."

"I did not know that."

Chaika's revelation stunned Pankeshev. His father had been killed in North Vietnam in November 1970. He was a Soviet advisor to the North Vietnamese Army near a village called Son Tay, south of Hanoi. One night, the Americans had launched a big raid on a prisoner of war compound nearby, a place where they believed some of their countrymen were being held. One of the American helicopters landed at the advisors' compound by mistake. When they realized they were in the wrong location, they withdrew. As

81

the helicopter lifted off, the Russian and Chinese advisors who lived there opened fire. Of course, the Americans fired back and their helicopters were armed with mini-guns. The advisors didn't stand a chance, maybe a hundred were killed and another two hundred wounded. His father died the next day. The POW camp didn't even have any prisoners; they had been moved weeks before. He and his mother were devastated.

We didn't even know he was in Vietnam.

Pankeshev stood quietly for a moment before he spoke.

"What is the item, Comrade Colonel?"

"All I can say is it's a technical device of some sort that our engineers very much want to inspect. You will be met and briefed on all the necessary information when you arrive at the base. An aircraft is going to be standing by to take you, so get everything together. You leave in four hours and won't be back here anytime soon."

"Thank you, Comrade Colonel. Thank you for the opportunity."

Pankeshev turned and strode from the office with a grim sense of purpose he hadn't felt in a long time. When he was outside the building, he stopped and pulled a knife from his pocket. It was an old folding knife that his father had given him on one of their last hunting trips together. It was made from an antique Damascus steel blade. He flipped it open and looked at the inscription on the blade; it said simply:

To my son, Dad.

14

It was mid-January and Landau knew he was in the right country when he walked into the arrivals terminal and saw the "students" the intel analysts had told him about. Most of them looked too old to be students but they weren't professional soldiers either. They carried their rifles with either studied indifference or the casual negligence characteristic of most undertrained militias. He suspected it was the latter. Most all of them wore beards—some full, some scraggly, all unkempt—and wore leather jackets or military field jackets. They could have passed for anti-war protestors back home and, having volunteered for and served two tours in Vietnam, Landau had a very low opinion of anti-war protestors, just as he had a low opinion of the "students" he now encountered in Iran. But he was not about to be lulled into a sense of complacency by thinking they were not a credible opponent. He had no illusions about Western military superiority in situations like this. There were just too many of them for one, and they were in control, which made them dangerous by default.

Besides, I don't have a weapon; not yet anyway.

He was also sure that somewhere in the country there was an intelligent group of minds that knew exactly how to manipulate and direct this untrained collective to do what was required, which might include mass martyrdom. He would warn the planners when he returned that they should be prepared for resistance, a good deal of it, if they spent too much time on target.

In preparation for the journey, he had cleaned himself up. He bought a nice German suit made by the same company that designed *Schutzstaffel* uniforms during the last world war and an Italian silk sports coat; he was, after all, an investor looking for someplace to park some good German D-marks to make him and his fellow risk-takers even wealthier. Or so his elevator pitch went, but he was confident. His cover was solid and he had good backstopping. It was all about getting in the door and having good reasons for doing what he needed to do.

McKay was coming in separately; Landau had only himself to worry about for now. He cleared customs and immigration and a couple of revolutionary guard checkpoints manned by kids who just wanted to show they were in charge. But the Iranians didn't hate all Westerners yet, just those from the land of the Great Satan.

If they only knew.

McKay would be a buyer who wanted massive quantities of pistachios for his non-existent distribution network in the United Kingdom. His visit was all about business licenses and export permits. Landau knew McKay would need his prodigious ability to sell that snake oil and survive the gauntlet he was about to enter. He would wear tweed, of course.

On this trip he would only see McKay once or twice, the better to maintain as much of their security as possible. Their return trip would be another story. For the moment, he would concentrate on his mission, reconnoitering the embassy compound and making contact with "Bob" who would be key to their success. Bob wouldn't do the target reconnaissance, but he could acquire the things they needed for the mission.

Landau had chosen the Park Hotel as his base. He wanted to be as far from the journalists and other foreigners as he could and the Park was not where any of the news people wanted to stay. A taxi ride and a quibble over the fare later, he was at the entrance. He carried his own bags from the taxi into the hotel as the porters seemed to have disappeared from the foyer. The interior of the Park was decorated in a typically anodyne style. It was designed so that once you stepped inside, the strangeness of being in a foreign land fell away to be replaced with the reassuring modern sameness, sometimes dullness, that Western businessmen needed. There were dashes of culture, Persian paintings and large bronze pots, arranged around an otherwise sterile reception area that any traveler would recognize as soon as he walked in the door.

At least that had been the case before half the members of the new government moved in while waiting for more permanent accommodation. The hotel had since taken on the controlled bedlam of a caravanserai. The sitting area became a de facto debating stage with some of the couches doubling as overflow beds. It had become the socialization and living area for a bunch of bickering politicians. The only things missing were the camels and goats.

What better place to stay than among the locals.

At least he didn't have to share his room. He was paying in hard currency after all. The room he was given was unremarkable. The bed looked as if its previous occupant had only just left. A photograph of the mountains above the bedstead and a painting of horsemen on the opposite wall were the only decoration, unless peeling paint was included in the description. A plastic chair and a plain wooden desk made up the other furniture, but the towels in the bathroom appeared to be fresh. He had brought his own small bar of soap and wash cloth, something he'd learned to do traveling back and forth across the United States, and set his valise up on a suitcase stand. When he sat down on the bed, its springs squeaked out a protest at first and then the mattress slowly tried to swallow him. A bit too soft, but it would do, he decided.

A mental review was in order. His first task in the city was to visit an international lawyer to establish his presence and reason for being there. Then he planned on looking for "interesting" investment opportunities, which would allow him to openly traverse the city for the next several days without ever committing to a specific agenda. Within that cover, he had many other things to accomplish sub rosa, things that would not be apparent to any observer.

***

The next day, Landau drifted out of the hotel with a portfolio in hand to see an Iranian lawyer someone in Frankfurt had dug up. He spent an hour explaining what he was looking for, talked about investments, and gave the man a retainer so that he would remember his visit if questioned. He doubted he would need to return. Then it was out the door to make his first operational contact.

"Bob" was an old hand at the game. One of the Agency officers had described him as a "veteran," another as one of the "originals." One of the originals seemed more appropriate in Landau's appraisal. He knew Bob had started out as an infantry officer during World War II and had quickly been recruited by the Office of Strategic Services because of his language abilities and experience overseas. His father had been a diplomat and Bob had grown up in a number of European cities before ending up in Beirut where he added Levantine Arabic to his French and Italian. He was a natural and hung on after the war to join the Central Intelligence Group, later moving on to the Agency. Service in more interesting places followed, mostly the Middle East although he did one tour with Partisan Forces Korea, sending agents into the North, many of whom were never heard from again. But there were a few successes. Then it was back to "ME," dealing with whatever crisis was happening at the time. Because Bob had never been to Iran before, and had a passport from a neutral European country, he had been sent in several times since the January 1979 crisis to deal with logistics issues. He was a fixer the Agency used to move things in and out of countries like this quietly and quickly. This mission was one of his biggest. He'd been working on it for over a month.

Landau made his first pass by the embassy compound en route to the meeting, taking a moment to establish a semblance of rapport with the students outside, asking questions, listening to the canned rhetoric denouncing the "Great Satan," and showing a feigned solidarity.

I'll be back.

Bob had chosen his car pick-up site well. After an hour of walking through neighborhoods and markets, Landau turned into a street and saw the car rolling toward him, a gray Mercedes sedan displaying a blue folder on the dash. Landau switched his portfolio to his left hand as he approached the car. It was a safety signal; he could just as well ignore the car if he thought the situation dangerous. The driver's sun visor was pulled up at the last moment and the car came to a stop long enough for Landau to open the door and hop in. Then the car accelerated, turned down the intermediate cross street, and was swallowed up by the city.

"I'm Bob."

"I was hoping you were. I'm Rolf, a business investor. I hear you have a storage facility that might be available to rent."

"A pleasure, Rolf. I do indeed and would like to show it to you."

Bob was as careful about driving as Landau was about his walking. He skillfully used his knowledge of the streets and his mirrors to ensure he wasn't being tailed, but he also didn't show behavior which might attract interest. Be bland and unremarkable—of course, that was why Bob was still alive after thirty-five-plus years of clandestine work. While Bob drove, Landau was doing his best to catalog all the streets and directions as they went through the town. Bob called out major landmarks and cautioned against driving through certain areas. There would not be many chances to learn the route. At one key point, he pointed to an intersection on the map that lay on the center console. There was a black dot next to it.

"We're here. Find this spot and it's an easy shot to the warehouse. Just remember everything I point out as we go."

Bob didn't call out directions or street names, which were either not signed or in Persian script when they were. He used buildings, advertising signs, and shops to indicate specific turns and way points. Landau looked in the mirrors to watch behind him as well as in front. He needed to remember how the route looked, both coming and going.

The area became more industrial, the streets dirtier, the people fewer, and the abandoned vehicles more numerous as they drove. Finally, they turned onto an unpaved street and bounced down the rough road, passing building after building marked with small signs and few windows.

"These are all warehouses or small industrial shops. There's little traffic and not very many folks pass through unless they are going somewhere on this street, and even then no one pays attention. Perfect for your purposes, I think."

He parked the car adjacent to a garage door and got out. Landau followed him to the entrance and looked around while Bob unlocked the front door. It was dark inside. The only window had been covered with plywood and there were steel bars behind that. When the door was shut and secured, Bob hit a switch and the fluorescent lights flickered as their starters warmed up.

"It's pretty secure."

Landau looked deep into the space. It was not too wide, around 15 meters, but it looked to be nearly 30 meters deep. Seven vehicles were parked in the space. There were two up front: another Mercedes sedan, this one pale yellow, almost the color of an old German taxi, which it probably was, and a Volkswagen LT-35 transporter. The transporter was the right size for the MFA team. Behind them were the five Mercedes 508 vans that would be needed to move Delta's ninety-some assaulters. Landau knew them all well as they were the same vehicles the unit used in Berlin.

"How did you find these?"

"They belong to a Turkish front company that we set up a long time ago for moving things in the region. They're all in good running condition. New oil, fully tanked up. The keys are under the floor mats of each one."

"I like them because unlike your Mercedes, they're all nice subdued colors."

"Believe me, the only people who drive dark Mercedes sedans, especially black, are the secret police. I didn't think you wanted to be confused with one of them."

"No, I suppose you're right on that one."

Bob handed Landau two sets of keys. "There's a set for the warehouse doors and the inside locks, and a spare set of keys for the trucks. The sedan has two sets of keys in the console," he said.

"And the other stuff?" Landau asked.

"Back here," Bob said as he walked past the big vans.

In the back was a set of locked cabinets covered with a tarp. Bob pulled off the tarp and unlocked the middle door. He opened it to reveal a kit bag inside and handed Landau the cabinet key.

"That bag has your two PSC-1 TACSATs and two PRC-90 radios plus batteries. There is also a set of maps that cover most of the areas in and around Tehran. Last but not least, you've got three suppressed High Standards and six loaded magazines for each."

"I'm not sure I want to know how you got this stuff into country."

"Let's just say it was courtesy of a friendly embassy who consented to forward our mail."

"Whoever they are, I love them."

"One last thing is inside as well. Very important, so don't lose it."

"What?"

"In the folder with the maps you'll find the equivalent of a hundred thousand US dollars in Belgian francs and two E&E belts, each holding twenty gold sovereigns. It's for contingencies, like if anything bad happens."

"Do I need to sign for it?"

"Why? I didn't."

It was about the only thing Landau liked about the Agency: they didn't mess around with silly stuff like accountability in tight situations. The army probably would have made him sign in triplicate in his true name and get it notarized by an Iranian judge.

He climbed into the front seat of the Mercedes and fired it up as Bob opened the warehouse door. He maneuvered it out onto the street behind Bob's gray sedan.

People might think we are running a taxi company with all these ugly colors.

He went back inside to help Bob close up. After locking up the inside doors, Landau turned to his new, if short-term, partner.

"When are you leaving?"

"I'll take off in two days. There's not much more for me to do here. After I get home, I'll be on standby for anything that comes up. But hopefully, you won't see me in Iran again. How much time do you have?"

"I'm planning on leaving in about a week. Then we come back a couple of days before the action, but we don't know when that will be exactly."

"How many are you?"

"That's still up in the air. Right now, we're just two, but at least one more guy is coming. He's going to meet the four Iranian expats who have been recruited to drive the trucks and he'll lead the main force to the embassy."

"Going with the bare minimums I see. I hope this thing goes well."

"Me too. I'll buy you a beer after this is all over."

"*Inshallah sadiqi.*" God willing, my friend.

Bob turned away and stepped out into the bright sun, closing the front door behind him. There was a dull thump of a car door closing followed by an engine turning over. The gravel on the street crunched as Bob's Mercedes drove slowly away. Landau's gaze turned back to the trucks and he envisioned over 100 men in the warehouse, waiting quietly deep in enemy territory, waiting for the signal to load up and drive out across the city to do their job. He thought about the immenseness of the task that lay ahead. It would be Game Day soon, but there were many things to do first.

***

The following days were filled with what must have seemed like a chaotic schedule to any surveillance team that had reason to follow Landau. But he doubted one was out there. The "student" occupation of the embassy was probably too exciting for the Iranians to even contemplate that the Great Satan's Special Forces operators might be outside the fence clandestinely collecting data—looking for every tidbit of information the satellites couldn't see to help an assault force. On the other hand, Landau was sure the journalists would be interested in what he was doing, so he was avoiding them at all costs.

He continued the same pattern of action he had begun days before. Set up an appointment that required him to pass by the embassy compound or another key point. He preferred to walk the routes; using the car was dicey. For one, the local drivers had no fear and being on the road risked the precious car. He would drive only when absolutely necessary, he decided.

As with the first walk by, he attracted little interest. There were a number of foreign journalists on hand and the students seemed ready to give their practiced condemnations of America and its den of spies. When Landau turned on the small movie camera he had secreted inside a shoulder bag, he was able to walk by several times, once across the street and once next to the perimeter fence, to film the goings on. Another time, a student asked him to take a picture with his friend's camera. Landau obliged then asked if he could take one with his own. The students were happy to pose next to the gate with the locks and chains well in view.

He didn't need to ask questions or elicit information; it was on display for all to see. He didn't take notes; he didn't need to, he would remember. He went through the target analysis formulary several times to get everything needed for the mission—well beyond what the planners in Frankfurt had requested. Happy with his work, he pushed back. He didn't want to burn himself by being greedy.

***

On day four, he went to the Intercontinental Hotel for a drink. It was the headquarters for most of the journalists and had one of the only bars still serving alcohol. The *mullahs'* edicts hadn't been fully enforced yet. It was also Ewen McKay's base of operations.

Thinking about McKay, *mullahs*, and alcohol, Landau didn't have a real comfortable feeling. That said, McKay had his share of good luck.

There were a number of occasions that Landau could think of—and maybe many more kept secret by whichever of the Fates protected McKay—that should have spelled his doom at the hand of the sergeant major. And one other thing bothered him: McKay was almost always in a good mood. That irked Landau who had a visceral certainty that most people did not deserve to be in a good mood all the time. It made him suspicious. Even when given bad news, McKay would laugh it off and head off somewhere to get a beer. That was probably why he didn't mind doing stake-outs on the street dressed as a German workman. There was never a time when a German work crew in Berlin did not have a case of beer standing by. There they would be at ten in the morning, their tools in hand, beer at the ready. When it was break time, they'd all have a nice warm Schultheiß. Landau hated Schultheiß like he hated all *Berliner* beers because they tasted like foul dishwater, which he assumed was because the rumors of formaldehyde being used in the brewing process were true. He much preferred Kölsch or Budvar.

He also worried about McKay's problem-solving ability, which was one facet of why he was so often in trouble—or nearly so, had it not been for his good luck. Going off "half-cocked" did not describe McKay's approach, because that hinted at his not being prepared. McKay generally went around on "full-cock," fully prepared to screw up with a hair trigger. Everyone—well almost everyone—in the unit remembered the infamous "shootout at the OK Corral" as a case in point.

The incident had revolved around an outing, one of those rare events when more than five unit members decided to descend on a bar in the British sector, a bar usually frequented by members of the British Army. Now, soldiers of the British Army have never been known to drink heavily, nor have the men of the unit, so what happened could be written off as an isolated incident. Except McKay was involved and the British soldiers were drinking heavily, as were the Americans. And it went downhill from there.

So when a rather rude British sergeant decided he didn't like McKay's accent, it being from Scotland and all, McKay took umbrage. Rather than challenge the man to a duel or fisticuffs, as has been the time-honored tradition among soldiers, McKay, who was sitting down at a table at the time, pulled his snub-nosed Smith & Wesson .38 caliber revolver from his belt and shot the man.

Two things saved McKay that evening. The music was loud and he failed to take into account the table was hardwood. The bullet was an 80 grain Glaser safety slug designed for people, not wood, and it lodged in the table's hard walnut belly. His teammates, who realised what had just happened and understood the potential implications of shooting a supposed ally, exfiltrated McKay from the bar before he could get a second round off.

His protective Fates also confounded the British soldiers to the fact they had been shot at by somehow muting the report of the pistol. Only a favored few knew the real story, which meant the entire enlisted strength of the unit was aware. Except for his team sergeant and the sergeant major. Had they found out, McKay would have been fed to the officers to be flogged and reassigned, but that never happened.

Landau almost choked on the memory but cast his lot in with inevitability and hoped that the Fates would look out for them just a while longer.

Looking around as he entered the lounge, he saw mostly Westerners. A few locals, perhaps translators or helpers, sat with the newsies. As expected, Ewen was in place inside the lounge at a small table in the corner and, after acquiring himself a drink, Landau walked up to the table.

"May I take a seat with you? It's rather full tonight." He sat before Ewen could even acknowledge his presence.

"How are things with you?" Landau asked after they had reminded each other of their traveler names and exchanged pleasantries.

"I'm doing well. I have found a path through the arcane world of the Iranian government trade regulations." Ewen pulled some official forms out of his briefcase and set them on the table.

"This is what you need to do business in Iran. I picked these up from the Foreign Ministry. I am going back to talk with someone about the pistachio trade tomorrow. Should be enlightening. I do want to buy the best varieties of nuts for my business."

He returned the forms into his case.

"I walked into the MFA and after I got the information, some guy in a suit with a preacher's collar introduced himself as the second deputy minister of whatever. He wanted to know if I'd been well served. He was very helpful and showed me around the ministry's art collection on the first floor. He walked me out to the street and I asked the policemen to take our picture by the front door. Then I took theirs. It was all great fun. Beautiful architecture, by the way."

Landau decided that McKay could indeed BS his way through most anything.

Landau said, "My business here has also been successful. My connections have been expanding and I have some good investment possibilities on all sides of the city. I think everything is well covered and I plan on doing some driving around town tomorrow, maybe sightseeing."

McKay knew exactly what Landau was talking about. They would be able to return to base with a bunch of valuable material.

But they had one more thing to do together.

"Have you looked at our car site?" Landau didn't mention that he had already checked it out. He was also a perfectionist.

"Yes, it's good to go."

"Day after tomorrow, I'll meet you there at 0740. The car is a yellow Mercedes sedan, it looks like an ex-German taxi."

They had set up basic meeting protocols before they left Frankfurt, only the locations had to be verified once they got into country. Picking up McKay would give them the opportunity to make sure they both could accomplish the most critical element of their mission, being able to drive the routes.

Landau decided he'd spent enough time in the fishbowl environment of the Intercon. He stood up to go and gave McKay a brotherly admonition.

"Don't stay too long behind that glass."

"Why? I'm fine and I don't have to walk home. I'm already there."

"Just be careful my friend. I'm sure there are people watching us."

McKay gave an involuntary glance toward the crowd and then came back to meet his comrade's eyes.

"I got it, Hans. Don't worry, I'll be out of here in a bit."

"Rolf. I'm Rolf, remember?"

"Sorry, Rolf."

Landau turned and walked out of the lounge thinking of all the things that could go wrong with the operation. He didn't want poor judgement to be one of them.

***

Landau got up early the next morning and was outside the hotel before the sun had broken the horizon, glad that he had not dulled his senses by staying in the lounge too long. He used all of them along with some simple moves to make sure he was clean before he approached the car, applying the tradecraft he had learned in Berlin as well as his acute ability to sense someone's, anyone's interest in him.

It was in Vietnam when he first realized he had what he heard called precognition or sometimes premonition; maybe it was just plain old intuition, but it was a feeling he got when danger was near. He first felt it when he was with the infantry, a feeling that always came before contact with the enemy or just before a sniper fired a round.

He became fully aware of his ability when he and his Ranger buddies were in downtown Saigon one night. A certain little cafe bar was a favorite of GIs. The waitresses were nice for the most part, meaning they didn't try to rip you off too much, and they were easy on the eye. But when one of Landau's squad wanted to go there, he felt uneasy about the place. Something warned him off and he said so. By that time, his close comrades knew to trust him. Others said he was paranoid, but his buddies knew better. An hour later a kid on the back of a motorbike tossed a satchel charge onto the patio. The blast killed four GIs and a Vietnamese woman, and wounded many more.

In the jungle, Landau developed his skills even further, focusing on being in the moment, sensing when the enemy was nearby. It is said that hunters and snipers often mentally telegraph their intent to the animals and men they intend to kill. Landau listened to those signals and learned what they meant—or perhaps it was instinct; anyway, it was his sixth sense, and it kept him alive. Always being in the present was fine with him, there were too many things in his past he did not wish to revisit and even fewer things in the future that interested him, especially if he was not going to be alive to enjoy them. Whatever the future had waiting for him, it would be there when he arrived.

Landau had left the car on a side street that had no parking restrictions. This evening it would be parked elsewhere. He surveyed the area and the car quickly as he approached, looking for any signs of disturbance and saw nothing. The door creaked open, evidence of its long, hard life, as he slid in and started the engine. He took a moment to survey in front and to the rear before he drove off away from the curb. He appeared slow, deliberate and methodical, but there was one thing about him that was in constant motion: his eyes. He was always looking around him, a habit disconcerting to people he talked with, because he often looked not at the person, but at what was happening around them. It kept him out of trouble.

He headed south, then east, then south again. Slowly, carefully he followed the route he had memorized off the map. Nearing the edge of town he headed into the neighborhoods away from the main roads and picked his way through many nameless streets and closely packed buildings and homes. Freshly washed, dingy clothing hung from the windows and balconies of many apartments, while carts, old cars and trucks filled the road, requiring several switchbacks before he came out on the far side. Before him was open terrain. Several small roads led off into the distance and he picked the best one and followed it until it intersected the main highway heading to the southeast. He was well beyond the city limits and he knew the probability of encountering a police checkpoint dropped off commensurately. He drove onward, clocking off the kilometers until he saw the side road he was looking for and turned onto it.

Thirty-five minutes elapsed.

Then it was sixty-five minutes, and finally an hour and forty minutes from the time he had turned onto the main road. This smaller road traced a path around the base of a hill in front of him. It was more of a plateau, flat on top. An old track led up the hill. He stopped the car, got out and stood looking around him for several minutes.

The next hour would confirm what he needed to know and what the planners wanted to know. They had looked at hundreds of square kilometers of terrain on maps and satellite photographs with their magnifying glasses and stereoscopes to choose this location.

He walked up the path, a 35-degree incline that was not too rocky or difficult to climb. It would be interesting walking down carrying rucksacks, weapons, ladders, and other equipment at night. Climbing over the ridge at the top, he saw what almost looked like a caldera but it was too shallow. It was also empty, not a sign of human activity anywhere. Several hundred meters across, he knew it would host up to ten helicopters. It would be sufficient. This was to be the *laager* site, Desert Two.

He trotted down the hillside to his car and headed home, logging the waypoints, the landmarks, and kilometers into his head as he drove. He would have to explain the route to McKay and the drivers who would drive the route out of town and back for the mission.

***

McKay was at the CPU site at the correct time the next day. Signals in both directions were seen and registered before he grabbed the door handle and injected himself into the car. There was silence for the first minutes as Landau watched for any interest behind him. There was none.

"How'd the route check out?"

"It's easy. I'll be able to put it down on a map when we get home. I have all the mileage numbers in my investment notes and everything else will be on the imagery."

For all intents, they were partners. Not because they were friends or comrades, but because the sergeant major and fate had made it so. McKay, on one hand, was indifferent to working with Landau. Landau was his assigned partner and that was all he needed to know. McKay was content to be part of the pack; he followed his team sergeant's guidance and played well with his team mates. Landau, on the other, was a solitary operator and he was good at being a singleton. He could work with others but he was constantly assessing and evaluating everyone he worked with. It wasn't because he felt superior but because he needed to know what his teammates would do in any given situation. He wanted to survive. Landau was a leopard, wary and self-isolated, an operator attuned to the streets and the convoluted ways of gypsies and policemen alike.

With the exception of the route from the *laager* to the warehouse, they drove every road and the alternates they planned to use for the mission at least once. McKay had been limited to either walking or taking a taxi, so he didn't have a feel for driving on the street. Landau handled that part. McKay gave directions to Mashq Square around the corner from the MFA, their staging area on the night of the assault. Then they drove from the MFA to the embassy. And, just in case, they drove from the MFA to Mehrabad Airport.

Always have a back-up plan. And a back-up to the back-up.

Landau dropped McKay a ways out from his hotel and let him walk back to his room. If anyone asked, they were two businessmen who were discussing mutual investment opportunities while sight-seeing. They had even taken exterior photos of several museums and gardens they had visited—which just happened to flank the MFA complex.

But it was better if no one had a reason to ask questions.

Landau was ready to get out of this middle-eastern version of a Dodge City. He had been on edge for the entire time he'd been in Tehran, not to the point of triggering his "danger close" sense, but his nerves had been stretched tight nevertheless. On one hand, the edge was good—it kept him focused—but it drained his body and mind of energy. It would be good to get out, decompress, and retool for the return trip just before Game Day, whenever the hell that might be.

***

The taxi ride to the airport was followed by the usual involuntary tensing of muscles, pounding heart, and anxiety while waiting in the passport control lines. There seemed to be more checkpoints going out than he had encountered coming in. Landau put on his best demeanor. He was who his documents said he was and, despite his desire to extinguish all the "revolutionaries" in the airport, he played nice, smiled and joked with them. Only one customs officer balked at the several sheets of Iranian stamps Landau had collected. The stamps had the hated Shah's image on them.

"Why do you have these?" he asked.

"I thought they'd be worth money after he was hung."

The customs officer was delighted and told his comrades who laughed. It was a fine joke and Landau was their new friend. No one looked deeper into his suitcase.

When he was finally settled into business class on the airplane, he waited and only relaxed when the airplane lifted off the runway. It was time for a Cognac, a large one at that or maybe two, but then who was counting?

First Zurich, followed by Frankfurt, and then it was debriefing time. McKay and Landau gave their obligatory renditions of how each got into country, what they saw at the airport and the kind of things that made the Agency happy, while the military was hungry for the details a Farm-trained case officer never looked for, or even thought about.

"What kind of locks? No, who *made* the locks? What kind of rifles do they carry? How many? Are they loaded? Are they in uniform? Where are the police? The military?"

Details on the enemy, details on the friendlies, details on the city.

"How long does it take to drive from there to there? How wide is the street? Where are the power lines? What is the gradient of the hill at the *laager*? How much fuel do you have for the trucks?"

Details. Everyone wanted details, for the strength of an operations plan is in its details. Plans are the life blood of staff officers. Of course, when the first round goes off—as stated concisely in Murphy's Law—the plan goes out the window. But first, you must have a plan. The more detailed and complex the better. Then you can throw it away and make stuff up.

McKay and Landau played the audience like virtuosos, with numbers and sketches, bits of data, maps with lines and arrows, but saved the best for last. First the films of the embassy compound and the MFA from the street; then the photos of the gate, the doors, inside the MFA building.

"But taking photos inside the embassy compound did seem a bit risky," Landau said.

At the end, the staff officers sat back. The planners from Delta sat back. The general sat back.

"This is almost like cheating. You've given us very useful information. Thank you."

Jelinek and Bergmann sat back, a satisfied "I told you so" look in their eyes.

"But we still have to go back and you need to get there to finish this thing," said Landau, deflating everyone's mood.

***

Two more men joined the debriefing: one named Rich Fields and a young man known only as "George." Fields was former MACV-SOG, an army major who was on the Son Tay raid in 1970. Landau knew *of* Fields. He had a good rep as a hard-charging field soldier. He had retired a few years earlier and Beckwith had asked him to come back to work as a civilian consultant with the "Big D." It was a good deal for both Delta and Fields. "George," however, was an anomaly. An enlisted air force technician who spoke Persian by virtue of being one, he was an expat who had joined up after coming to the States with his family only a few years before. He had volunteered and would be Fields' translator and assistant. Totally untrained in any kind of fieldcraft or tradecraft, he was either the bravest or craziest member of the Joint Task Force.

He said, "I need to do this for my adopted country."

The four men became Team "Esquire." When the mission went down, they would be at the *laager* to bring the troops into the warehouse and then split into two teams. Fields and George would go to the embassy with Delta; Landau and McKay to the MFA with their fellow *Berliners*. They were the guides, and they would get the assault force to the targets.

Landau thought they should have a name for their tour company.

Maybe we'll call it Esquire Excursions. He practiced his delivery in his mind, *On your right, you'll see the national museum…*

15

"MISSION: Joint Task Force conducts Operations to rescue US personnel held hostage in the American Embassy Compound, Tehran, Iran."

"That's it?"

"That's all. The mission statement is simple and to the point. The actual operation will be another story. Our task is to get the three men out of the Foreign Ministry. We'll launch from Saudi with Delta by MC-130 to a forward refueling point inside Iran called Desert One. The helicopters will meet us there and fly us onward to Desert Two, what we are calling the *laager* site, on the same night. When we get there, we meet our advance team and they'll move us by truck to a hide site at a warehouse in the south of the city. The next night we split off and conduct the assault on the MFA, grab our folks, and get the hell out."

"Simple it is not."

"No, not at all simple. Delta is at ninety-two men, but they have fifty-two people to get out. We are all restricted—because White House forced the mission planners to cut this thing to the bone. I'll go as the MFA element commander. Charlie is leading his embassy element in and I don't want him messing with our people. An air force colonel will be in command until we leave Desert One."

"It's all too complicated. Too many variables that can go wrong."

"It is what it is, Jeff. I want you to put together the team, the other eight. A team sergeant who has good experience and seven steady operators."

"I have some men in mind."

"We've also been tasked to have one team on standby as an Escape and Evasion recovery team. They'll be forward based in Turkey. 10th Group is going to field four of its teams as well for E&E support."

"Do we have a name for the mission?"

"Right now, they call it 'Operation *Rice Bowl*' but that's just for planning. We'll have to come up with something a bit more aggressive when the time comes."

Bergmann could think of quite a few good code names he remembered from the old days.

Too bad they're all in German.

***

Master Sergeants Jock Sheldon and Kim Becker stood before the sergeant major's door.

"I think it's decision time," Sheldon said as they walked in.

Bergmann was standing to the side of his desk looking at the world map. Next to him was Colonel Jelinek pointing at the Saudi peninsula. They turned to face the two team sergeants and Bergmann spoke.

"The colonel has decided and this is the way it's going to be, gentlemen. Both your teams are ready for this mission, but we have only room for nine men. Some of your guys will be disappointed, but the team not chosen will be forward based during the operation for E&E support if needed."

"I hate being second." Both Becker and Sheldon agreed on that. One team was going to get the mission of a lifetime, while the other would be condemned to wait at the firehouse for something bad to happen.

"Now, these are the folks that will go: Team 2, that's you Sheldon, along with Ritter, Pavlovich, O'Brian, Sam, Holden, and Adler. And Jock, because you're short an engineer, I'm going to borrow Fitzpatrick from Kim and loan him to you. Team 5 gets to cover the E&E contingency out of Turkey. It was a difficult decision, but the main reason I chose Jock's team is because one of his guys, Landau, is already committed and leading the reception team in country. The other is that Sam speaks the language."

Sheldon, who was concentrating on the names and his fingers, looked up.

"Wait, that's only eight men," he said.

"I am number nine. I am taking you in," Jelinek said.

Sheldon and Becker looked each other. Leading an eight-man squad wasn't normal for a full colonel, but Jelinek was going to be out front.

Becker was deeply disappointed but accepted that for once language skills weren't going to tip the scale and, all things being equal, the two teams were the best prepared in the unit.

"Kim, your team will work on the train-up with Team 2. If Sheldon loses anyone before we commit, you will provide a replacement."

***

The unit conference room had once again been converted into a mission planning room. A big target model of the Ministry of Foreign Affairs building sat on two tables that had been pulled together. It was the product of a special shop back in the States that made everything from tiny model replicas of Soviet tanks to complete cities in small scale. There was a similar model sitting on top of an even bigger table back in the States. It was of the embassy compound and it was being studied by members of Delta in the same way. On another table were maps and high-res satellite photos that were so clear, the registration plates on the cars out front were almost readable. Everyone's attention had been glued to the model but the sergeant major had it now.

"Okay, you guys have been working on this for a while. What's the plan?"

Sheldon spoke. "On the first night, we get picked up by the reception team at the *laager* and are moved to the warehouse by truck. We lie low all day and launch into the city just after sunset, which is 1945 hours. We will move in a closed van to the MFA and stop at the corner of the building. Two of us will get out and approach the police post near that entrance to ask directions. According to McKay's intelligence, there are always three policemen on duty. We'll take them out with suppressed weapons and get the gate open. At the same time, the rest of the team, minus Landau and McKay who stay with the vehicle, will rush the entrance and enter the building. As far as we know, there are only two security guys inside the building so we don't expect much resistance, but we'll be prepared for more. The three hostages are on the third floor in the ministry's formal dining room, so we will clear and hold the stairwell all the way up, grab them and return to the van. After that it's a fifteen-minute drive to meet Delta at the soccer stadium exfiltration point."

"Simple."

"Not really, we still are figuring out the contingencies for what happens if things don't go according to plan. What happens if the warehouse is compromised? What if the truck breaks down? What if we can't make the link-up with the helicopters? We may just have to make the run from the MFA to Mehrabad Airport and link up with the Rangers who have secured the airport for the exfiltration aircraft—the C-141s. It's actually almost as close as going the other direction to the soccer stadium where Delta will be picked up by the helos."

"Maybe as close distance-wise, but probably more security controls."

"It's hard to say. Once Delta goes over the wall at the embassy compound, I expect a lot of Iranians will be headed in their direction to see what's going on. Our little side-show at the MFA should be a whole lot quieter and we'd be heading in the opposite direction."

"Sounds like you have Plan A and Plan B then. Maybe another option would be to head for the coast where you can steal a *dhow* and sail across the Persian Gulf," Bergmann said.

"That's 800-some kilometers, we'd be better off heading for Turkey. That's where most of our E&E pick-up points are anyway," Sheldon said.

"True, but remember you better have one more plan than you actually think you need, maybe two."

"I hear Kazakhstan is nice this time of year," said Pavlovich.

"Too many Russians," said someone in the back.

16

Military Intelligence Colonel Harry Pennington looked up to see his counterespionage chief knocking on his office door.

"Come in, Frank."

Major Frank Wallace strode in to the office with a note in his hand. He was agitated. Pennington couldn't tell if he was excited or angered. Maybe both.

"What's up?"

"Our *Verfassungsschutz* friends sent us a security notification. They were surveilling a clandestine meeting of a suspected Soviet agent and identified another guy that he met with. At least they got his automobile license plate."

"And how does this concern us?"

"The car had private US Forces Europe registration plates."

"Has it been run yet?"

"Yes, I just got the trace back. It belongs to a Ralph Spurgin. He's a staff officer in G-3 Plans, a 74 Alpha, a Chem-Bio specialist."

"Damn, what else did the Germans give us? Anything we can use to positively connect him with the Russian?"

"No, but they got a photograph of the subject getting into his car," Wallace said as he offered the paper he held. "It's dark, but it matches Spurgin fairly well."

Pennington stood up and stretched. It was his way of changing gears mentally. Moments before, he'd been looking over intelligence requirements from the Defense Intelligence Agency that basically asked for everything from the main gun caliber of the latest Soviet tank to the number of condoms shipped to the Group of Soviet Forces Germany. Some poor fool in Washington had to assign each requirement with a number and list them in a six-hundred-page directive that was more an albatross than an aid to his collectors.

His gray-streaked hair was starting to evidence the stress he felt being the commander of the brigade. Thoughts of retirement were starting to intrude into his thinking process, at least until the excitement of an actual operation popped up. It kept him going for another week or so.

"We can't move on 'matches fairly well.' We need substantive proof that he's done something. But for the moment, we can mount an investigation. Get his background data and take an especially hard look at his finances. Set up full coverage on him at work, at his home, and wherever the hell he goes at night. We are going to need to bring in other assets to cover this and I'll inform the commander and FBI legal attaché. I'll talk to the G-3 and coordinate everything. If this turns out to be true, we are going to nail this guy to the cross," Pennington said.

"How about notifying the Agency?"

"Not just no, but hell no. When do they ever share with us?"

17

The teams standing in front of Colonel Jelinek had been told by the man codenamed "Heavyweight 51" to bring the bare minimum of assault gear. Assembled on the edge of the field, they were dressed in olive-drab coveralls with submachine guns and pistols as their only weapons. The sky had gone dark as the operations officer laid down beacon lights in the field in front of the men. Jelinek's words caught them off guard.

"Gentlemen, tonight, we are going to practice the MFA takedown. We have already practiced in small elements at 'Doughboy City,' but tonight we'll do it all together. The next time we have a chance might be for real. To avoid traffic in the city we'll be moving by helicopter and the birds should be inbound about now. Break up into your designated elements for loading. Once we get to the target at Doughboy, we'll run through the operation twice, once for the primary team, once for the back-up team. Let's get ready."

The dull thumping of the Hueys' rotors was becoming louder as they approached the field. As everyone looked toward the sound, they could barely see the flashing red marker lights of the three-ship formation flying low over the forest.

Twenty minutes before, it was just growing dark when three UH-1H helicopters took off from Tempelhof Airfield, circled it once and headed west. To anyone watching on either side of the Wall, the sight and the noise were unusual. Rarely did the US Army Berlin Aviation Detachment launch a helo at night, and it was even rarer when it launched three of its six helicopters at the same time. The only nod to air safety regulations was that the aircraft kept their marker lights lit over the city.

It was a short flight from the airfield to the landing zone inside Rose Range in the southwestern corner of West Berlin. A strobe and three dim lights marked the corners of the area inside which the helos would land.

The first two ships settled onto the ground. Two groups of men ran forward, each splitting into two smaller elements as they streamed around the noses of the birds to avoid the man-killer tail rotor and climbed into the cargo compartment. When full, they lifted off and began to circle about a kilometer away. One more bird came in and picked up the command group. It lifted off and joined the others in trail.

Together, the air element flew east toward the landing zone, an open area on the edge of a grouping of tall, empty concrete structures. It was the Berlin Brigade's combat in cities training area and the field on its southern edge was the ideal landing spot for the helos. About one kilometer south of the LZ was the Berlin Wall, which snaked around the city with its looming guard towers that stood as silent sentinels and warned East Germans to stay away under the penalty of death.

The birds did a fishhook and turned on a short final approach, lined up and descended quickly over the field. They came in hot—there was no hover or maneuver—they flew in fast and hit the ground hard, sliding forward on the dirt as they slowed to a stop. The men bailed out of the birds and ran, some toward the buildings while two small groups moved toward either end of a road to set up security points. The rotors on the birds kept turning, waiting for their cargo to return.

Sheldon's Team 2 recovery element stopped on the edge of the gravel road in front of a five-story building as if they'd just arrived from inside a truck instead of a helo. With a silent command, two men moved forward and approached a barrier fence set up with three mannequins to simulate the normal security element. With a map in hand to cover the suppressed weapon he had at the ready, the first man walked up to the closest "guard" and shot the mannequin three times. His partner pulled his pistol and helped him finish the task.

The three others of the assault team moved quickly to the entrance. The designated breacher attached an explosive charge to the door handle while his comrades found cover behind a corner wall. He connected the wires to a M57 "clacker" he pulled from his pocket, a firing device originally used with claymore mines that had been adapted to its new purpose. He stepped behind the wall and looked at the team leader who gave him a thumbs up.

He squeezed the handle and, with a bright flash and a dull bang, the door splintered into pieces and disappeared in a puff of smoke while the door handle went flying, pinging and bouncing off the concrete. The team stepped out from their cover and entered the building, racing up the stairs, clearing the way ahead with their weapons at the ready. Just as Chargé Long and his partners had reported from their confinement in Tehran, there were no guards. There was no opposition.

On the third floor, another closed door was encountered. This one was opened with a heavy rubber sledge hammer that substituted for a key. Flashlights attached to their weapons illuminated the way as the team rushed into the room. There they found three men sitting on the cots, trying to shield their eyes from the glare. The team leader came forward and identified each of the three as they were handcuffed and hustled out the door and back down the stairs. They burst out the door on the ground floor level and ran with their "precious cargo" to the first helo and loaded them on board.

The recovery element leader reported to the force commander, "Heavyweight, this is Bandit One. Bingo, I say again, Bingo."

The force commander took the cue. "All teams, this is Heavyweight 51, execute Angel Flight, I say again, execute Angel Flight." The two-man security teams folded back in on the helo, loading in well-practiced order.

After a short break to reset the scenario, Team 5, the back-up element, practiced the takedown. The entire session took less than forty minutes.

After the helicopters departed, a quiet fell over the area. The East German guards in their towers next to the Wall had no idea what had just happened on the other side. All they saw and heard were dark shadows flying by and two explosions. They reported their confusion to the sector command but by the time an officer reached the area, it had turned quiet once more.

Heavyweight 51 was pleased. Even with no previous nighttime rehearsals, the first practice run was close to perfect, a function of all the preparations done by each team. They couldn't do a second run in any event; their security profile was already elevated. Instead, they would wait for the order to deploy forward to some as yet unknown base. There, training and rehearsals could continue in a more secure environment.

***

Back at the building, the teams cleaned up their gear and prepared to go home for the night. Becker walked into the team room.

"You all did well tonight. One way or the other, this is going to be a good mission. That is, if it actually comes off. Now get the hell out of here. We can finish cleaning up in the morning. First formation is 1000."

Everyone did their best to stuff the gear into their lockers and scramble out of the team room as fast as they could.

"Paul, I almost forgot," Becker said, "the sergeant major wants to see you. He didn't tell me why, so don't ask."

Paul got out of the room before anyone could say anything stupid and walked down to the sergeant major's office, wondering what his team sergeant hadn't told him. He knocked on door frame and announced himself.

"Come in, Paul," Sergeant Major Bergmann said.

Paul stood in front of the desk and waited for the man to finish reading a file. Finally Bergmann looked up and clasped his hands together.

"How's your leg?"

"It's fine, Sergeant Major. It only hurts when it rains."

He was lying, of course. Despite the doctor's assurances he wouldn't feel them, two steel rods in his tibia and fibula constantly reminded him they were there with a dull, cold ache.

Bergmann seemed to smell his pain. "Well, next time remember: feet and knees together."

"I am trying, Sergeant Major. I've done six jumps since, seems to be working."

"Good. And that friend of yours? Sarah?"

"She's doing well. We're okay, but she's getting ready to PCS back to the States and attend the operations course at the Farm, thanks to your intervention."

"Ah, don't worry about her, Paul. You two will be okay one way or the other. But I have something for you right now. It seems the Agency folks have not been entirely candid with us. They left an item in Tehran and one of their officers is babysitting it somewhere outside the embassy. It's a very sensitive piece of equipment and we need someone to go in and link up with the Agency guy. That will be you."

"Damn, Sergeant Major. It seems like we've had to help the Agency guys out a lot lately."

"This time it's only because there really is no other choice. The rescue mission is the only viable option to get their man and the package out of country."

"Thanks for your confidence in me, but can't Landau or McKay handle meeting him? It's not that I don't want to go, I was just wondering."

"No, those two have enough on their plates with their reconnaissance tasking. You'll have to go in, find the guy at his safe house in the north of the city, and then get him and the equipment to the MFA when the raid goes off, that's all. Then our team will take you both with them to the exfiltration point."

"No small task."

"No, but I'm sure you can handle it."

"And the Agency folks are happy with me going? They seemed to think I was too young for the businessman cover."

"They're fine with it now. Besides, I told them you're the man to handle the job."

"I hope so."

"Don't hope, you have the background, the training, and the street sense. First thing tomorrow, go and see Admin to arrange travel to Frankfurt. You're going back to the same Agency place as before and they are preparing your documentation. They will give you all the details on their guy and the item down there."

"What's the item? Why is it so important?"

"Have you heard of Green Light?"

"Only whispers, Sergeant Major."

"First, do not discuss this with anyone but Landau. Got it?"

"Roger, Sergeant Major."

"Green Light is the code name for SADM, the trash can nuke."

"Jesus, we have to get a nuke out?"

"Yes, it's almost as important as the hostages. If the Iranians find it first, it might go off in the States."

"Great," said Paul without conviction. "Can I take back my thanks, Sergeant Major?"

"Ha! You'll do fine. *Jetzt hau ab und gute Reise.*" Now get lost and have a good trip.

Paul was elated.

I'm in.

18

The plane landed at the airport called Eleftherios Venizelos east of Athens and Paul Stavros passed through customs and immigration easily. A long, 30-kilometer taxi ride took him to the Psirri section of the capital and his hotel, the Euripides. Some sightseeing would have been on his list as it was his first time back in Greece in a number of years, but he didn't have much time.

The first thing was to get his travel documents in order and that required a meeting. After he settled into his room and scoured his belongings once again for anything that could compromise his status, he placed his passport and wallet into a small pouch and left the hotel. He decided to walk the distance as it wasn't far to his destination, the Bakaliarakia o Damigos, an old, very old, taverna in the Plaka. The citadel of the Acropolis towered above him and the narrow streets were crowded with tourists and locals alike. It was a rabbit warren of streets and alleys and, had he been worried about surveillance, it was an easy place to detect the opposition.

In Frankfurt, Cavanagh had told him not to worry about a hostile service—the Greeks were firmly in the pro-America camp this year and the Iranians didn't have a strong presence. Besides, he had not even told the Iranians of his interest in traveling. That would come soon enough.

That said, he watched his back well enough that he knew he was clean when he entered Kidathineon Street and took the stairs down into the restaurant. It was what some might describe as cozy; others would call it homey or plain. The old walls were painted white with an odd hanging collection of framed photographs and poetry, a guitar, and a couple of *Kariophili* flintlock muskets and pistols. An ancient marble column stood in the center of the room holding up the ceiling like an Atlas turned to stone. Stavros decided it was an eclectic place.

His contact, as arranged, was already seated at a table. He had a rather garish blood-red jacket thrown over his shoulders. He was a big man gone somewhat to seed in his early fifties. He looked Greek, but Stavros would soon learn from his life story that he preferred being called Macedonian, inferring something about vague family connections to a royal father and son duo by the name of Philip and Alexander, a tenuous two-thousand-year genealogical leap that Stavros didn't even try to question. The man may have imbibed too much ouzo from the look of the nearly empty tumbler in front of him. There was only a small puddle of milky liquid left in the glass. They ordered dinner.

He called himself Demitri and Stavros went with that. He was an odd character, with a bushy unkempt moustache, a deep voice, and olive-green eyes that were sad even when he told a joke. Demitri casually looked about him to make sure no one was watching and pushed a leather pouch over to him in the middle of dinner as he mentioned the owner was a friend of his. Stavros wasn't sure if that meant the owner was a friend of the Station or really Demitri's personal friend, but decided it was the latter when he swung by and exchanged a joke with them, and also dropped a third carafe of retsina onto the table without having been asked.

Demitri explained that the passport that had been fabricated for Stavros in Frankfurt was in the pouch along with a newly minted international driver's license, national ID card, and a scattering of pocket litter he could either take or leave. Stavros planned on acquiring more in any event, as he would be making some stops around town over the next days, including a visit to the company that was providing his very thin cover for doing business in Iran. His own small pouch was passed over to Demetri, whereupon Stavros assumed his new identity. Since they were already speaking Greek, no one noticed.

As he dipped a piece of his deep fried cod into the skorthalia on the plate, Stavros absorbed Demetri's rendition of recent Athenian political and social gossip. He got a chance to wedge in an explanation of his own origins from the island of Crete. At least half of him came from Crete, but he didn't mention that the other half was from the Peloponnese, knowing the possibilities of a conflict between a Spartan and a Macedonian, although he was sure he could kill Demitri if he needed to. Stavros knew he had a long night of drinking ahead but was happy that tomorrow was mostly an open day and he could sleep in a bit.

**

One task down, Stavros visited his cover business the next day. One of his Agency handlers in Frankfurt had opposed his suggestion of carpet buyer as an occupation until Stavros baffled the man with an extemporaneous exposition on tribal rugs. He had, after all, traveled extensively in the Persian Empire, if only through his reading of *One Thousand and One Nights*.

The next task was more onerous but necessary above all the others: a visit to the Iranian Embassy. He presented himself two days after his arrival wearing his new, but well-practiced persona of Greek citizen, a purveyor of fine carpets entrusted by his employer to travel to the markets of Iran, and politely asked for a visa to visit.

The Iranian consular official behind the glass looked his passport and Stavros over thoroughly while checking off each line of the official application and then made sure the two photos were of the proper size and orientation.

"Where were you born?"

"Chania on the island of Crete."

"When?"

Stavros recited his own birthdate, the one the expert suggested he use for the passport. "It's easy to remember when you're under pressure," the Agency guy had said.

After five minutes of silent examination, the official finally smiled with what looked more like a scowl and told him it would only be a short wait and to take a seat.

There were only three chairs in the room and two were occupied by what looked like an elderly married couple who had brought most of their worldly possessions with them in cheap plastic tote bags. Stavros took the remaining chair and promptly began to meditate with his eyes closed. An hour went by and the elderly couple went to the window and took care of whatever paperwork they needed and left. The clerk looked at Stavros and left. It was eerily quiet in the room and getting close to lunchtime. Stavros suspected he had been forgotten and decided it was time for the squeaky wheel routine. He rang the bell at the window until the clerk came back.

"Yes?" he said. He seemed to have no recollection that Stavros had been there before.

Stavros knew it was time for a convincing argument and flashed his wallet with some bills conspicuously visible.

"It's been an hour and a half since I dropped off my application. Your sign says you close for lunch from noon until three in the afternoon. That's ten minutes from now. I can't wait here for another three hours for someone to finish my paperwork!"

The clerk mumbled what could have been an apology or an epithet and left his booth. Another ten minutes went by until he came back with the passport.

"The consul left for lunch and forgot to put your passport in the finished box. I found it for you." He gave the excuse as if Stavros owed him a debt of gratitude.

It made Stavros wonder if they were trying to check his cover story, but then he always was paranoid.

Stavros leafed through the document and read the visa. Valid for one year with multiple entries permitted. He looked up at the leering official. *I guess I better say something nice.*

"*Sas efcharistó*," he said as he dropped a one-hundred drachma note through the slot—he tipped more for a cup of coffee—and left the building.

Later in the day, he called the telephone number Demitri had given him. He spoke the short parole they had agreed upon.

"I have the visa and will depart on time."

***

"Olympic Airlines flight to Tehran is now boarding."

Stavros had finished his greasy souvlaki at the airport grill and waited for an hour for the announcement. He wasn't sure if eating had been a good idea as his stomach was feeling uneasy. This was his first undercover deployment into a hostile country, trips into East Germany notwithstanding, and the implications of failure were as ominous as anything he could imagine.

The Ossies generally don't hang spies.

He settled into the business-class seat and was grateful the military wasn't paying for the ticket. If they had, he'd be sitting in the back in a non-reclining seat next to the toilet.

At least the Agency treat their people right.

Shortly after takeoff, Stavros did what most soldiers did when faced with three and a half hours of enforced monotony: he took a nap.

He woke up when the stewardess nudged his shoulder a couple of hours later.

"Snack, coffee, cocktail?" she asked.

"I'm fine, thank you." His thoughts turned to meeting Jonny Panagasos. He had to find the Agency man somewhere in a city he did not know without compromising the man, the safe house, or the reason he was there. He had a photo, an address, and a telephone number, all of which he had committed to his memory, and a few simple written clues that passed for a carpet buyer's notes.

As the airplane descended for its landing at Mehrabad International Airport, Stavros peered out of the scratched and crazed oval window. He saw the white-capped mountains north of the city and searched at the base of the hills for the twenty-five-story Crown Hotel which would be his home for the next few days.

The Boeing 707 touched down lightly on the tarmac and he thought of the upcoming operation.

In a couple of days the Rangers will seize this very airport.

Mehrabad was the key to their getting out. Once the Rangers had it secured, the helicopters with the hostages and the assault force would arrive and a couple of air force C-141 Starlifters were to carry everyone out to safety.

Stavros reflected that he only had a small part to play, two guys and a trash can nuke, among a cast of thousands.

If we can pull this thing off...

Stavros decided he had worried about the airport formalities too much. He got through the customs and immigrations inspections without any problems. The militia and security heavies in the terminal were not half as threatening as some he'd seen in Africa, but his experiences there seemed so long ago and far away as walked toward the taxi queue.

Hanging on to his seat as the taxi swerved and wheeled through the traffic to his hotel, Stavros decided whoever said or wrote that taxis snake through a city had never visited the Middle East. In Tehran, they're more akin to stampeding antelope, just without their grace.

Deposited in front of the Crown, he stood on the sidewalk for a moment to reduce his blood pressure and to get his bearings.

He turned to go into the hotel but looked upward on a whim. Twenty-five stories of American-financed grandeur recently confiscated and delivered at no cost to some local disabled veterans' foundation courtesy of the Islamic Government of Iran.

Well, in this part of the world, you pays yo' money and you takes yo' chances.

19

KGB *Rezident* Oleg Ignatyev yelled at his deputy to bring in the goons. Not that he called them "goons" to their faces, but in his mind that's what they were. A couple of back-alley types, thugs from Service "A" sent down from Moscow to do the dirty work his academy-trained officers couldn't, wouldn't, or shouldn't do.

Ignatyev called them "Mischa" and "Arkady," their not-so-very-clever cover names. He didn't care about their real names, Sergei Todorov and Maxim Solov, or their connections to the *Bratva* back in Moscow. He just knew the message from the Center told him they were to be given all assistance necessary and their reporting was to be direct, no officers from the *Rezidentura* were to be involved. That suited him fine. If they screwed up, he could disown the entire operation.

Goons with guns. Exasperating.

The two sauntered into the *Rezident's* office and stood before him, neutral expressions on their faces. One was short with overly long arms, a gorilla—no, a monkey—in a cheap suit, dark, greasy hair, and a five o'clock shadow at nine in the morning. The other was taller, just shy of 2 meters, thin, with a wire-thin moustache below a long thin nose and beady eyes that were set too close together.

He has whiskers, he's a weasel. A weasel and a monkey with guns.

He sighed. Together, they made an unlikely tag team.

"I don't really know why you're here and I don't care, so don't tell me, but I am supposed to help you. So, what do you need?"

"Not much," said Mischa, the monkey. "We are looking for something the Americans have and we need information from inside the embassy compound. If you have anyone that can tell us what's going on in there, that would be about it."

"Do either of you speak Persian?"

"I do," said Arkady, the weasel.

"And you don't?" Ignatyev indicated he was speaking to Mischa.

"Why? I don't need to talk to these people," he said. A slight smile crossed his simple face as if he was making some insider joke that was lost on a *Rezident* who chose to ignore the comment.

"I will give you one of my agents who has good contacts inside. He is part of the Islamic student movement, but he's one of ours, a member of *Tudeh*. You know what *Tudeh* is?"

One nod, one shake of the head.

"*Nyet*," said Mischa, clueless.

"He's a communist," said Arkady.

"You've studied up, I see," said Ignatyev.

"I've been around a bit."

"All right, so that means you also know not to burn this man. He is important to our operations," Ignatyev said. His statement was made without conviction because he had at least three other assets with comparable access. Not quite as good as this agent, but good access nevertheless. He figured he should give his guests a decent source just so they would have a better chance of success and he could have them out of his country as soon as possible. He hated having to clean up messes that Service "A" tended to leave behind.

"His name is Ervin Rajavi. Get his file from my deputy; it has all the information you will need and he can help you get in contact with him.

"And one last thing, I know your orders say you don't report through me, but if you are going to do anything active, like with

125

guns or anything, let me or my deputy know beforehand. I don't want to get caught flat-footed if anything goes bad. Understood?"

Mischa was about to protest that they didn't have to tell him anything, but Arkady, who had played the game before, knew better.

"Understood, Comrade *Rezident*." A little deference wasn't a bad idea, especially when you didn't know just who the boss knew or was related to back home.

"Perfect," said Ignatyev. He turned and resumed his habitual place behind the desk and began reading papers and ignoring his two visitors. Mischa and Arkady clearly understood that they had been dismissed.

20

Minus much of his previous anxiety, Landau walked back into a familiar scene. The airport greeters and checkers looked to be the same as the ones he had encountered on the last visit. He regarded them mostly as undisciplined and a therefore dangerous bunch of fundamentalist thugs. As he studied his surroundings, he began to notice a few more men in the crowd who looked serious. The analysts had mentioned reports that some former Iranian SAVAK agents had been "rehabilitated" by the new regime to serve again as gate keepers, investigators, and agents of persecution. Behind the dark sunglasses, he saw them for what they truly were, professionalized suspicion and evil. These were worse than the fundamentalists, they were agnostic to the regime, beholden only to reward and perhaps the lure of power and violence.

The more things change, the more they stay the same.

After he cleared the airport, he headed back to the Park Hotel. He saw no reason to change his lodging. It was familiar territory.

The visit would be different this time. He would recontact his lawyer once to discuss ostensible investment possibilities and recheck the Foreign Ministry and embassy compound to make sure the situation hadn't changed. McKay was due in shortly and he'd make contact with him later.

The big change was that one more man had been added to the mission. Along with Fields and George, Stavros was coming into town with a role on the fringe, perhaps less important on the humanitarian scale of things but a major national security issue. He would tell the others only that Stavros would be bringing another American to the MFA for exfil. He wasn't planning on mentioning the device, at least until the mission kicked off.

***

Meeting McKay was the first thing he had to do; afterwards, they'd find Fields together. They had to coordinate their activities closely now. Only three days left to recheck and recalibrate their plans if necessary. Then it would be game time.

Once again, McKay was at the proper location. To Landau, it seemed that even if McKay did forget the meet plan, he would inadvertently wander into the correct site while trying to remember where he was supposed to be. And it would be at the correct time and well within the four-minute window. He had to give McKay credit or maybe just chalk it up to sheer luck. And now, there McKay sat, waiting for his comrade-in-arms, living his cover as a world-class pistachio buyer in a hostile land far from home. Landau just shook his head as he sat down.

"What's up?" McKay said.

"Not much, just the usual vacation in Tehran thing. Tomorrow, I'll pick you up at 0800 and we can run the routes. Then we need to do one last close look to make sure everything is still good."

"I am ready to lather, rinse, and repeat," said McKay.

"What's that mean?"

"It means we're going to do the same thing all over again, ad infinitum. You know, the Department of Redundancy Department."

"Yes, if that's what you want to think, but it's vital we know that nothing has changed. I will pick up our new partner, Fields,

128

afterwards. We need to go to the warehouse and run the routes out of town and back, since he's leading the big group to their site."

"Today is Monday. Tuesday and Wednesday for rechecks. What do we do on Thursday?"

"After we have confirmed everything is ready, Fields will send the 'ready to receive' message Thursday morning. Then we sit back and wait until nightfall."

"Maybe I should be getting nervous."

"You should have been nervous a while ago."

***

It was Wednesday and McKay watched the city map and gave out the occasional directions as they retraced the routes one last time. It would have been monotonous except for the large number of men in civilian clothing with guns and uniformed security forces who now congregated at every large intersection. Even the traffic cops seemed to have back-ups who watched from the sidelines. Security had increased some since their last visit.

"We need to do a run at nighttime to see how things look," McKay said.

"A dry run, yes," said Landau.

"Right, that'll give me time to hit the lounge afterward."

"I doubt it'll be open that late, because we'll need to see the location shortly before midnight."

"I can deal with it. I have some 'cola' stashed in my room."

They drove on through the late morning, the sun streaming down, turning the dust kicked up by the vehicles into a backlit fog. The traffic got heavier until just before midday when it dropped off quickly. For several hours, the volume of cars and trucks would diminish while their drivers took a break. Some went home, others stopped for food. Some just went into the park to eat a packed lunch, maybe *kuku sabzi*, a local kind of frittata, or the ubiquitous kebab and flat bread. Landau and McKay stopped near the National Museum and walked through Mashq Square.

"It would be a nice place to visit if it wasn't for all the Iranians," McKay growled.

"It's not the Iranians, it's the zealots. They ruin everything they touch no matter what religion they think they are. Most of them are hypocrites and some are just dangerous."

"They're still all a bunch of 'WOGs,' the whole uncivilized lot of 'em."

Landau glanced at McKay to see if he was serious and it appeared he was.

"And you think you Scots are more civilized."

"I know we are."

"Haggis," said Landau.

"Haggis? What are you talking about?"

"Any nation that calls stuffed goat stomach its national dish is not civilized."

"It's a sheep's stomach."

As they sat on a wall in front of the National Garden, which lay across from the MFA building, McKay pulled a paper bag of pistachios out of his coat pocket and poured some into Landau's hand. They sat husking the nuts and pitching the shells over their shoulders into the grass. Munching while watching the scene in front of them, McKay started to reveal his new-found expertise in the field, "These are Akbari, super big, one of the best varieties."

Landau just nodded as he worked a stubborn nut, trying to coax the precious fruit out of its shell. For once he had to break the nuts open before he could eat them, unlike his beloved hardboiled eggs or the peanuts that he ate, shells and all. The two, ignored by the locals, talked in generalities about the mission and the timetable.

Across the wide road, the three policeman at the gate on the southern end of the compound stood together next to the guard box and chatted. The gate was wide open and once in awhile someone would walk through it without being challenged.

Ensuring that no one was close enough to hear them, McKay spoke softly: "I hope it will be this easy on Friday."

"It won't be; they'll lock up after hours. We'll re-confirm that tonight. What weapons did they have?"

"I saw only a single G3 rifle in the guard house. It looked to be loaded and they each have what I think are Colt .38 revolvers or a clone. I couldn't get them to show me, but I also didn't see a single spare magazine for any of the rifles."

"Fire superiority shouldn't be a problem then. At least until the enemy cavalry gets here."

Together they studied the plaza in front of the MFA. A museum on one side, a military club across the street, the police headquarters down the road—but hardly any visible security. People drove past or walked along the street without a care. The constraints and the fear one would expect in a totalitarian state didn't seem to exist. They apparently hadn't perfected that part of repression yet.

After watching for patterns and routines, it was time to go. No sense in burning the target at this late date, they agreed wordlessly.

McKay got to his feet and crumpled the paper bag in his hand. He was about to toss it on the ground when Landau's voice stopped him.

"Don't drop it, look around you." With the exception of a few pistachio shells, the grounds were pristine, maybe the only part of town that was actually clean. "Littering is probably a capital offense these days."

McKay stuffed the bag into his coat pocket.

***

Fields, the Delta guy, was waiting near the pick-up site. Landau spotted him from far off as he approached with the car.

Perhaps he got there a little early but no matter.

The recognition signals were there, the safe signal showed that all was well. The door opened and closed quickly. With Fields in the back seat, Landau took off watching all directions at once while his second passenger settled in.

"We're going to do the warehouse first. The route is simple. You can look at the equipment there and then we'll do the run to the *laager*."

"That's fine. I went over everything before I came out and since I arrived, I've walked the routes to the embassy compound and the key intersection in the south. Now I need to see it through the windshield," said Fields.

"We're doing that. When do the drivers show up?"

"I'll bring them to the warehouse Thursday and we'll all be locked in. Are the route maps there?"

"They are. But we'll be with them so I'm not too worried."

"We only have one shot to do this."

"You don't have to remind me. That's why we've run everything through so many times."

"This is pretty mundane stuff though. Getting bored yet?"

"You are going to have to learn patience when you're out here alone because there's nothing Ninja-cool about this kind of work. It's repetitious, but not boring as long as you look at it like a puzzle. You have to find all the little things that are just waiting to trip us up."

Before long, their warehouse loomed ahead of them, one of a series of unremarkable buildings.

"This street looks familiar. It's probably burned into my brain because of all the photo and map data I've memorized."

Once inside, Landau showed his comrades the vehicles and equipment before giving Fields a set of the warehouse keys. He would need them to bring the drivers to the trucks. He also grabbed one of the PRC-90s from the bag. Holding it for Fields to see, he said,

"Our man Stavros will need to know when to bring the Agency guy down to the MFA."

"Where is he now?"

"He's staying in the northern part of the city at the Crown. I'll meet him tomorrow night so we can talk and I can give him this thing."

"Tell him to be on top of a building or something before the mission. That thing is meant to be used for ground-to-air commo not ground-to-ground."

"Hopefully he'll be on the twenty-fifth floor of his hotel, that will have to do."

***

The mundane did kick in on the road trip to the hilltop *laager* site.

"Nothing but miles and miles of nothing but miles and miles," said Landau. "Maybe you were right about boring."

"Maybe, but I can see your point about possible trip-ups too." Three sets of eyes strained to see what, if anything, was in the distance. It was always better to see the checkpoints long before the police could identify you.

The only thing that moved was the trash and weeds that blew across the highway, a dusty two-lane blacktop that headed toward the holy city of Qom further to the southwest.

"What did you worry about most on the Son Tay raid?" McKay asked.

"Not anything like this, that's for sure. We worried about the flight path, how we were going to fly into country. The North Vietnamese had a very good air defense system—all set up by the Chinese and Russians, of course. So our biggest concern was not getting shot down on the way in or out. This time we have further to fly, but the Iranians haven't got anywhere close to the same kind of missile coverage along the route the aircraft will use."

"No, but we have an incredibly complicated plan just to get everything in place and that's even before we get to the launch point in town."

"One little wrench in the gears will stop the machine, I know. Even perfect execution won't prevent something bad from happening."

Fields thought back to the raid deep into North Vietnam ten years earlier. Everything went right except that the POWs had been moved some time before they arrived. One detail, one intel failure, and all their work had been for nothing.

Well, almost nothing. Life in the prisons became much easier once the North Vietnamese realized we were serious about our men.

McKay seemed to sense Fields' thoughts.

"At least the POWs were treated better afterwards."

"I just want this one to go right."

The *laager* hilltop was in front of them when Landau slowed the car to a crawl.

"I think we can skip the trail. We won't learn anything new." He saw that no one had been in the area since his last visit. The trail had not been disturbed.

"Yeah, let's go home."

"We'll do the route from the warehouse to the embassy."

***

The traffic was heavy in town as they inched north toward the compound. McKay directed Landau onto a street he had not driven before.

"This will get us there?"

"Yes, I walked it several times as one of several alternates."

"Traffic isn't much better."

"Just stay to the right, we have to turn in a block or two."

Landau should have realized something was not quite right. Two buses were in front of him and they stopped in turn to pick up passengers. Then a man in a blue uniform appeared out of the crowd. The cop stared at the Mercedes for a moment, tugged his coat down to straighten it and walked up to the front of the car and started haranguing the occupants in a loud voice. It was then that Landau noticed the international sign that told him he was in the wrong place.

"Damn it, a bus lane."

There was no way out. They had been channeled into the restricted lane and short yellow poles in the road held them inside. He couldn't reverse or change lanes; he was condemned to follow the buses while a cop yelled at him. The cop came around to the driver's side window and realized he was dealing with foreigners only when Landau told him in German he didn't understand what the officer was talking about. A pantomime ensued between two grown men trying the theory that volume and hand gestures made for better communication. It didn't. But it drew attention as several of the officer's colleagues gathered on the sidewalk to watch the entertainment.

The policeman switched to some form of pidgin that approximated English in an attempt to express his displeasure with this foreigner who was speaking some metallic-sounding language.

Landau heard, "Passport and driver's license."

That I can do.

He turned to the back seat but couldn't find what he needed.

"Where's my briefcase?"

"I put it in the trunk. It's on the left side, but the radio is out in the open," said Fields. His anxiety level spiked when he saw the look on Landau's face.

"*Mist,*" a pause, a deep breath, "*jetzt geht's los.*" Crap... okay, showtime, said Landau. "Neither of you two move. Just stay in the car." A new persona enveloped him.

He opened the door and got out of the car slowly, his hands spread in front of him showing good intent, with a smile on his face to confirm that. He looked at the cops on the sidewalk and smiled at them too, showing he respected them and their occupation very much, while he cleared his mind of the thought of killing them. He had no weapon after all.

Their demise will just be postponed for a bit longer.

He turned back to his principal tormentor. And let loose.

"Why have you stopped me? I'm not doing anything wrong or illegal! I am a visitor, a businessman who brings commerce and money to your country. I do not deserve this kind of disrespect."

His speech went on and on in a mixture of bad English and perfect German, delivered with an authority and force that left the policeman bewildered and a bit cowed. Even his comrades were mesmerized.

"Passport and driver's license," was the only response.

"Yes, yes, they are in back." He made the policeman understand with hand gestures and pointing as he walked to the back. He was smiling and talking quietly again. Doctor Jekyll had returned.

The key slipped into the lock and the trunk popped open. Landau caught the lid before it opened too far as he quickly reached in, grabbed his briefcase and pulled it out. The trunk thudded shut and became his desk as he pulled out the documents and presented them to the policeman, smiling all the while.

The policeman was joined by a supervisor who took the documents and made a point of inspecting them closely while speaking in a better form of Police-English for tourists, telling Landau that what he had done was upsetting to the equilibrium of the Iranian nation. He pointed at the bus-only sign and wagged his finger at the Mercedes as if it was an interloper at a family funeral and pulled out a citation book and began to write down the details of the crime. When he was finished, he ripped out the form and handed it to Landau.

"You will pay the fine at the airport before you leave the country. Now go."

The newly obsequious Jekyll smiled, mumbling in German something along the lines of "I apologize for my transgressions, but don't be out Friday night or I will have to kill you."

Landau was not quite livid but steaming when he got back into the car. He looked at McKay. Understandably, McKay didn't return the stare; instead, he gazed at the dashboard of the car. Landau held his breath and counted to five before he spoke while he steered away from all the policemen who were still gathered on the curb nearby. When they were away, he spoke. Quietly.

"You almost got us arrested. You should have known that it was a bus lane. And you..." he turned to face Fields in the backseat, "I'll say this once because I know you're better, but you almost got us killed."

"I'm sorry, I moved your case when we were at the warehouse because I needed the space. I should have mentioned it."

"You remember what I said about the small shit? That was as close as I ever want to come. If either of you do that again, I will personally shoot you."

The deafening silence would last for quite a while.

***

It was nighttime and the unusual had become the norm in the city. Landau had sat on the outdoor patio for a while listening. There was the steady hum of traffic along with the usual noises of a city still very much alive. He could hear crashes and bangs of machinery and trash bins and the occasional loud voice or yell. Earlier he had heard the call to prayer and once there was a staccato burst of three rifle rounds, a machine gun perhaps, but nothing more. Never, not once, a siren or wail of an emergency vehicle.

When they hit the streets again, it was only for a short trip. The three men came together in steps: Landau got the Mercedes and began to drive the route, Fields came next, stepping into the street as the car slowed and then climbing in, barely a stop; then around three more corners, McKay followed. Silently they drove south to the key intersection and then retraced the route to the embassy, past the soccer stadium, around to the MFA. This time, Landau was more careful about which lane he was in, but these streets were familiar to him now. Compared to daytime, the students were small in number behind the walls of their enclave, with more perhaps inside the buildings, but few on the street itself. Those who were out appeared awake and somewhat vigilant, probably more concerned with sharing stories as their faces were briefly illuminated by flaring matches that lit their cigarettes. The MFA was well lit; apparently the city's power plant was working that night. Three policemen stood behind the gate near the museum, another three at the entrance at the other end of the block. They posed a challenge, but not as large as the one at the embassy.

"I think we've seen everything," Fields said.

They all agreed: time to rest. Tomorrow was Game Day.

21

Stavros looked at himself in the mirror. He wasn't sure if his dark blue Adidas sweat suit would mark him as a German "fun boy" when he was out on the street, but so much the better to cover his true purpose. The face in the mirror stared back. He didn't think he was ugly, but he also didn't know if he was good looking. Certainly, he wasn't Sean Connery, but he wasn't Peter Lorre either. Aside from his curly hair, he was ordinary looking, he thought. No scars—visible ones anyway—and no tattoos. Tattoos, so common with the regular troops, were *Verboten* in the unit. He also didn't look very American, in dress or manner, which he supposed was good. Especially when you don't want to be taken for someone from the Land of the Great Satan, like right now.

He had found running to be an effective way to do a recon in a city. It was generally very obvious if someone tried to pace you either on foot or by vehicle. The only downside was that it was difficult to keep it up for very long unless you had the endurance of a wildebeest. He had endurance but, at this altitude, only enough to run seven or eight clicks before he started losing focus on his task.

He had been outside the hotel several times already and noted that there were a lot of walkers in this, the northern part of the city. Many were businessmen, but he saw plenty of idle older folks who seemed to be well off in spite of the regime. Or maybe they were the regime. The women were correctly dressed: they all wore the required *chador* as was recently decreed. The word was appropriate because it literally meant "tent" in Persian. His mind started to wander toward an old saying about camel noses and tent edges, but he stopped himself. He had also seen a lot of hikers a little further to the north when he came close to the trails of Darakeh in the foothills. And he saw a few runners, all male, all young, probably students or military, maybe athletes. He wasn't sure if Iran would be entering the Summer Olympics or not or even whether they had much of a team, but his running should not look out of place.

It was early morning on his third full day in Tehran. Stavros walked through the lobby, monitoring the faces he passed to gauge their interest. If anything, there might be a spotter to alert the exterior team that their rabbit was on the move. He saw nothing, not even a studied lack of interest. Outside he found a place to do some stretching before he took off, as much to give his muscles a little warm-up as to look for any opposition who might care if he was there.

Then he was off, slowly at first. He would maintain a comfortable pace as he had a long way to go. He knew the route because he had laid it out on a map and then walked it in individual sections. Now he ran the whole damned thing at once.

Even after several days in Tehran, Stavros still felt a bit like a fish out of water. He was on his own in a city that before he came was unfamiliar to him except for the several hours of map work and a quick review of the 1969 edition of a Library of Congress tome called *Iran, A Country Study,* which told him very little about what was happening at present. He was, for all intents and purposes, a singleton. Of course, Landau and McKay were also in town, but they were of little help for this task. He had no support, no network, no assets, nothing except his brain and a certain amount of discipline to get the job done. It was lonely work and the tedium could be overwhelming; he didn't even have any good war stories to tell himself. Just stories from training group and his first tour which were about as interesting as watching paint dry.

Well, maybe there was one story...

He had filled his time with walkabouts and a number of meetings with carpet merchants. He did have a feeling of being in another era when he was in the bazaars. There, he sat with the owners and sipped endless cups of *qahveh,* coffee heavily sweetened and infused with cardamom, while young men took carpets off huge piles, unfolded them with a flip of the hands and then quickly refolded them after he nodded in appreciation or dismissed them with a wave. He lost count of how many carpets he had agreed to buy, although he planned on leaving quickly before he actually had to pay for them. He just hoped the planned direct exit by helicopter courtesy of the US Air Force would come off without a hitch. Only two more days until Game Day.

When he saw the site, he knew it from the photographs. For once, the Station had sent location files on one of its safe houses out to Headquarters. Usually the files were kept in the office safes in case there was an emergency or another officer had to service the site, but apparently the chief had realized there might come a time when they would be needed by someone from outside. Then again, the Perses thing was a compartmented project and therefore critical and, for that reason, was primarily controlled from Langley. If it hadn't been done that way, no one would have a clue where the safe house was, except maybe the students occupying the embassy if the original files hadn't been shredded or burned.

Had the files been destroyed?

He realized he had no idea, which meant the safe house was in danger of being compromised from inside as well as out.

He ran past the safe house briskly and into a nearby park where he throttled back to a fast walk. He kept moving and then stopped and did some stretching. He had to come up with an approach plan and when he had decided on one, he started off again, picked up speed and headed back to his hotel on another roundabout route. He would be back later.

***

Even after dark, the streets were still busy. Many of the small shops had lines of lights hung under the canopies that protected their wares. The twinkling lights swung back and forth in the breeze and gave a festival feel to the neighborhood. The smoke from the braziers cooking meat or boiling beets drifted over and around the people on the sidewalks into the street. Despite the unease that gripped the center of the city there was still fun to be had in this section of Tehran, just no alcohol.

Along the way, Stavros decided he was hungry; he wasn't sure when he'd get a chance to eat again that evening. Diving into a line of vendors, he looked over what was available. Liver kebabs, nope, he had no desire to eat any kind of poison filter. The fava beans didn't look that appetizing either. There were a few other things that were difficult to identify so he decided on a bowl of noodle soup, *âsh reshte* they called it, and paid for it in a pantomime of hand signals in an exchange of words that neither the vendor nor Stavros seemed to understand.

He took the bowl and spoon over to a bench and sat down like most of the other customers. It was much preferable to spilling the soup all over himself and the other folks. He tasted and thought it wasn't bad, noodles and beans with lots of garlic and onions in a slightly spicy broth topped with something that looked like runny yoghurt but didn't taste like it. He never did figure that part out but he ate it anyway. While he ate, he watched the locals on the street. More women seemed to be out at night, still well covered although many of them walked with their faces visible. He was struck by their eyes. They appeared almost Asian, which made sense from the illustrations he remembered from *One Thousand and One Nights*, but with the heavy eyeliner that most wore they looked dark and often brooding.

He was sure he didn't look Iranian because he seemed to catch people's interest, sometimes for a moment, sometimes longer. When he saw one of the women look at him for more than a second he felt his pulse quicken. She was, after all, very attractive, at least what he could see of her, but he tried not to stare, he didn't want anyone to become a victim of an honor killing. Thinking of Sarah instead, he went back to watching the drifting smoke before he turned his gaze up over the mountains where the stars were flickering in night sky. He missed Sarah. He liked having her around to talk with and even argue with. It had been a couple of weeks since she went back to the States and for a moment he wondered how she was doing in training. A pang of loneliness struck and he felt very out of place in Tehran.

Focus on the now! Don't think about anything else.

For a moment, Stavros felt he was in a world between reality and dream. He couldn't quite reconcile the beauty that surrounded him with the fact he was essentially deep in enemy territory. If he was detained and arrested, he would be guaranteed some unpleasantness at the hands of whoever was in charge of security these days. Earlier in the day that reality had come to him when he walked past what he first took to be a warehouse, albeit a well-protected one. The stark walls of the facility were tall, perhaps 10 meters high, but there were few windows, just small air vents in the white-washed concrete that reflected the morning sun with an angry glare. Then he saw the sign that showed a simple symbol of a camera inside a red circle cut in two with a red line. He knew the meaning instantly: no photography. But why no photographing a warehouse? Then he saw the flag, the rolls of razor tape that topped the walls, the lights, and last, the men in blue uniforms with guns strapped to their belts. Men who had nothing but bad attitude and cruelty written across their faces. He realized what he was looking at, a location he had seen on the map back in Frankfurt and the small letters that described the place: Evin Prison.

He had not meant to walk there; he was wandering, looking for different ways to get to the same place. He felt a cold shiver down his spine. He wouldn't come this way again. As he walked away, he felt like there was a long piece of toilet paper stuck to his shoe that screamed "Look at me!"

He vowed he would not do anything that didn't make sense for a foreign businessman until it was time to go operational, which was in about an hour. He shook his head at his thinking. There was no one single game day as some said, it was game on at every moment. Every second was an opportunity for things to go bad. He just had to make sure they didn't.

For the second time that day he began to think too much about the situation he was in; he thought about the similar events he'd seen depicted in movies and felt truly alone. The only time you were alone in training was when you were on a cross-country walk or undergoing POW training, otherwise there was generally a teammate around who you could talk with. Even working alone at nighttime on the streets of Berlin, he felt comfortable. There was small chance of being arrested, more a chance of being jumped by criminals.

Nothing like what awaited behind the walls of Evin. The stakes had become a lot higher.

He wasn't sure if he should be scared or not. He did know that he had to be on his best game. He also wondered if the adrenaline rush would disappear or if he even wanted it to.

Stavros walked the bowl and spoon back to the vendor's cart and tossed a couple of coins into his cash cup before he turned back to the street. Although the warm soup had filled him up he bought a couple of *sambosehs* for later.

Just in case.

***

The final approach to the safe house was critical. It was a smaller building set among some high-rise apartments. The key thing that had made it attractive to the Station was that it was set on a corner lot and had easy access from several directions as well as good visibility from inside. That meant it could be easily escaped from as well.

Stavros walked down a narrow alley and into a small area behind two of the apartments. He looked at the safe house through the trees and bushes at the edge of the lot. There was no wall that separated the properties, which would make the next part easier. He watched the darkened lot until he was satisfied no one else was around before he made his way to the edge and slipped carefully through the parked cars. The only sounds he heard came from the major streets several blocks away. There was no music, no yelling, no noise coming from the surrounding buildings, just quiet. He wondered if there were block wardens like in Germany, old women who sat at their windows and reported the slightest infraction to the *Polizei*. He decided it was best to assume there were watchers and kept to the shadows until he was able to make his way through the bushes and onto the back patio of the safe house. He stepped quietly; it was very dark in the shielded area and he didn't want to accidentally kick something and get shot by whoever was inside. There was a spare set of keys hidden behind a brick but he didn't bother with those either. The sound of a lock being opened would bring the same result as kicking the cat, so he decided to resort to his teenage method of summoning friends. He pulled a small coin from his pocket and pitched it against a window pane.

He waited.

Nothing.

Another coin came out and this one was pitched against a window on the other end of the house. Again, he waited, standing about 3 paces from the door. A few minutes passed and the curtain moved to the side slightly. There was no light inside so he couldn't see who or what made the curtain move. Stavros tapped the button on the tiny flashlight he held and a short flash of red light lit up his feet. He waited. The curtain dropped back into position, swaying back and forth a bit. Then he heard the slow click of the lock. The door opened slowly and a face appeared from behind the wood.

Stavros thought it best to introduce himself. In Greek.

"Jonny. *Eímai το ippikó.*" I'm the cavalry.

After a moment, Jonny Panagasos stepped outside. "Are you all there is?"

"For the moment. We needed to find you first."

"You did. Would you like to authenticate yourself?"

"Your folks didn't really give me a way to do that but I'm here to get you and Perses out of here."

Jonny considered Stavros for a second. There was no way headquarters could have provided a code word because there wasn't one. *But he mentioned Perses.* He decided it couldn't be a provocation and slid his pistol back into the waistband holster.

"Maybe you should come inside."

Stavros stepped around Jonny and entered the house. It was dark inside except for a bit of light streaming out from under a door to his front. As Jonny relocked the outside door he said, "Head for the light and go in that room."

The room was windowless, being in the center of the building, and could be well isolated from the outside.

"This is my headquarters now. I abandoned my apartment and moved everything I needed up here, which wasn't much. So who are you?"

"You should call me Pavlos—Pavlos Nikos. I'm a businessman on a Greek passport, here buying carpets."

"Are you going to take me out rolled up in a load of *Isfahans*?"

"No, but I do have purchase orders for carpets all over the city. I will need to leave before someone actually makes me pay up. Anyway, I'll get to our plan to get us out of here but where's the thing?"

146

"The *thing*? The thing is in a warehouse about twenty minutes away by foot. But it's not anything we can just lug around town."

"I understand that, I've got a pretty good picture of what it is. You have a truck though?"

"Yes, what are we gonna do with that?"

Stavros felt his mouth get dry. The sometimes hazy, clandestine world he had been living in was beginning to come into focus and he was parched.

"Got anything to drink? I've been walking for a while now. It's thirsty out there."

Jonny left the room for a minute, returned and set a big bottle of soda water and a couple of glasses on the table. Stavros had pulled his bag of *sambosehs* from his coat and put them on the table.

"I'm hungry too. My dinner wasn't enough tonight."

"I have plenty of surplus C-Rations if you want. We took everything the military advisory group left behind when they bailed out last year."

"I can do without those right now, thanks."

"You said 'your folks.' You're not Agency are you?"

"No, I'm army."

"Special Forces, I assume? A volunteer, right?"

"Yes to the first. As to the second, who'd be crazy enough to volunteer for this shit?"

"I'm thinking maybe you did."

"Maybe."

Stavros poured some water and drank it down before pouring some more into both glasses. He took one of the meat and lentil pastries from the bag and pushed the rest across to Jonny. As he chewed on the snack, he pulled a piece of paper and a pencil out of his pocket.

"This is the plan..." he said as he scratched four squares under a line he had drawn. He turned the paper to Jonny. Pointing at the line he said, "These are the mountains. This square is you, this one is the American Embassy compound, this is Mehrabad Airport, and this, in the middle, is the MFA."

"OK, good geography lesson."

"Indeed. First, we have two days before we move. Tomorrow evening, a rescue force will launch by air from somewhere down around Saudi Arabia. Early Friday morning, it will land in the middle of Iran and meet helicopters. Then the whole force will move by helo to a location south of Tehran. You with me so far?"

Jonny was silent for a second. "You're not kidding me are you?"

"No, I am totally serious," Stavros said. "The next night, the force will move by truck into town to the embassy and the MFA and pull out all the hostages. Once that happens, they'll move the people to a soccer field, here," he scrawled a circle next to the embassy compound square, "where the helos will come in and pick everyone up and take them to Mehrabad for exfiltration by transport aircraft."

"Jesus."

"When I get the word that the force is on the move into town, you and I will take your truck and meet the force at the MFA. We'll take the device and go with that team as they move to the soccer stadium."

"Not much that can go wrong on this operation, is there?"

"There aren't any other options and the experts at the Pentagon give us a fifty-fifty chance."

"Of failure?"

"Does it matter?"

22

"Okay, we are a go. There's no call back this time," Jelinek said. Jock Sheldon and his small team listened intently. The sergeant major, the S-3 ops officer and the S-2 intel sat nearby. They had already seen the message. It was simple and to the point.

"Execute Mission as Briefed. We are Ready and Able. God Speed," signed Vaught, Commander JTF.

"God speed, indeed," Bergmann said.

"The nine of us are going in as part of the main force," Jelinek said.

They had just deployed forward from Wadi Qena in Egypt, which was every bit as desolate as the place they were in now; hot, dusty, and godforsaken. Masirah Island would never be a tourist destination despite the fact that it was surrounded by water—unless, perhaps, you came from Wadi Qena.

Up to this point, the deployment had been "iffy." No one had an idea whether it would happen or not. The deliberations at the White House and the Pentagon may have been heated and divisive, but those discussions never made it down to the troops. Instead, the soldiers wandered around the big hangar and the tents, renewed old acquaintances, talked shop, and wondered aloud whether or not they'd be better off in their comrades' unit because the grass is always greener there.

Everyone knew what the selection criteria for Special Forces were, as well as for the leap into Delta Force, but no one, other than the *Berliners* themselves, knew how someone was selected for SF Berlin. So, when someone asked, "What's your selection criteria?" Brad, a long-time member of the unit, explained the super-secret way into the unit as only he could.

"First, you have to do a meeting with a stranger in a *Kneipe*, a bar downtown. He questions you on your cover in German while giving you lots of schnapps to drink, then after about three hours, you have to take the subway to three different locations around town and you make a final meeting in a gay bar at an exact time. If you make it without getting lost or throwing up, you've passed the first phase."

"That's a weird selection process."

"It is, but it's also *very* special. And I forgot one thing: you have to send Mrs Palmer at Headquarters DA a box of chocolates and some flowers."

"Why?"

"Because if she doesn't like you, you ain't going nowhere."

Whether or not the listeners believed Brad's BS was a good test of their gullibility, however. There were members of SEAL Team 2 who could at least attest to the truth of the drinking part of it.

Inside the big olive-drab tent, it was hot. Outside, it was even hotter, but at least there was a wind. It was not a cooling wind, but it blew continuously and made the air feel a tiny bit cooler. Of course, on the down side, it also carried half the fine sand, dust, insects, and desiccated camel dung blown from the mainland across the channel onto the island. The question was whether to sit inside and slowly steam to death or stand outside and have your skin kinetically exfoliated. The intelligence officer made the decision for them. No one could be outside because a Russian reconnaissance satellite was due for a pass and security dictated no one would have their photo taken from space.

Everyone in the tent had heard the colonel say the same words before, only to have the mission delayed. This time it was different. General Vaught said it was a "go" as he stood on the podium inside the big reinforced concrete hangar. That meant the green light had been given and only a last-minute change by the president would stop them. That wasn't likely to happen now since the secretary of state had resigned in protest. The rest of the president's advisors were supportive of the mission.

It was still going to be a close-run thing. The assault force was in pretty good shape, but Delta had just enough people; Berlin had barely enough. And the Rangers, who would seize Mehrabad, the exfiltration airfield, on the night of the assault, were ready. The question remained: would the equipment needed to get them all the way to the target suffice?

There were many questions about that and nobody wanted to think about it too much. The navy helicopters had not been stress tested before the operation despite a directive by the Chairman of the Joint Chiefs. No one knew what their limits were. Marine pilots had replaced the navy pilots who couldn't meet minimums for the mission. The Marines were much better than the navy, but they had neither the training for a long-range night infiltration nor the time to prepare. The ideal, the air force special ops pilots and helicopters that should have been there, were left in the States because… well, no one really could articulate that clearly. Something about security profiles and having green helicopters on an aircraft carrier instead of gray ones.

I guess they could not afford to repaint them.

Vaught and Colonel Kyle, the air force commander, were worried. So were Beckwith and Jelinek. But then again, who wouldn't be worried. Not one rehearsal with the helos in Nevada had gone well. And now, they were on the verge of launching a rescue mission deep into enemy territory with unknown odds all around them.

151

And with only eight helos committed, the margin of failure was very tight.

***

At around 1700, the troops loaded the MC-130s sitting on the tarmac nearby. Colonel Kyle, Colonel Beckwith and the Delta Blue element, along with an air force combat control team and the Ranger road watch team, climbed on board the first aircraft. Colonel Jelinek and his eight-man MFA team, along with Delta's Red element, climbed onto a second MC-130. Delta's White element loaded onto a third airplane.

There was a mix of weaponry and demolitions. Explosives to breach the walls and the doors, weapons for the shooters. Delta carried CAR-15s for the assault teams along with M-60 and HK-21 machine guns for the security elements, Colt M-1911A1s for everyone. The Berlin MFA team was going in light, carrying only their Walther MPK submachine guns and silenced High Standard HDMS pistols. There were also a few more esoteric weapons thrown into the mix, hidden among their personal gear.

The mission was a "go." Onboard the aircraft, the mood was electric. The men were quiet, subdued, waiting to go into action, as is the lot of soldiers everywhere. Precisely at the OPLAN's stipulated time of 1800, the lead aircraft released its brakes, rolled down the runway, and lifted off into the early evening light. Thirty minutes later, the second and third aircraft lifted off and headed north on the same track as the first bird. Three EC-130 refueling birds followed in trail. They flew low across the water and would remain low, crossing the coast line and evading Iranian radars until they reached their destination, an isolated piece of terrain chosen as the rendezvous and refueling site 1,600 kilometers away in hostile territory, a location called Desert One.

Somewhere to the east in the Indian Ocean, at 1900 hours, eight US Navy RH-53 helicopters lifted off the deck of the aircraft carrier USS *Nimitz*, turned north and disappeared into the ever-darkening night. An encrypted radio call went out and was heard in several crowded control rooms around the world.

"Eight birds off the deck."

The helos and their crews had 900 kilometers to go, all of them in harm's way.

23

In Tehran, Mischa and Arkady were at a loss on how to locate the device. They hoped their new asset, Ervin Rajavi, could help them. The small cafe they sat in was not far from the American Embassy compound but far enough that Rajavi probably would not be seen by his fellow hostage-takers. When he came into the shop, he saw the only other men present were the two he had been told to meet. He sat down with his back to the door. The two Russians had already taken up the obvious spots that let them watch the entrance, but they were not worried. The Soviet Embassy had yet to be put on the list of enemies of the Islamic Republic.

As he sat down, Rajavi rubbed his eyes. His right eye had a tic that flared up as soon as he got nervous and it was now in high gear.

"This guy's eye is driving me crazy. I want to strangle him," Arkady said. He was smiling but he had little empathy for spies although it was his job to deal with them. It was enough that he had to do all the heavy work, since Mischa couldn't talk to or understand Rajavi at all.

"I hope he doesn't speak Russian," Mischa said.

"The deputy said he doesn't."

Arkady turned back to his new agent. Still smiling.

"We are glad you can help us, Mister Rajavi," he said. "I don't want to keep you away from your responsibilities too long but we need something that you should be able to get from the American files."

"I may be able to help. What is it you need?" His head began to swivel, which, along with the nervous tic, was even more distracting.

"Don't keep looking around. You look like a criminal."

"I'm sorry. We never met in the open like this before. Your colleague would see me in parks at night."

"We don't have that luxury, there is no time. Now, do you know where the American spies had their offices in the embassy?"

"Yes, and we have many of their files that they could not destroy."

"That's very good. Now what I want you to find for us is simple, but it may be hidden somewhere among those files."

Arkady leaned in to talk softly with Rajavi and outlined what he was looking for. Satisfied the other man understood, he leaned back. "I will make it worth your while if you are successful."

"I hope so. I may have to leave this place if the *mullahs* continue on their path. They may make it very difficult for us to live here."

"Communists, you mean?"

"Anyone who is not one of them." Rajavi stood to go. "When will I see you again?"

"Call this number when you have something," Arkady said, sliding a card across the table. "We can meet here again after that."

"I will do that. I just hope you are thinking of my future security."

"Don't worry, comrade. We want to have a long relationship with you."

Rajavi had his doubts but he knew he had little choice. He pushed the door open and headed down the street, his head on a swivel. He was beginning to feel like a wanted man.

24

About twelve hours before the helicopters were scheduled to lift off the rolling deck of the *Nimitz*, Stavros was contemplating the steaming cup of coffee sitting in front of him. Tonight was the night; the arrival of the rescue force at Desert One. He was sitting in the restaurant of the Intercon waiting for Landau. A brief meeting was all that was required for final coordination. It was early enough that not all the news crews were crowding the place, just a few. Mostly it was populated with businessmen who were still trying to figure out how to make a buck off a new regime that had no qualms about nationalizing anything that was American or "un-Islamic." Stavros had no more cover meetings to make; his only real job now was to await the signal to move. He was at peace with his fears for the moment.

Landau approached and sat adjacent to Stavros, nodding with a smile. He slapped a copy of the *Frankfurter Allgemeine* onto the table and glared at the waiters until one took his order.

"Third World service still." A theatrical aside to bring Stavros into the conversation.

"I know, it took them three tries to get my coffee right. I guess all the experienced workers got fired."

"Or they left the country. Have you been here long?"

"Five days. I'm buying carpets but that's all finished and I hope to be leaving tomorrow night if my flight holds."

"Me too. I have one more meeting at the Ministry tomorrow and then a Friday departure."

"God willing."

"If you read German, I'm done with the newspaper."

Landau placed the newspaper over a small cloth bag on the chair closest to Stavros and rose to leave. He tossed some money on the table but before he left, he turned to his comrade.

"Macht's gut und sehen wir uns bald wieder." Take care and see you again soon.

When Stavros was sure no one was paying attention, the newspaper and the bag underneath it went into his carryall. The bag was his link to the team. It was also the one item that, if discovered, would tell the Iranians he was a spy.

When Landau was gone, he pulled the newspaper out and looked at the three-day-old headlines but nothing captured his attention. He noticed that Landau had circled all the German football teams that won their games on the sports page, but Stavros' thoughts were racing and he could only think of one thing.

We're coming down to the wire.

***

Team Esquire—Landau, Fields, McKay, and George—met at the warehouse around midday. Three of the expat Iranian drivers recruited in the States showed up one after another and slipped into the building. Fields took them off to a corner, briefed them on the route to be driven and gave them instructions for what to do in case of breakdown or emergency. He was wondering where the fourth truck driver was, when the man pounded on the door about ten minutes later. Once inside, he announced breathlessly:

"They're coming, they've found us!"

"What are you talking about?"

"The police are blocking the front entrance so we can't get away," the driver said. His eyes were wide with fear. Despite the fact he'd signed up for a possible suicide mission, he was not quite ready to be a martyr. There wasn't enough of a cause to die for just yet.

Fields whispered, "Be quiet!"

Landau went to the door and opened it a crack. Disjointed noise from machinery and loud voices filtered in as he peered out.

"A construction crew is digging a trench along our side of the road."

Fields took a look himself and turned back to the drivers. "Just be calm. I see no police out there. We'll wait a bit and see what happens."

The drivers sat together in a circle talking among themselves. Two played on the small backgammon board one of them had the foresight to bring, the clack of the chips and the rattle of dice comforting compared to trying to divine what the noise outside was all about.

A couple of hours later when it was quiet, Fields opened the door. After a quick check from the door frame, he stepped outside. A couple of minutes later he came back in.

"It looks like they're digging a pipe trench. The workers are gone, but we can't get the trucks out."

Fields stood looking at everyone who quietly watched him back. With hands on his hips he looked very much like a commander considering a new battle plan.

"George, where are those oranges you bought?"

"Here," George said, pulling a crate from the trunk of the Mercedes.

"Give me about ten."

Puzzled, George put the oranges in a small box and handed them to Fields.

"There are some kids outside," Fields said.

Fields headed back out the door. Soon a different sort of noise was heard, the yelling and screaming of children.

Landau had to look and stuck his head out the door.

McKay asked, "What's going on?"

"He bribed the kids. They're competing to fill in the trench with rocks."

"I think he's trying to buy his way out of perdition."

***

The view from the room was good and the altitude wasn't bad either. Stavros had managed to talk the front desk into giving him a room high up and he ended up on the nineteenth floor facing the city. The rooms on the other side had the more scenic mountains to look at but radio reception was lousy.

He studied the simple code word list that Landau had passed him along with the PRC-90. He knew he had to monitor the radio twice, tonight for word that the assault force had made it, and on Thursday for the "execute" time when the assault would commence. He hoped Landau would remember to describe Jonny's truck to the team. He and Jonny had to arrive at the MFA just as things started happening and he damn sure didn't want to be met by a hail of friendly fire.

Sarah would really be pissed.

When he received the confirmation he would need to pass the message on to Jonny. They had devised a telephone code for that. No words, just a series of calls to the safe house and the number of rings would indicate which way things were going. It was the best they could do under the circumstances.

***

The first truck pulled out of the warehouse as the early evening slowly stole the light of the day. Fields gave the Iranian driver directions as they moved slowly toward the southern edge of the city. George had the second truck with McKay in third position.

159

Landau brought up the tail-gunner slot in the number four truck as he knew the route best and would make sure no one deviated. Two trucks were left behind at the warehouse; they wouldn't be needed until the following night.

It was quiet, but Landau just wished he had more weaponry on board. As it was, the three High Standards would have to suffice. Still, he was better off than Stavros who had nothing but his wits to defend himself.

Once again, the route unwound itself before them. The tight turns and unease that came with driving in the crowded urban areas soon gave way to the relative freedom of the open road once they were clear of the city.

As they drove, the headlights of each truck threw a flat cone of yellow light down the road. It was monotonous except for the occasional desert owl that flew across the road in the front of the truck, perhaps hunting bugs or just because they were mesmerized by the beams. As the evening progressed, the ground ahead became a dark blue that was split by the horizon, black on one side of the road and a fiery red-orange on the other as the sun set in the West.

Landau opened the passenger side window not so much because the air inside the cabin was stifling or the air outside was beginning to cool off, but because his driver was a smoker. He was a smoker with terminal cancer who decided he was going to enjoy his habit even if it killed him. Which it had.

"I will be dead in six months, maybe a year," he told Landau at the beginning of the trip.

Landau decided the driver was trying to take him along with him. He needed the fresh air and leaned closer to the open window. He hated the smoke. The cheap Iranian cigarettes reminded him of the smell of burning bamboo, the fires that raged after a napalm run. Those were times he would rather forget because there was the memory of another smell that came along with the bamboo smoke, that of burning flesh.

The convoy finally came to the unpaved turnoff and the distance between each vehicle increased as clouds of dust rose to obscure the following drivers' vision. They drove on, east against the night, taking as much care as possible on the gravel and dirt road. No one wanted to be the one to accidentally go off-road in a big, heavy Mercedes van without a really good reason.

The road snaked and rose steadily as they came into the foothills. The vans, without a load, had no difficulty climbing the grades as the diesels sang the smooth tune their German engineers intended. Then they reached the path at the bottom of the *laager* hill site. Fields and Landau hopped out and directed the drivers to turn their trucks around and line up some 100 meters away, out of sight of the main road.

McKay and George joined them and, once the rucksacks were adjusted and comfortable, they began the trudge up the path. The temperature dropped quickly in the desert; there was nothing to hold warmth. The heat escaped from the earth and sparse flora much faster than it would return the next day. Still, the climb was enough for them to break a light sweat. When they reached the top of the path, everyone stopped to pull on a jacket or an anorak to shield them from the cold and wind. They were in position, on top of the hill, as close as they could be to the trucks and ready to receive the flight of helicopters when it arrived. Marker lights would go out once they knew the birds were within thirty minutes of landing, but for the moment, all they had to do was wait.

McKay and Fields unpacked one of the PSC-1s and began to set it up.

"We're shooting for the Indian Ocean bird, the Fleet Sat 72E."

"Never seen one of those SAT things before," said Landau.

"It's still experimental."

"Not so experimental that it doesn't work, I hope," McKay said.

"They work. We used them in Nevada."

Fields unfolded the antenna and attached its cable to the main box, still marked with its factory labels. The antenna looked like two flat spider webs, one set on top of the other with a rod in the center. "It's directional. We need to shoot a 135-degree azimuth and keep it on a 35-degree angle or we won't hit the satellite." He carefully oriented it with his compass and set it on the ground.

"Too complicated. What happens when the satellite moves?"

"It doesn't, it is in a stationary orbit over the equator down there." Fields pointed vaguely into the southeastern sky, where the stars were just starting their nightly light show. "At least we've got good weather."

McKay watched closely as Fields dialed in the frequency and turned on the radio. "Because it's high angle and line of sight, the Iranians can't intercept our signal."

"But they could pick up the satellite's, right?"

"Yeah, but we won't say anything they can use."

Fields grabbed the handset and pushed the talk switch and released it. There was a click and a hiss and then a moment later came an answering click.

"That's the bird talking. Got the splash on the first try."

"Your teacher would be proud," Landau said.

Landau couldn't see Fields glare, which was a good thing. Fields pushed the switch again.

"Foreman, Foreman, this is Esquire, over."

He waited. A moment later, he repeated the call. There was a static hiss on the radio and Fields turned down the squelch until it disappeared.

"One more time," he said and pushed the switch to talk. "Foreman, Foreman, this is Esquire, over."

A moment passed and then, faintly, "Esquire, this is Foreman. Go ahead, over."

"Foreman, this is Esquire. Pass to Bowshot, we are Kingpin, I say again, we are Kingpin, over."

"Esquire, how does it look from your end?"

"Foreman, it's going to be a piece of cake, over."

"Esquire, good copy. We'll pass your report to Bowshot. Bowshot is moving now and will confirm onward movement as scheduled, over."

"Foreman, roger. Tango Uniform. This is Esquire standing by."

Fields set the handset down on top of the radio and sat back.

"That's it. Now we wait."

"Kingpin?" said McKay. "I remember that name from somewhere."

"It was the codename for the Son Tay raid. This time it means we're in position and everything is a ready. And Foreman is General Vaught at Wadi Qena. Bowshot is the main force. The next call we get will be when the helicopters leave Desert One."

"How much time do we have?"

Fields looked at the glowing hands of his watch. "Roughly three hours." He was excited. "I can't believe we're part of this operation. We're going to be making history tomorrow night."

Landau was not impressed.

"That's tomorrow. Right now, I'm going to take a nap. Wake me when they take off."

25

The Desert One landing strip had been checked out several weeks before when two Agency pilots flew a de Havilland Twin Otter into country with only one passenger on board: an air force major, a combat controller who knew a thing or two about improvised airfields. Specifically, he understood how hard the strip needed to be to support the landing weight of several big Hercules aircraft. It would not do to stick a bunch of big C-130s into a giant sand trap deep inside a hostile country.

After unloading a little motorcycle from the Otter, the major rode up and down the strip looking it over. The location had been chosen by analysts using map and satellite photos along with the personal experience of someone who had driven through the area once long ago. At one point, the major stopped and peered unbelievingly out into the empty darkness that surrounded him. The day's heat was still percolating up from the hard sand that had been baked by an unforgiving sun all day. It would only be relatively cool a couple hours before sunrise and then the cycle would repeat itself. The major didn't want to be caught in the desert during the day for too long. He'd heard the stories of the American pilots who crashed in the Libyan desert during World War II. Those who were found years later had been preserved like beef jerky. On a lighter note, he was still amazed at his situation.

I'm in the middle of a desert in Iran at night on a motorbike all by myself checking a runway for a secret mission. No one would ever believe me if I told them.

He stopped at several points and pulled a device from his backpack, a long rod with a sharp point and a gauge on the other end. It was a penetrometer, and he pushed it into the dirt to test the underlying hardness. Satisfied with his findings, he pulled out some small boxes and buried them in the ground—remote-controlled infrared landing lights. He took one last look around the strip before he headed back to board his ride home. The Agency pilots were playing cards under the wing waiting for his return.

***

On April 25 in the very early morning, that same air force major is on board "Dragon 1," the lead MC-130. As the combat control team commander, he is responsible for moving and arranging the aircraft as if they were chess pieces on a big game board. As they approach their landing strip, Dragon 1 does a circular fly-by looking for anything unusual. Nothing. A switch in the cockpit is flipped and the landing lights marking the center line of the airstrip come to life, their green glow visible only through the lenses of the pilots' night vision goggles. The game is on and the Combat Talon sets down heavily. The pilot reverses the angle of the propellers and the loaded bird comes to a quick stop, the rear ramp already open. Combat controllers rush out on Yamaha motorbikes to set up a more robust lighting system for the follow-on aircraft, while the Ranger road watch teams set out to secure both ends of the dirt track that runs the length of the runway. It is 2245 hours.

Before they can secure the road, a civilian truck bumbles into the zone. A snap decision is made and a Ranger fires a light anti-tank rocket. The truck is disabled, but the driver escapes, jumping into a pick-up that was following. Unfortunately, the truck was a fuel tanker. It flares into a burning beacon; it looks like World War III has started.

What had been an empty track a few minutes ago now seems to be a major thoroughfare. A bus appears from the darkness; it is stopped and the frightened passengers onboard are offloaded by men who, with their guns and night vision goggles, must look like visitors from an alien world.

The second MC-130 lands, then the third, and they offload the troops. Two aircraft take off. They will return to Masirah for the night. Then the refueling birds land. Their engines cannot be shut down for fear they won't restart. Everyone waits expectantly in a strange darkness. They stand inside a bubble of dust kicked up by the propellers, illuminated by the bonfire of an unlucky fuel smuggler's truck.

They wait. The helicopters should arrive in thirty minutes.

They don't.

***

To the south, six helicopters struggle, flying at low level through an intense dust storm called a *haboob*. It doesn't matter what the name means, all the pilots can think of is that the dust of the storm is so fine it seeps into every part of the aircraft, coating everything, but more importantly making navigation nearly impossible. The pilots have never experienced anything like it and it requires all their skills, attention, and physical reserves to continue the course. They are nearly overwhelmed.

At first, they could see the other aircraft flying in formation. Then it got darker and visibility closed down to 200 meters, then less. The lead helo risked turning on his bright red marker strobe, the others followed suit. The visibility got worse, 100 meters and then nothing. They could not see each other. They were on their own to navigate over the desert and through a pass in the mountain range that lies between them and their destination.

Two helicopters have already given up the struggle, one with a warning light that indicates a rotor crack. They know it might be fatal to continue so they land in the desert. A second drops in and picks up the crew of the first and decides to return to the mother ship.

Finally, six helicopters arrive at the Desert One refueling point. It is 0100. The pilots are exhausted physically and mentally. There is concern among the command group, but with six, they can proceed to Desert Two, the *laager* site. Six helicopters are the minimum for continuing the mission. The mission could continue.

Until it can't. Upon landing, the last helicopter lost a critical system; its hydraulics are "Tango Uniform"—broken and not repairable. Little time remains; the night is fast turning to day.

A leaders' meeting is called. Eight helicopters had started, only five can continue. It is not enough as one more bird is predicted to fail. The minimums are not met. There is but one solution: abort and withdraw to try again later.

Abort. It's an ugly word. From the high the men of the force felt on departure from the island, everyone is in the depths of disappointment. So close.

***

The command group is centered on the airstrip between the four remaining airplanes and the helicopters. By now everyone is covered with the fine dust that floats above the ground. The ghostly light from the bonfire of the fuel truck makes the men look like warrior spirits freshly emerged from the underworld.

Colonels Kyle, Jelinek, and Beckwith confer briefly. The helos will be refueled and they will withdraw to the carrier to fight another day. The men despair but are resolute: they'll return to finish the job. Jelinek calls Jock over.

"The mission is off—delayed. Gather the team and be ready to reload the aircraft. We'll depart once the helos are topped off and have lifted off."

Jock Sheldon nods and walks back to his men. "We're going home. We'll try again later."

The Rangers continue their road watching as the men of Delta and SF Berlin stand by. The helicopters do their slow dance among immense billowing clouds of dust. Each flies in a low hover to the refuel point, each sits like a nursing chick to receive its 15,000-pound fuel ration of JP-5 which will take it back to the *Nimitz* where they will await another attempt.

One helo moves off and another settles into place, guided by a ground crewman with lighted batons. The dust swirls around its rotors. The pilot struggles to see and fly at the same time, his hands moving the cyclic and collective in well-practiced motions. Only the motions are wrong. The helicopter maneuvers somehow as if the pilot were flying it while looking in a mirror. He wants to go left and back, the helicopter slides right and forward. Horribly, like a slow-motion movie clip, things go wrong. The pilot can't see that the long rotors of his RH-53 are inching closer to another EC-130 that is preparing to depart. Closer and closer, until finally one connects just behind the cockpit of the airplane with a loud *crack*. The momentum of the turning blades pulls the helicopter forward, even closer, and its blades smack the fuselage several times, cutting it open. Sparks shower inside and out of the aircraft and flames begin to lick the insides of the big metal tube. A big rubber fuel bladder inside the C-130, which serves as the resting place for a group of airman and soldiers, becomes a bomb waiting for an already burning match.

The men onboard had fully expected their airplane to take off. That thought quickly evaporates. They can instantly hear and see the danger, and quickly come to the conclusion that something is very wrong. Controlled pandemonium results. With the fire taking hold, everyone races for the exits. An oxygen tank explodes, showering the men with metal shrapnel. Some fall, others pick them up and throw them out the open hatchways.

The helo slams into the hard-packed sand, the pilots frantically trying to power down, then leaping through the open windows as it too began to burn. The fuel-fired, aluminum conflagration is intense: there are only seconds to escape before everything explodes.

Several men on the outside run to the burning aircraft and help the wounded and injured away from the fire. Two brave souls climb inside and pull crewmen, some horribly burned, from the aircraft. Everyone is stunned. The mission goes from an abort to catastrophic failure in a matter of moments.

One hundred meters away, Jock Sheldon pulls his pistol from its holster. He had cleared it for the ride back to Masirah, but now he jacks a round back into the chamber and checks his submachine gun. It too is ready.

"What are you doing?" Robert asks.

Robert isn't alone. The rest of the team want to know what is going on with their leader.

"It's a long walk out of here. If we meet any Iranians, they're gonna regret it."

Colonel Kyle takes charge after a short radio conversation with Foreman. He speaks with the army commanders and makes the decision to abandon the site as fast as possible. The helicopters will be sacrificed. The White House has denied permission for a fighter mission to destroy them.

"Get everyone out now. An airstrike would be too dangerous," they say.

For whom? This place is already dangerous.

Inside the two burning aircraft, eight men had no chance. Trapped in the wreckage or killed outright by the explosion, there is no way to get to them out of the inferno. There is no time.

Eight brave men are left behind.
Eight families will mourn.

***

The next morning the mood on Masirah is bleak. An oppressive despondency drifts over, around, and through the tents like an invisible cloud. Embarrassed, humiliated, pissed off—every other possible bad feeling haunts the men, despite knowing they did their best and could do little to change the course of events. Most men are silent, except Beckwith who rages. Vaught and Kyle try to calm him.

Around noon, an airfield tug arrives from the other side of the airfield pulling a cargo trailer. The British advisors to the Sultan's air force have sent a package. It's a pallet of cold beer. Attached to the delivery is a note written on a cardboard box flap.

"At least you had the guts to try," it says.

26

Landau's gaze swept warily over the Intercon's small lounge. There was a scrum of newspeople in one corner talking among themselves and a few isolated guests, but no one close enough to eavesdrop. Fields, McKay, and Stavros leaned in to listen.

The previous evening sitting on the hilltop had been tense. The time for the helicopters to launch from the refuel point had come and gone. Several lifetimes went by as they waited. Then the message finally came.

"Not tonight. We'll try again."

What happened? When was again?

They had no idea until that morning when Landau was listening to *Deutsche Welle* on his Grundig World Band radio. When he heard the lead, his stomach sank. It sank further when he heard the newsreader describe the mission in detail.

Amerikanische Rettungsversuch gescheitert...
American Rescue Attempt Fails

The four Americans had chosen to meet in the Intercon, one of the only places left where more than two Westerners could get together without looking out of place.

"Where's George?" Landau asked.

"He's gone to ground. He heard about what happened on the news this morning and called me in the room to say he was going to his uncle's village. That was his way of saying he was going to make it out on his own. He is resourceful," Fields said. "He'll most likely make it out on a smuggler's route."

Looking at his comrades, Landau said, "This is going to have to be our last meeting in the open."

Before anyone could ask why, he continued.

"We have been screwed by the Pentagon. Not only did they give a press release on the failure in the desert, some idiot gave a deep background brief and said there were Americans still in country. That means we are in a bad way. Our documents should hold up to scrutiny, but we need to avoid being linked together. From here on out, we need to have individual meetings to coordinate when we get out of here. I think the best way will be just like we went out before—by air. Our tickets are good and trying to go cross country wouldn't make any sense."

"Then we wait a day or so?"

"Yes. I told the drivers to make their own way out as well. I gave each of them five thousand dollars at the warehouse. Everyone let me know when you're traveling after you get your tickets changed, but stay cool. Don't rush."

Then the meeting broke up but Stavros remained, sitting until Landau was alone.

"I won't be going out with you. I still have to get the trash can out," Stavros said.

"Why?" said Landau. "It's the Agency's problem, not ours."

"You're right, it's not your problem. It's mine. I was given orders to get it out. There's no telling what might happen if it's found."

"They should send their own team, not risk any of us."

"I'm here now and this will probably be the best shot we have. Besides, if I can get one American out, it will be worth it."

"You're crazy, you know."

"This whole thing was crazy to begin with, but we accepted that."

"Do you have any idea on how you can pull it off?"

"The Greek knows things went south so he's lying low. He'll wait for me at his safe house. My plan is to go for one of the 'bus stops,' the E&E points, but we never did final plans for a specific place or time because it was only a contingency."

"It's real now."

"Thanks, I know that. I need to figure out the best location for a pick-up and you'll have to get that to the boss for me. Since we can't go out through the airport, crossing the border on foot with the device is our last option."

"And how do you get there?"

"The Greek has a fully kitted out truck, so we can use it to head for the Turkish border or maybe a seaport. We'll pick up a load of carpets as a cover cargo from one of the vendors I was dealing with. If we aren't picked up at the E&E site, we both have Greek papers and should be able to exit on those. Getting the device through customs will be tricky though. It's not like we can pass it off as a can of pistachio nuts."

Landau looked at Stavros closely and saw a bit of himself, a younger version, much like he was a long time ago. A young, untested man on his first solo operation who wanted to do it right. Maybe scared underneath it all, but pressing on nevertheless.

If you're not scared, you're lying.

"Come up with a plan for your best option and get it to me right away. I will brief the boss when I get out. We can support you better from outside anyway. You can use all the gear we have stashed at the warehouse, including the Mercedes. And don't forget the gold."

Stavros felt like a kid whose dad had given him the keys to the car.

"I'll work it out and give you the specifics. Meet you at Bravo?"

"That's good. Let's meet at 2120 tomorrow."

*****

173

The next evening, Stavros crossed the Park Hotel's crowded lobby and slid unobtrusively into the lounge. There wasn't any alcohol being served as the hotel had been mostly taken over by the petty theocrats of the regime who had yet to find permanent residence in the city. The lounge still looked strange, like a Howard Johnson version of a *hammam,* with ornate wall-coverings and modern plastic furniture. It was filled with cigarette smoke and the heavy smell of cardamom-laced coffee being consumed by a malevolent-looking clientele. Ninety-five percent of the people staying here were Iranians, the rest were foreign businessmen, mostly Middle Eastern, and not a woman among them, he noted.

He wondered how Sarah would handle the situation and decided she wouldn't have given it a second thought. She'd walk in and sit down, openly daring any of the men to give her a hard time. He cleared the thought from his mind, enjoyable as it was, and got back to thinking operationally. This wasn't the time to be missing his girlfriend.

He sat at one of the few empty tables until, finally, a surly waiter asked him what he wanted. Stavros thought his presence was being challenged but resisted countering with his own bad attitude. He did not wish to be remembered.

"*Qahveh siyaah, loftan.*" Ordering coffee exhausted most of his Persian, but the waiter was impressed and lightened up before he marched off to get the order. While he was waiting, he looked around the room. Most everyone was in animated conversation and no one seemed interested. He relaxed a bit and shook out the well-worn copy of *Kathimerini* he had picked up in the Athens airport the day he left Greece. It was as good as anything to get people to ignore him.

The coffee came. Stavros paid right away and went back to reading.

2107 hours. Stavros sipped the last dregs and stood up, folding his newspaper. He left the lounge and kept to the left, entering a hallway to a staff elevator where he waited. When the door sighed open, he entered and pressed the button for the twelfth floor, two short of the top. He got off and walked the hall to the opposite end, then pushed the exit door, making sure it was unlocked on the inside before he stepped into the stairwell. A moment passed as he waited silently sensing the environment, then he walked down three levels. It was still quiet. He hadn't seen a person since the first floor. On the ninth floor he again walked the length of the hall hoping his luck would hold out. There were stairwells on both ends, a concession made to fire safety in the last ten years. He entered and again stood for a moment listening to the emptiness, then walked up.

"Everything okay?" Landau asked on the half landing.

"I'm okay, no problems. I met with the Greek and this is what we came up with," he said, as he passed a small envelope to Landau. "We're going to head for Safe Area TIBET using the main road network toward Tabriz. We'll be there in not more than four days. We'll monitor the E&E frequencies for as long as we can. There's a designated E&E airstrip up there and if we can get picked up there, great. If not, we'll move the last 30 kilometers and cross the border on foot near 'Dog Bone.' It's all in there."

"Dog Bone? What's that? And why not just cross the border with the truck?"

"Dog Bone is someone's very clever codename for the only crossing point foreigners can use to get into Turkey. Its real name is Dogubazet. Dog Bone, get it? Never mind. As to crossing the border with the truck, the Greek doesn't think we'd make it through Iranian exit procedures. They search too well looking for drugs and contraband."

Stavros handed Landau another piece of folded paper.

"This is the address of Jonny's warehouse, just in case. You better eat that after you memorize it, that's the last thing we want anyone to find. We'll most likely be out of town in no more than two days."

"You'll keep us up to date?"

"Yes, I have the radio and Jonny told me the truck is equipped with some type of tracking rig called OMEGA and he can plot our position pretty accurately."

"Send out your coordinates and your ETA at TIBET on our channel anyway. I don't trust the Agency to share anything with us. They have not been very helpful in that regard."

"They better share if they want their toy back, not to mention their man."

"One would think that would be the case, but don't count on them." Landau put the notes in his coat pocket and checked the stairwell again out of habit. "Listen, we'll be gone soon and you'll be on your own. I'll get your plan to the boss and we'll do everything to get you out."

"I certainly hope so," said Stavros.

"No worries my friend. Now, I have one more request of you. McKay and Fields are leaving from their hotel going straight to the airport. I need a ride and the taxis won't come to my hotel. Too many *mullahs* hanging around, I think. Would you pick me up tomorrow at 0900 with the Mercedes? After that, you're on your own."

"Is that safe?" Stavros didn't want to question Landau's judgement.

"Not the best way, but there's not much choice. Just a quick pick-up and drop-off."

"Okay, no problem. How are you flying out?"

"Swiss Air to Geneva and then I'll call in and go wherever they need me."

Landau grabbed Stavros' shoulders and squeezed hard.

"*Geh mit Gott, Kampfgenosse.*" Landau handed Stavros the keys to the warehouse and the car, the keys to the kingdom as it were.

"Stay safe, brother, and see you in the morning."

Stavros headed down the stairs. He didn't hear Landau go but knew he was gone.

***

The next morning, Stavros got up and tried not to think about the danger. Instead he focused on what he needed to do immediately. Pick up Landau. He had the Mercedes and headed through town. Landau was at the edge of the driveway when Stavros approached. With a well-practiced move he popped open the trunk and tossed in his suitcase before he climbed into the car.

"*Los*," he said.

"You'll be out of here in a few hours."

"Two and a half, but who's counting?"

"McKay and Fields are gone?"

"They should be, hopefully. Ewen managed to stay out of trouble this long, I hope he didn't kill anyone on the way out."

"Hopefully. You'd have to be insane to stay here when you have a safe ride out."

"You mean like you? For the most part, but not entirely. I still have to run the security gauntlet at the airport. The only good thing about them is the guards don't seem to have had much training. Of course, they're liable to shoot anyone by accident."

"Well, you'll get out. Give everyone my regards," Stavros smiled.

"You'll be fine. I'll pass on your plan and you'll be out before you know it."

"I feel a bit like Odysseus right now."

"Why?"

"Because I'm Greek and prone to tragedy."

"He got home, didn't he?"

"Sure, ten years later."

"They didn't have airplanes back then."

At the terminal, Landau got out and grabbed his bag before he waved Stavros off.

"Safe journey," Stavros said as he wheeled the car out of the airport.

Landau watched him go and then walked inside.

***

Down the road from the entrance where Landau disappeared, Arkady sat on a wall in the shade watching things happen. He had thought this would be a good spot to watch for foreigners and he was pleased. The Mercedes looked like many others in town but he recognized the man who got out. He had seen him in the Intercon several times with several other Westerners. When the car drove past, he looked at the driver.

That face I haven't seen before. Strange that one businessman would be driven to the airport by another...

As the car passed he looked for something to remember. On a remarkably unremarkable car, the only thing he saw was a Persian Football League sticker on the trunk. And a registration number. He needed to find Mischa. There were finally some questions to answer.

Who is the driver and what is he doing in Tehran?

***

Rajavi beat Arkady to the punch for the next meeting. He was in the chair facing the window when the two Russians came in and he already had his coffee. He could see they were upset with him for stealing the chair, but he didn't care, what with the one guy talking bad about his nervous eye and all. He was a communist but he wasn't sure he liked Russians any more than he did the religious types. Even if they didn't know he could speak their language, they should show him respect. But he was still hoping to get out of the country so he could travel to the Iranian communist party office in East Germany.

It would be good to live there, maybe go to school.

A smiling but silent Mischa sat down while Arkady walked up to the counter and ordered coffee.

No patience, always in a hurry.

Returning to the table, Arkady sat down and slapped his hands on his thighs.

"You have something for me?"

"I do. I went through the personnel files in the spy boss's office. He had a list of his people with telephone numbers and addresses. There were four names. The only problem is we have only three of them hostage. One is missing."

"Did you question the American spies about the missing one?"

"We questioned all of them but they say he left Iran long ago."

"Damn it."

"Not to worry. I asked one of the secretary women if she knew. She said she had not seen him since the day before we took over the embassy."

"So he may still be in country?"

"Yes, no Americans have been allowed through the airport. He must be still here."

"His address and phone number. Give them to me."

"No need. I have already checked, his apartment is empty. That means he is hiding."

"How can we find someone hiding in a city this size?"

Then Arkady thought back to the airport. *Someone leaving town after the American disaster, someone staying in town, was there a connection? A yellow Mercedes with a football sticker, what else do we have?*

"Can you have your comrades look for a car? A yellow Mercedes; here's the license number. It's probably parked at or near a hotel."

"I'll try. Is it the American's?"

"It could be. But if you find it, don't grab the driver. He may not be the right guy and even if he is, he has something we want. If he disappears into the embassy with the rest of the hostages, we'll never find it. We need to talk to him first."

"Talk to him? I'll doubt you'll just 'talk' to him."

"Don't worry about what we will do with him. Just find the car."

179

27

Captain Pankeshev and his men were met on the flight line of 3624th Airbase as they disembarked from the Ilyushin 62. The airplane they had flown in on appeared to be an Aeroflot commercial airliner but in reality served only the KGB. As Pankeshev loaded his men and equipment onto a couple of trucks, a lieutenant hopped out of a UAZ-469 staff truck and walked up to Pankeshev, saluting as he approached.

"Comrade Captain, you are requested to report to your new commander. I am to take you to him."

Pankeshev returned the salute noting the junior officer was wearing the blue beret of the VDV airborne forces. He assumed the young man must be *Spetsnaz*.

"Who is my new commander, Lieutenant?"

"General Nikolayev, he came down here from Moscow specifically for this operation."

Pankeshev had heard the name before. A senior officer, Nikolayev had something to do with foreign intelligence collection. He didn't know much more, because no one really understood what it was that the First Chief Directorate did, other than steal secrets and maybe kill people.

The UAZ shook and rattled over the tiniest bump or crack in the concrete. Pankeshev decided it was probably twenty years past the end of its useful service life, but knew it would conceivably still be running twenty years on, like most army vehicles.

The lieutenant brought them to the front of a steel hut like all the others that flanked it except that it had been recently painted a dark olive green. Two troopers stood outside the front door with Kalashnikovs at port arms, shoulder slings relieving their arms of the weapons' weight. They came to attention as Pankeshev approached. He didn't acknowledge them; they were conscripts and well beneath his status.

Inside the hut was a large office that ran almost the entire length of the building. A single doorway stood closed at the far end. In between Pankeshev and the door was a gauntlet of desks and boards with maps and instructions pinned to them surrounded by a phalanx of junior officers and non-coms. A VDV major saw him as he entered, dropped the papers he was reading onto a desk and came to the front where Pankeshev was trying to decide who he should talk to.

"Captain Pankeshev?"

"Yes, Comrade Major. I was told to report to General Nikolayev."

The major returned Pankeshev's salute, "Follow me."

Reaching the far door, the major knocked once and waited.

"Come!"

The major pushed the door open and motioned for Pankeshev to enter first. A large metal desk covered with papers stood in the center of the room. There was a conference table surrounded by chairs to one side, a mobile cork-board stood on the other. Pinned to it was a map of Iran with a clear acetate cover reflecting the harsh overhead lights. It was unmarked.

"Captain Pankeshev reporting as ordered, comrade general."

General Nikolayev stood and came around the desk to face Pankeshev. He looked the junior officer over. He turned to the colonel who stood nearby. "This man led the assault on the presidential palace in Kabul. By all accounts, a very good operation."

"But somewhat costly, comrade general. We lost Colonel Boykov and some very good men," said Pankeshev.

Nikolayev looked at the young captain for a moment, assessing his constitution. Nikolayev had his own experiences, similar to Kabul but more numerous and some even more trying. His face bore the scars as did his memories. He took a long drag off the cigarette he was smoking and dropped it in the ashtray on his desk, then turned back to Pankeshev.

"Yes, captain. But their sacrifice is part of our struggle and must be borne by us survivors. You are a survivor, I think?"

"I hope so, comrade general." Pankeshev was staring at a fixed point on the pale green wall in front of him. He wasn't sure where the conversation was going.

"Good, because you are about to get another chance to prove yourself. I am sure you heard that the American rescue of their hostages failed, yes?"

"Yes, general."

"When their mission failed, the Americans were not able to retrieve their device as they apparently planned. Our agents inside Tehran have been able to discover that there are two Americans in Tehran trying to get the device out. My men are tracking them and keeping me informed of their location. When they are able, they will ambush the Americans and take control of the device. When that happens, you will infiltrate Iran, meet our people outside Tehran, and bring the entire package—our agents, the Americans, and the device—back to the Motherland. Understood?"

"Yes, sir, but we have not been told what we are looking for. Before we left Kabul, Colonel Chaika told me we would be briefed on the device."

"You will be. Colonel Surkov here will ensure you have all the information and maps you need to plan. Now are you satisfied you can do this, captain?"

"We are ready, Comrade General."

"I would say I hope so, but that is not what I feel. This is an imperative. Failure will not be tolerated. Now, get your team settled and be ready for my order to launch. You are dismissed, Captain."

Pankeshev saluted and wheeled about. As he walked purposefully through the hut, he felt uneasy about only one thing: what was this device that no one was willing to tell him about?

28

The American soldier and Russian mole, Ralph Spurgin, made the call from a public telephone as his handler, Klausen, had instructed him. He let the phone ring three times and then hung up. A minute later he called back and someone picked up.

"Yes?" said Klausen.

"It's Robert," said Ralph. "We have the parts for your repair. Can you bring your car?"

"Yes, tomorrow."

"Not then, I'm traveling."

"Where and how long will you be gone?"

"A week, I'm leaving for Berlin tomorrow night."

Klausen thought quickly. He needed to meet *Vladyka* soon and a meeting in Berlin would be a good thing. He knew a place he'd used before.

"I know a very good place to eat in Berlin called Restaurant Stilbruch. It's in the Spandau district. You should go there the day after tomorrow at 2015. If you can't go that night, go the next. Same time. Got it?"

"Stilbruch in Spandau, 2015 hours day after tomorrow, I've got it."

***

184

Major Wallace stuck his head into his boss's office. He was about as excited as a counter-spy officer could get.

"*Verfassungsschutz* called me this morning. Their suspect got a phone call from someone speaking American English. It sounds like arrangements for a meeting were made."

"Anything that links it to our man?"

"The meeting will happen in Berlin at a restaurant either tomorrow or the following night. Coincidentally, our boy is going TDY to Berlin today."

Colonel Pennington jumped up from his desk.

"Hot damn, call Berlin on the secure line. Get them to cover this with all they have, then get your butt up there with Spurgin's photo. If he goes anywhere near the restaurant, nail him and his Russian."

"What about the Germans?"

"Take your contact with you. You'll have to invite him and we'll pay for him to be there 'unofficially' because the Federals can't normally be involved with Allied operations in Berlin. But they can observe and we can share anything that will help their investigations."

"They did say their Russian is an illegal. That means they could prosecute if we can get him back in the FRG," said Wallace.

"Talk with the MI Det when you get to Berlin. See if there is some way we might be able to help the Germans out," Pennington said.

***

Spurgin was pleased with himself. After he had massaged the ego of the slow-witted lieutenant in the vault to get access to the restricted files, he had found the basic plan of how the device was going to be recovered. He even made copies like his handler told him and returned the originals to their folders. He had no clue what the Russians would do with the information but that wasn't his concern. Paying for his Porsche 930 was. He had overextended

185

himself buying the thing—thirty-seven grand was way more than he could normally afford in his pay grade, especially paying alimony at the same time—but now he had steady money coming in from his "second" job.

As he walked toward the restaurant in early evening, cool night air was blowing across the Havel Canal. The restaurant was situated in a pleasant, upscale Berlin neighborhood just north of the old *Zitadelle*, a renaissance fortress built in the sixteenth century, completely separate from the prison nearby where Spurgin knew an infamous former Nazi boss by the name of Rudolf Hess was permanently residing.

He paused at the front entrance to read the menu, thinking perhaps that he had one last chance to watch for surveillance. He had no clue that surveillance was already there, inside the building as well as out. They were waiting not only for Spurgin but for the man they believed would be meeting him. They were patient.

Spurgin entered and found a table toward the back of the room. While he was waiting for his handler, he looked around at the other tables. It was a mostly older crowd and a bit more prosperous than what he was expecting, but he hadn't looked at the prices. The others were mostly couples; one large table was occupied with what looked to be a business gathering as there were two women and three men. He could hear them speaking German, laughing and telling jokes, none of which he could understand. At another sat a younger couple, in their mid-twenties he guessed. Finally, the door opened and Klausen walked in. Another older man was with him, a distinguished, heavily jowled, gray-haired man with glasses, perhaps fifty-five years old.

Klausen walked up to the table with a smile on his face.

"Hello, my friend. I would like to introduce my colleague, *Herr* Blaue."

Herr Blaue shook Spurgin's hand and sat down without a word. Klausen followed suit.

One of the women from the business dinner party stood up and walked toward the restrooms in the back. When she was inside, she clicked the transmit button on her radio three times and then did it again.

"How have you been?" Blaue said.

"Well, and I have had some good luck." Spurgin pulled out an envelope and pushed it across the table to Klausen. Blaue grabbed the envelope and pulled out the note inside. He read it carefully before putting it into his coat pocket.

"Tell me what you've found out," Klausen said in a conspiratorial whisper.

"You heard about the rescue attempt in Iran? Yes. The original plan was to get the device out with those forces, but the accident ruined that plan. Now, they will try to get picked up at one of three sites, which are listed in the paper I gave you. There are only two men and they have a cargo van of some sort. The only other thing is that the truck has some kind of beacon. The radio frequency is also in the notes."

"You've done well, my friend. Your reward will be deposited like your regular payments."

"I was hoping you might be able to give me something sooner than that."

Blaue nodded and Klausen pulled out a small brown envelope and pushed it back across the table.

"This should help," he said.

The front door opened again and two men walked in followed by two uniformed American military policemen and two West Berlin *Polizei* officers. The older of the two men in civilian clothing walked up to Spurgin and flashed his credentials. The business diners also stood up and formed a ring at a safe distance around Spurgin's table.

"Ralph Spurgin?"

Spurgin froze; fear, confusion, panic swept his face.

Again the man asked, "Are you Ralph Spurgin?"

Spurgen sputtered only, "Yes?"

"Please come with us, you're under arrest," the man said. The two tall, beefy MPs flanked Spurgin and pulled him out of the chair.

"And you two, may I see your identification?"

Klausen stood up and pulled out an identification card.

"What's this all about? I am a German national."

"Blaue" swore under his breath. He looked at his subordinate. *You're a bigger idiot than your American spy. You're in West Berlin. Where is your Soviet identification?*

"You, sir, are being detained under suspicion of espionage, as are you," he nodded to Blaue.

"You cannot detain me, I am a Soviet diplomat." Blaue pulled his real identity card from his pocket and held it out like a shield.

The *Polizei* officers grabbed Klausen and frog-marched him out of the restaurant behind the MPs and Spurgin.

Frank Wallace took Blaue's identification card and wrote down the name in his notebook. One of the business diners snapped the Russian's photograph; the flash blinded him and he closed his eyes momentarily. He glared at the photographer who took another just to annoy the Russian spy master.

"I have diplomatic immunity in West Berlin. I demand to be released immediately."

One of the diners spoke quietly to Wallace.

"Spurgin gave him an letter in an envelope and got one in return. We have it on film."

"Well, Mister 'Petr Nikolayev'… of the KGB First Chief Directorate, I assume?" Wallace said.

His question was met with a stony glare.

"You have something that the American gave you. It belongs to the United States Government."

"What he gave me is not of your concern. As I said, I am a diplomat. You can't touch me."

"Take him to Checkpoint Charlie and let him walk across," Wallace said to one of the diners. "You won't refuse our generosity of a ride home, will you? I thought not."

The three men of the business dinner gang herded the Russian out the back door of the restaurant. Wallace turned to his West German colleague.

"Unfortunately, we can't do anything about a Russian diplomat in West Berlin. His 'German' partner on the other hand…"

They walked outside where a handcuffed Spurgin and Klausen were waiting to be loaded into a Military Police van. One of the MPs handed Wallace a cloth pouch.

"We searched them. Their papers and belongings are in there, all inventoried of course. Spurgin had some notes and an envelope with ten thousand dollars cash. The other guy didn't have anything other than his probably fake identification and some Deutschmarks. They must have been driven here and I figure their driver probably split as soon as he saw us move in."

Wallace took the pouch, tucked it under his arm and walked up to Spurgin and Klausen. He leaned in close to Spurgin, who was looking pitifully at the sidewalk.

"I suggest you start working on your confession and tell us everything you've given your Russian friends. Otherwise, you're going away for a long time, slug."

Klausen looked at his former agent.

"You have nothing to tell them. You've done nothing wrong."

Spurgin seemed to gain strength and spit out in Klausen's face, "It's all your fault! You brought this down on me."

Spurgin shoved to the right and left and pushed his MP guards off balance momentarily to break free of their grip. He turned and bolted for a space between two parked cars and into the street. He looked behind him as he breached the gap and turned his head too late, just as he blundered in front of a big yellow Berlin BVG bus. A silent scream came from his mouth as his head slammed into the metal with a sickening thud like a ripe melon hit with a bat. The driver did not see him, nor did she brake when Spurgin bounced off the grill and tumbled onto the asphalt. The bus kept moving forward and bounced over the body which was run over by the big tires and dragged along the street. Only then did the driver manage to stop.

The MPs recovered their balance and followed up to the edge of the parked cars and then inched their way along the side of the double-decker bus. Spurgin's feet stuck out from underneath the vehicle. The MPs leaned over to look at the body with their flashlights. Wallace came up behind them after he made sure Klausen was well restrained.

"He's dead," said the MP sergeant.

"He's mush," said the other.

"Most definitively and legally dead," said Wallace. He was staring at Spurgin's shoes. "It looks like the 'Wicked Witch' just got a house dropped on her."

His German companion didn't understand the comment. Rather than explain, Wallace continued.

"Well, I think this makes it a matter for the German authorities. That Russian with false West German identification just caused a fatality."

"I'm not sure your legal interpretation of our laws is correct, Mister Wallace, but the Federal German government will happily take custody of *Herr* Klausen to look into this incident. And we will gratefully share the results of our inquiry," said *Verfassungsschutz* officer Helmut Beyer.

***

Back in Stuttgart, Wallace walked into Pennington's office looking through a folder of papers.

"We have zero information from Spurgin's office files, home, or pocket litter to indicate what he was giving the Russians. We know he had a hell of a lot of bills, especially paying for his Porsche, but not much else. The photographic record from the restaurant showed him receiving cash, evidently for the envelope he passed, but there's no audio of the event. We do have one tidbit though."

"Go on, don't make me wait for it," said Pennington.

Wallace continued, "When Nikolayev looked at the note Spurgin gave him, our cameras captured a frame of the paper that we were able to enlarge. It shows names and geographic coordinates of some places called 'bus stops.' I gave them to the G-3 to check. They're for a group of E&E extraction sites in Iran that were to be used during the hostage rescue operation."

"So he didn't give them anything that is really current?"

"Actually, he did. The sites are still active and they're tied to some special recovery operation. It's apparently so classified that they took the photo from me and they want all the film showing the document to be destroyed."

"You told the G-3 where it came from, I hope?"

"Yes, sir. That got them even more agitated. The current ops colonel told someone to inform Colonel Zakary at SOTFE that the sites had been compromised."

"That means the Special Forces are up to something. Whomever or whatever it is they're going after, I hope they get there in time."

29

Stavros had showed up at Jonny's safe house the previous evening. They had talked about the best time to leave town and how to get where they wanted to go. It was simple, up to the point when they had to drive the truck out of the warehouse, get onto the road to Tabriz, and run the gauntlet toward Turkey. Jonny had no idea what awaited them on Highway 2 as he had never driven that direction before. He'd been on the other half of the route all the way to the eastern border and beyond but that didn't help much. But he knew one person who could help them: Kemal Sayd. Jonny had recruited Kemal to be his team leader for Perses shortly after he arrived in Tehran. Meeting in a late-night coffee shop, Jonny had recognized him as an outsider although he didn't initially know how far of an outsider Kemal really was in Iran. Kemal was doing off-the-books work; he was an illegal. When Kemal confided that he was a Kurd, Jonny knew he had a keeper, someone who could help him get things done. But now Kemal was out of a job.

But Jonny's federal benefits were still being paid and he had enough of the contingency funds, around twenty thousand dollars, to pay off the team and keep Kemal occupied for a while, plus maybe another ten thousand for expenses. Stavros told him he had some money as well. Not how much, but apparently enough to get them across the border. They wouldn't need much: gas money, hopefully no repairs because the truck was in good shape, and maybe some money for *baksheesh* at the border if they had to go that route. Beyond that, he didn't care. If they failed to make it, it wouldn't matter.

Before he contacted Kemal, he needed supplies and maybe some news. His short-wave receiver wasn't receiving well and Iranian radio was well censored to make sure nothing he heard was informative. It was either the same old propaganda drivel or non-stop prayers. He wanted to hear what was happening, maybe something about the embassy and how his fellow Americans were doing. Even though he was outside and not a hostage, he didn't feel free. To be sure, there were no ropes and gags and blindfolds, but he still felt restrained. He had to consider the risk of every move he took. Moreover, he hoped the Station's files had been destroyed. As with every bureaucracy, anytime the Agency paid for a service, it had to record the cost and the justification and what it was all for. His safe house was no exception; but it wasn't safe if the files were opened.

He accepted that he was in a jam, and by the time "Pavlos" had shown up, he was beginning to question his motivations for saving the free world from whatever it was that threatened this week. Last year it was the Russians, this week it seemed to be the *mullahs*. Being a bachelor, he was just happy he didn't need to be concerned for a family. Today, as with every day he spent in Iran, he only needed to survive until tomorrow.

He knew one small shop across the street that was probably a safe bet, owned by an elderly man who kept his politics out of sight and his head down. He may have been pro-Shah but he didn't advertise, but then most people didn't talk politics before or after *mullahs* came to power. Most importantly, he seemed friendly. Not that he intended to confide in the man, he just wanted some things before they made their dash out of town.

Every time he walked out the door he felt he was taking a risk. He wasn't going far but it would take him a while.

In this case, the round-about route is the shortest way to get where I'm going and back without an interruption.

By interruption he meant capture, interrogation, and perhaps a very long incarceration. At best.

So he went out the back and walked through the same parking lot Pavlos had used the other night. The night air outside smelled better than inside the safe house, which was filled with the stuffiness of someone trapped inside, the smells of bachelor cooking, empty tuna fish cans and not enough cleaning. It was good to be out in the evening twilight and harder for anyone to notice him if they were watching. He felt freer on the streets.

Freer? Is that a word? Whatever, more free.

At least he was using his senses, his observation skills, and not just sitting, waiting.

The shop was actually on the front side of the safe house, across the street and visible from his front window. That was how he knew it was open. The lights hanging from the fringe of the canopy were on. He could see the bins of fruit out front, people checking out each piece carefully before putting it back and selecting another. On the inside, a small space, were the hard goods, the expensive things, the things he needed. And he could see the owner in the shop, behind the counter one moment, among the wares the next, flitting about making sure everything was in place and everyone was happy.

He came from behind the store, down a side street, and walked in.

Sohan was the shop's name, and the owner was Hamid.

Hamid looked up when Jonny walked in. He didn't know Jonny's name, but he knew Jonny. He knew the face, a polite young man who had shopped in his store before.

The old man smiled and nodded his head and went back to explaining where the canned sardines actually came from to an old lady who didn't quite believe him.

"I only sell good merchandise, madam, you can believe that. Would I still be in business if I didn't?"

"It depends. How long have you been in business?"

Jonny gathered the supplies he needed, some canned goods, some batteries for his radio and the flashlight. "Good Japanese batteries, not the counterfeits from Pakistan," Hamid told him.

When the store was empty, the man spoke quietly to Jonny and they stepped behind a rack of goods. Hamid was fingering a white silken piece of cloth he had pulled from his pocket. Jonny recognized the shape: it was a yarmulke.

Jonny looked at it, then looked at Hamid and nodded.

"You're Jewish?"

Hamid smiled a small smile and put the fabric back in his jacket.

Hamid said, "A strange thing happened today. Two men came in here and bought some bread, but one of them didn't speak Persian. He kept asking his friend something and finally the other man asked if I had any caviar sandwiches. I thought that was very strange. Then they stood outside looking at that house across the way, your house, no?" He gestured at Jonny's safe house with his a nod of his head.

"Yes. What language were they speaking?"

"Russian."

A cold chill ran down Jonny's spine as he walked back his convoluted route home.

Caviar sandwiches?

The last time he'd thought about caviar seemed so long ago. He had arranged an event for the ambassador back in the old days. It was at Leon's Russian Grill. Leon's was the spot where the chief of station used to entertain his contacts. He never said he was the COS, but everyone knew and that was okay with him because he relished the attention. He didn't do anything operational, he just ran the Station. And Jonny remembered the ambassador's meal because it was the last time he had eaten there. First, the borscht came, then the blinis with caviar and crème fraîche on top. And they drank vodka. It didn't look like vodka because the waiters served it from 7 Up bottles to fool the *mullahs'* watchers. He should have realized then what the future would bring.

Jonny approached the back door of the safe house with no small amount of trepidation. For one, he wasn't armed. He'd left his pistol in the house. Now he was wishing he hadn't. As he walked closer, he couldn't see anything out of place. The wind rustled through the pine branches above his head. The only other thing he heard was his own heartbeat.

He unlocked the door as quietly as he could and pushed it slowly open. He was thankful that he oiled the latches. Stepping inside, he stopped and listened… nothing, quiet. He moved again, forward, slowly. In the front room of the house, he saw the lights of a car through the window and he knew. The glass in the front door was broken. And then everything went black.

***

The safe signal wasn't there so that meant the open doorway was a danger zone. If there was a noise, the door was where everyone would look and gun barrels would follow.

No need to make it easy for them.

For a moment, Stavros listened and heard only the ticking of his watch. Time slowed and his senses sharpened as he focused on everything around him. When he first began training in close quarter battle, it seemed like each scenario was a jumble, moving too fast, his movement awkward, the targets blurred, shots taken before they should have been, malfunctions not felt or recognized. Then, as he became used to the speed, he felt he was able to take in a situation completely with a quick glance and could focus on his target precisely, his movements controlled by muscle memory that came from repetition and conditioning. He knew when to move and shoot as well as when not to.

He chose.

Stavros moved quickly, deliberately, a silent blur through the open space, and stopped in the shadow beyond, coiled, waiting. Nothing, silence, he didn't sense a living thing. Light from the next room fell through the door ahead of him. He extended his senses outward and picked up movement, muffled voices, life. He moved again, carefully, slowly picking his way along the hallway while focusing on the distant danger until he was at the next door. He looked into the room using the wall as cover, degree by degree, section by section, like cutting pieces of a pie, until he knew what was happening. Jonny was sitting stiff in a chair against the wall. He knew where the friendly was; now he had to pinpoint the hostiles.

He watched Jonny's face, which showed only a neutral expression. There was a line of dried blood running down the side of his face. His eyes were locked on the man speaking to him, a man Stavros couldn't see. A voice was speaking English with an accent. He fixed the position from Jonny's eyes. That's where one hazard would be, and there were probably others. He also knew the room, he'd been there before.

Stavros pulled a second magazine from his pocket and held it and his pistol with both hands extended in front of him. The High Standard HDMS was not the best weapon for close quarter combat, it was best employed to take out the lone sentry or guard dog. But it was all he had and he knew how to use it. With the hammer back and the weapon off safe, he leaned slowly into the light falling through the door. He could see more of the room and an arm of a man standing by the far wall. Two hazards at least, maybe more. He had twenty rounds in hand, more in his coat. Stavros was surprised at how calm he felt. He exhaled then inhaled slowly.

Stavros watched as Jonny tilted his head and looked at the floor. Then he saw Jonny's eyes dart toward him and back. Jonny lifted his head and looked in the blind corner and then back at the voice. Three hazards in the room.

197

Stavros committed. Three quick steps, pistol held level, shoulder high, firing as soon as he acquired the target. Before he stopped, two rounds hit the target belonging to the arm he had seen. The man's eyes grew wide as he looked down at his chest where a red blossom appeared. His G-3 rifle clattered to the floor.

Stavros swept his focus right to the man with the voice and fired one round before he swept on to the last man in the corner. Two bullets, these in the man's face. His head jerked back and he collapsed in a heap. Stavros swept his pistol back to the man with the voice. It was not a pleasant face. The voice was frozen, the eyes wide, he tried to speak but the voice never came. A red hole in his throat oozed blood. Stavros pulled the trigger twice more, the suppressed High Standard puffing its bullets the 2 meters that separated the muzzle from its target. The impact of .22 caliber Stinger hollow-points on flesh and bone was almost louder than the muffled report of the gun. The man dropped to the floor like a sack of flour. Stavros dropped the magazine and clicked a second firmly into place. Seven rounds in less than five seconds and a combat reload. He swept the room again. No more danger.

Stavros walked up to each body one at a time and fired a single round, a *coup de grâce*, to make sure they were not just merely dead, but completely and truly dead before he turned to his comrade. They looked like the "students" he'd seen at the airport.

"What happened?" He picked up the ejected magazine and stuffed it in his pocket.

"I am not sure. I went out to get some stuff we will need and when I came back these guys were waiting for me. I got knocked out and when I came to, they had me in a chair. Thanks for dropping by. I owe you one."

"How's your head? You need a band aid?"

"I'm fine, thanks." Jonny grabbed a towel and winced as he dabbed at the bump on his scalp.

"You can buy me a beer when we get out of this mess."

"What do you think now?"

"We get the hell out of here soon."

"We may have one other problem. These guys may have been sent here by the Russians."

"How do you know that? They look Iranian."

"They are," Jonny said, gesturing at the bodies, "But when I was at the shop, the owner told me about two guys who had been watching the house. Said they spoke Russian."

"You trust him?"

"I do now."

"That means this place is burned and we need to get out of here ASAP. I was planning on leaving here tomorrow. I think we need to move our departure and get out now. Can we go to your warehouse?"

"We can, but my biggest questions are how did they find us and what did they want? Did you drag them here or did something from the station files give away the location."

"Or both? That means I need to dump the Mercedes, but I need to get my stuff out of it."

"I have an idea. One last ride, we drive up the hill a ways and leave the car there and go cross-country on foot. Can you climb?"

"What kind of climbing?"

"Easy stuff, tourist trails. I've got everything here. One other thing, we're taking someone with us tomorrow."

"I can climb. Who are you taking?"

"My team leader. He knows the northwest provinces."

"All I care about is whether he's trustworthy."

"He's good, he's a Kurd. He doesn't have many Persian friends."

***

Mischa and Arkady came in the front door of the darkened house they had been watching earlier. Arkady was concerned that Rajavi hadn't reported back.

199

"I told you we should not have left."

"We needed to follow the Mercedes," Arkady said. "Besides, Rajavi is here."

"Somehow, I don't think he is here anymore."

Arkady stepped into the central room. He knew from the sweet metallic smell in the air that something bad had happened. Flipping the light switch confirmed his fears.

"Rajavi, you fool," he said.

Rajavi didn't respond; he'd been dead for at least an hour.

"So these Americans are not entirely stupid," said Mischa.

"And now they may know we're after them."

"Probably. What now?"

"We find the Mercedes again."

***

Jonny and Stavros both grabbed their rucksacks from the car and hefted them into a comfortable position on their backs for the walk.

"Where we going?"

"Up. This is the trail to Darband village and the mountains. It's a favorite weekend spot for walks and picnics. There shouldn't be many people and we don't look out of place except for the fact that hardly anyone climbs the hills at night. But it will get us away from town and we can traverse the foothills to above where the warehouse is located."

"What about your team leader?"

"I'll go get him and bring him in tomorrow. Then we can blow this joint."

"Dated," Stavros said.

"What's dated?"

"You, your vernacular: 'blow this joint,' where's that from anyway?"

"So maybe I've been out of the country for a while."

Abandoning the car, they headed up the street to where it joined the upward track. True to Jonny's word, there were hardly any people on the trail except for a few making their way up to one of the restaurants that sat along the route. They proceeded slowly, leap frogging, one moving on ahead while the other remained behind to ensure they weren't being followed.

"Thanks, Rabbit," Stavros murmured under his breath, thinking back to the long days of surveillance training in the city. Jonny shot him a curious look, but Stavros just grinned and shook his head.

After about thirty minutes, Jonny turned off the track onto a smaller path that headed across the hill. The trees were close to them and the ground covered with pine needles. The foliage seemed to absorb the noise of their passing. A series of steps appeared, which Jonny bounded up.

"Watch out, the wood is slippery."

It was a bridge over a small river. The cold mountain water splashed and gurgled down the slope toward the city. Stavros grabbed the handrail and looked up the small valley the river had cut in the hill and then turned to watch the water disappear down the slope below him.

"The water goes underground in a park down the hill, I think."

Jonny continued over the bridge and stopped at the bottom of another set of steps.

"This is our first stop. It's called Koohpaye. Good food. I used to come here a lot."

Stavros saw before him a rustic restaurant set on multiple levels, part inside, part outside terrace. It was half-filled with guests who made it up the trail, but there were people who obviously hadn't climbed the hill. Old people, far too old for the hill.

"There's a road on the other side. Some people drive up that way. It's also where we'll head across the slope."

Jonny switched from Greek to Persian as he spoke to the man behind the podium. Stavros could see that Jonny had a well-established rapport with the man. The maître d' was wafer thin, with slicked back hair, dressed in a banded-collar white shirt and black slacks, and he was trying hard to show off his position. With a flourish, he picked up a couple of menus and led them across the red-tiled terrace to a table next to the railing. Over the railing was the river and up from that was where they had crossed it.

"We'll break here for a bit and then press on. We can see if anyone approaches, but I doubt the Russians will know the trails well enough, especially since you took care of their local guides."

"I hope they don't have more. We need the time and space to clear out of here."

Stavros let Jonny order some food. Tea came and he stirred in a little sugar before he took a sip and, although he didn't really like tea, it was hot and fragrant. He preferred coffee but accepted that it was probably not as healthy for him. Then again, he wasn't really worried about his health right now. The clinking of his spoon on the cup was a comforting sound and dispelled some of his anxiety for the moment. Music drifted out of the interior and across the hills, a plaintive Persian melody, probably a folk tune, a mellowing sound, played on an acoustic guitar that somehow didn't fit his mood. He looked around at the restaurant and saw a bunch of locals, most of whom looked to be fairly well-off but not very happy. He was sure they were concerned with exactly what direction their country was heading. His concerns were of shorter term, like surviving the next forty-eight hours. He heard the wind rustle through the mountain pines and turned back to Jonny, who was watching the trail intently as if he expected a squad of soldiers to burst into view.

"I think we can relax," Stavros said. "They won't have any idea where we are unless they find the car and, even then, there are ten trails to take. What are the odds?"

"Small, probably, but then I don't have control over the script."

"Script? Are we in a movie?"

"Have you ever read *The Quiet American*?"

"Graham Greene?"

"He wrote it, yes."

"What about it?"

"Nothing much, just sometimes I think we're chasing shadows. Fighting a war that can't be won."

"And that reminds you of the book?"

"Kind of, this situation... our conflict with the Russians is reminding me of the book."

"I don't agree. Unlike Vietnam, this war, even if it's a Cold War, can be won."

Stavros sipped his drink and decided to ask because no one had told him what he wanted to know.

"What was the device for?"

Jonny turned his attention away from the trail and looked at Stavros for a moment before he spoke. It was hard to discern what he was thinking, dark eyes hid his thoughts and the beard hid his facial expressions.

"We were going to dissuade the Russians from invading Afghanistan by destroying their river crossing site at Kushk."

"With a nuke?"

"Yeah, it would have taken out their bridge and whatever was on either river bank."

Stavros sat back, incredulous; all he could say was, "That's fucking insane."

"They never would have figured out who was behind it. We had a solid plan. The engineers back home devised a sled for the thing that would float just under the surface of the water and hide it. We were going to put the sled in the river about a mile upstream and float it down with the timer set to go off right as it got to the bridge."

"Who figured out the timing?"

"I did."

"Like you went there and tested it?"

"Just once. I went in with Kemal and looked at the site."

"So, then the thing goes off and everyone thought the Soviets wouldn't figure out what it was when their dosimeters spiked into the red and the mushroom cloud appeared? And who would they blame it on, India? Who came up with the plan?"

"The head of Russia House, but everyone above him signed off on the finding."

"Bad, bad, stupid bad idea. Russians don't think like we do and if you expect they will react the same way as us, you're wrong. Who knows what they might have done? Direct provocation is not the way to beat them."

Jonny didn't have a ready answer. He stared up as if he was trying to see through the dark blue fabric of the pergola over their heads. It was quiet, seemingly the entire restaurant was waiting for Jonny to speak. Stavros sensed he had probably wounded several sensitive spots in Jonny's psyche.

"We'll never know."

Stavros came to a sudden realization.

"Jesus, I just thought of something. They know about the device. Why else would Boris and Rasputin be looking for us?"

"Who are Boris and Rasputin?"

"The two Russians watching your house, the ones following us. They needed names."

Jonny sat up in his chair, thrust back into the moment.

"Let's get going."

"I'm not going anywhere until I finish my kebab."

***

Then it was time to go. As they walked out of the restaurant, Jonny grabbed the maître d's hand with both of his and shook it once, hard. He held the grip for a moment while he thanked the man, discreetly passing a five-thousand-rial note. Although the note displayed the

Shah's face, Jonny was certain he would accept it. It was still legal tender after all.

"He was always helpful and you never know when I might be back," Jonny explained.

"Unlike MacArthur, I know I'm not coming back."

***

"It's not quite what I envisioned your warehouse would look like," said Stavros. "It's more of a garage."

"You're right but I didn't think 'garage' would sound very impressive in the reports."

Stavros looked around. Behind him was a door to the small office where they had entered the building. In front was Jonny's Mercedes van parked in a space just long enough for a row of tool cabinets to fit behind it. To get to the cabinets, you had to turn sideways to slip through the gap. But Stavros was only interested in the truck. Jonny unlocked the cab and climbed in, Stavros following on the other side. The front section was roomy, with a bed behind the two seats which would accommodate them all comfortably. The rear section was walled off from the front but Stavros could see a hatch. He turned the handle and it opened into a dark empty cargo bay.

"The device is hidden in a compartment under the bed. You can get to it from the cab or through a concealed door in the wall. There are two Kalashnikovs in there, as well."

The cab had little colored cotton balls that dangled from the tops of all the windows. Colored pictures of Bollywood stars and singers were plastered to the walls and ceiling. Jonny pressed a spot on the ceiling and a concealed tray dropped down a short way. "My commo system," he said. "I tested it about a month ago, it's good."

Jonny pulled out a small headphone and mike set and rewrapped the cord around it before he shoved it back inside and carefully closed the compartment.

"It looks like something from a Gypsy caravan," Stavros said.

"It's appropriate, we're going to be on the Silk Road, after all."

Stavros hopped out of the cab and walked slowly around the truck inspecting. New tires, he noted, deep clean tread but appropriately scuffed and aged. They would hold up for the rough road ahead.

Hopefully.

The exterior was well banged up. Stavros wasn't sure if it had earned its stripes on the road or at the hands of an artist in a shop. It certainly looked the part of an average local transport vehicle. He was having difficulty categorizing the truck's color. It was an amalgam of shades and tints, from an off-white to light rust brown with dusty mid-gray accents; an urban camouflage of sorts. On the rear bumper was a Turkish registration plate and a rectangular blue and white shield with the letters "TIR," which he knew from his time in Europe to mean International Road Transport, the convention that allowed trucks to pass through a country without being taxed. In this part of the world it didn't necessarily mean anything, other than possibly lower bribes.

Jonny came up behind Stavros, momentarily startling him out of his thoughts.

"I have all the necessary paperwork to forge and we'll put 'official' seals on the doors so the local police won't be tempted to inspect us. Kemal will handle the talking anyway." Jonny made finger quotes around the word official as he held up the pliers that would crush the lead seal on the doors' to show they had been properly inspected.

"Kemal is your guy?"

"Yes, he would have led the team into Afghanistan."

"He's lucky, there's better job security in this gig than the old one, I think. When will he get here?"

"I have to go meet him. He's never been here before."

"Does he know he's going to take a trip?"

"He will, there's nothing else for him to do right now. He travels light anyway."

"How light?"

"The clothes he wears, and a shoulder bag, that's it."

"He's a Paladin then?"

"Maybe a Kurdish version. He's been with the *Peshmerga* a long time."

"And he's survived in Iran?"

"Rather well. He's a ghost and it's time for me to go bring him in."

***

After Jonny slipped out the back door, Stavros wandered from room to room partly in an attempt to ward off boredom, partly to figure out what he had for options. He decided there weren't many. Despite his feelings about the stupidity of Jonny's mission, at least its being aborted by the regime change may have been a blessing.

Now, I just have to get the damn thing out of the country.

And Jonny.

And me.

The plan he had passed to Landau had no doubt already started the process and now people, his people, would be getting ready to place themselves in danger to help them escape. That meant he had to get to the exfil point to meet them. He had an obligation to be there, to complete that part of the mission for them.

He found himself staring out the front office window through a gap in the tightly closed curtains. The area had been dark and empty when they arrived earlier in the day but now he could see a few people moving along the street. The building was still in the foothills of the mountains, further up the slope than his hotel but not as far as the restaurant they had visited. The neighborhood was also much quieter and more prosperous than where their mission warehouse had been located in the south of the city. He watched the street for a while, then turned away deciding he didn't like being on the run. He looked at his Seiko Diver. Several hours to go. He tried to relax but his mind was racing again and instead he reflected on his memories of Berlin. He realized that Sarah knew just what she was doing when she gave him the watch. It was part of his job to know exactly what time it was and he would look at it often and remember her. And now he missed her.

When he heard the scrape of the key in the lock, Stavros was reclined on the couch with his eyes closed. He rolled off and took a position in the corner with his pistol at the ready and waited. As the door squeaked open, he heard Jonny's voice quietly say in Greek, "I'm home, dear."

"You're funny," Stavros relaxed. "Where's your man?"

"Waiting. Is that how you greet all your friends?"

Stavros returned the pistol to his bag. "Only bearded gnomes like you."

"All is well I hope?"

With Stavros' confirmation, he walked over to the curtain and swept it open for a moment and then closed it again. He turned to Stavros. "It's quiet out there. Nothing out of the ordinary."

A couple of minutes later a rap came on the door and it opened. In came a tall, athletic figure with long black hair framing his face, which was a well-toned bronze influenced by both his heritage and the sun, much darker than either Jonny's or Stavros' Mediterranean skin. He was also graced with a shorter, more disciplined beard and moustache than Jonny's. What surprised Stavros were his piercingly bright blue eyes.

Perhaps a Circassian somewhere deep in the family wood pile.

"This is Kemal. Kemal, this is Pavlos, my partner." Jonny was speaking English.

Stavros walked the seven steps across the room to meet Kemal and shook his hand. Kemal noted the gesture.

"It is good to meet you." He touched his hand to his heart as he said so and Stavros returned the greeting. Stavros noted that Kemal's

English was precise, with an accent learned in a school that probably didn't teach Arabic or Persian.

True to Jonny's description, Kemal was carrying only a simple bread bag, a cloth shoulder bag with a flap. He slipped it off and placed it gingerly on a table. Stavros heard the telltale clunk of a metallic object. Kemal looked at Stavros and smiled. "It's my guardian angel."

"I think we all have one to rely on."

Jonny picked his own bag up and set it on the couch. He opened the flap and began to pull his gear out of it.

"What now, do we just leave or wait a while?" he said.

"We need to make a run into the city. We need a cover cargo, and there's one rug dealer on the way out of town who can give me what we need." Stavros watched Jonny as he went through his gear. Most of it was the usual everyday stuff that all former Boy Scouts turned action guys tended to carry: flashlight, a folding knife, a small pouch with documents and money, a couple of Long Range Patrol rations, some canned fruit, and a cloth-wrapped bundle.

Stavros picked up the knife and opened the blade.

"It's a Gerber Silver Knight. It was issue at a previous office I served in. I forgot to give it back," Jonny said.

"Nice. I have a knife in my bag, but I don't even know who made it. I got all my kit from the guys who bailed out. What's your pistol?"

"CZ-75, it's Czech, similar to the Browning Hi-Power. They always did make good weapons." He unwrapped the bundle and revealed the pistol in a dark brown, leather concealment holster along with four magazines of 9mm ammo.

It was about to become show and tell time as Stavros opened his heavier rucksack and started to pull his equipment out. Then he realized something was wrong.

"Crap," said Stavros. He stood with his hands on his hips, cursing silently.

"What?"

"I left the Prick 90 in the car."

"What's that?"

"The survival radio."

"You have the other radio don't you?"

"Yes, but it won't communicate with the airplane. We don't have the right antenna."

"So what do we do?"

"Only one thing to do. After we pick up the load, we have to blast past where we left the car. I go grab it and then we hit the road. We'll have to be careful though, Boris and Rasputin may be watching the car."

"This is getting to be almost as complicated as a family trip the beach."

"Except without the kids."

"We are the kids."

Kemal listened to the exchange with a bemused look on his face. He wasn't exactly sure how, but he was beginning to think he might be involved in some kind of satire.

"I have a Stechkin pistol," he said.

"Where did you get that?"

"It once belonged to someone who no longer requires it."

"His guardian angel switched sides?"

Kemal smiled again. "Yes, that would be a good way to describe it."

***

Downtown, Kemal was supervising the boys loading the rugs into the van while simultaneously watching the street for any signs of interest. Stavros was trying to speed up the transaction with the merchant without stepping all over the time-honored requirement to drag out every transaction with his hospitality.

"You chose impeccably, my friend. Thirty-two of my finest carpets, some ancient, some new, all quite valuable and very unique. I have given you a very nice discount because I hope you will come back and buy more."

Stavros was actually surprised at the amount he had charged; it was reasonable compared to most of the other price gougers he had dealt with and the shop had very good coffee to boot.

"I can't pay you in Iranian currency because the banks could not change so much money quickly," Stavros lied. He had not wanted to risk going into a bank and flashing his passport at this stage in the game. Luckily, he had the operational funds that Bob left at the warehouse that were in Belgian francs. He had been told by the briefers that the Iranians preferred them to their own currency. He showed the old man a crisp thousand-franc note.

"Those will be fine, but just give me some small money for my needs here. The rest I would like you to pay my son. He lives in France. Here's his address, send him the money and give him this number." The old man handed Stavros a note.

"You would trust me to do that?"

"It's a variation of *havala*, a very old way of moving money. Above all, life is all about trust, my friend. If you pay me here, you'll be giving the government money. Outside, my family gets it. I would prefer to trust you."

Stavros dealt out the colorful notes until the carpet dealer finally said stop and then put the wadded-up remainder back in his pocket.

As they climbed into the van, Jonny asked, "How much did you give him?"

"About three hundred dollars."

"For thirty-two nice carpets? I shoulda bought a couple."

"I'm not sure. Someone at headquarters will have a fit when they find out we bought a bunch of carpets that may not even get out of the country."

"I call it the price of freedom."

"You do that. Maybe I'll call it cover support expenses."

"I think you should keep your op fund and tell my folks to pay the bill."

"An even better idea."

Jonny drove the first leg back up into the foothills, up Shemiran Road parallel to the street they had parked on the previous evening. When he came to Jafari Street, he turned into the darkened lane and stopped by the curb.

"The car is parked to the right of the next intersection. I'll wait until you turn up the street and then roll across and stop about 50 meters further down this same road."

"You know the city well."

"That's kind of what they pay me for."

Stavros got out and headed down the sidewalk as Jonny turned off the motor. Kemal crawled out of the back section and hopped into the vacant seat.

"I'm going to shadow him."

Jonny didn't ask why. "Go. Make sure he makes it back to us."

Kemal slipped out and crossed the street to give himself some distance and then followed Stavros up Darband. He stopped for a moment to watch Jonny drive the Mercedes van further down Tajek Street and then slowly followed Stavros, watching the neighborhood.

Stavros approached the yellow sedan carefully, looking for any sign that it had been disturbed. Seeing nothing, he quickly unlocked the passenger side door and reached under the seat. Pulling the small bag out, he stuffed it in his coat pocket, and shut the door. He looked around as he pretended to lock the door and then returned down the street to meet the truck.

In the car parked up the street, Arkady elbowed a napping Mischa.

"We got one. Let's go."

Mischa waited a moment before he let the brake off and rolled out of the parking spot without starting the car. Only when Stavros turned right onto Tajek did he turn the key and start the car. They didn't see Kemal as he slipped through the shadows on the opposite side of the street.

Stavros climbed into the cab.

"Get in the back. Kemal is coming."

Now in front of them, Kemal dashed across the street and followed Stavros in.

"We may have company. Two guys in an old, dark red Peugeot followed your friend Pavlos after he left the Mercedes. They're at the intersection now, so watch for them."

"They see you?"

"I don't think so."

Jonny put the truck in gear and started off. "I'll drive the first leg and then turn it over to you, Kemal. In the meantime, make sure you're both locked and loaded."

30

They periodically checked the mirrors for the Peugeot, but it was difficult to see clearly through the road dust and all the other traffic. They just assumed the Russians were there.

"I am still wondering if it was your car or the Station files that led them to us?"

"A combination, I think," Stavros said.

"We could stop and ask them," said Kemal.

"Then we'd have to kill them," said Jonny.

"That may be necessary in any event."

"More importantly…" Stavros was thinking aloud. "What are their plans? They have a reason to be after us and it must be the device, otherwise they could have turned us in or just kidnapped us."

"They probably want to ambush us now that they have our trail. Question is: do they have backup and do they know where we're headed?"

"I think they can assume we're headed for Turkey. And right now, our only advantage is that we know they're there."

"I'm starting to like Kemal's plan."

***

It was dusk as they got onto the road. Route 2, it was called, and it was heavily traveled by all manner of cargo trucks going in both directions. They fit right in with the possible exception that theirs was *probably* the only truck with a nuclear weapon on board.

Earlier Stavros had asked Jonny if Kemal knew about the weapon.

"I briefed him generally, but he figured out what it was as soon as I described it. He studied engineering at Cambridge in the UK, he's very intelligent."

"And now he's fighting the Soviets?"

"He's very disappointed that he won't be able to kill any. Now he'll have to go back to killing Turks. For him it's all about freedom for the Kurds. Engineering comes later."

The truck hummed along the road with the constant growl of its diesel becoming just more background noise to be ignored, although voices were raised to be heard. Stavros felt relieved to be working as part of a pack instead of the lone wolf. The days on his own had worn on his psyche. He was also happy that Jonny seemed to be something of a kindred spirit. Then he noticed that Kemal was eating something. He was hungry again.

"Kemal, what are you eating?"

Kemal swallowed what he had in his mouth. "*Zalobiya*, it's a Kurdish pastry. Here, try." He handed the remnants of his piece back to Stavros, before pulling another out of a bag.

"I get the leftovers?"

"Yeah, in case you don't like."

Stavros took a bite. "Good, like a sweet Danish," he said.

"If you say so."

"Where do you get them?"

"From a friend. They don't sell them in Tehran."

"A friend? Not family? Where's your family?" Stavros asked.

Too late he saw Jonny's look. It was a 'don't ask that' look.

Kemal was quiet. He stared out the windshield for a long moment.

"They are all gone. My father and mother were killed by the Turkish *İstihbarat*. I have one sister still. She's a nurse in Kurdistan. I never see her now."

A quiet set in that no one wanted to break.

Eventually, Jonny's curiosity got him.

"Pavlos, your father was in the army?"

"He served in the Greek Army during World War II. He fought the Germans and ended up on Crete and stayed there through to the end. It was his home. That's where I was born after the war."

"Was he there when the Germans invaded?"

"Yes, he fought with the *Andartes*, the guerrillas."

"Communist or Republican?"

"You're kidding, right? He was Republican, of course. How about your family? Where were they?"

"On the mainland, my dad went into the hills like yours while my mom kept her head low. My family left Greece in 1946 just before the civil war. I was born in Virginia. My dad was working for the USG by then," Jonny said. "Why did your family leave?"

"We left because of the communists. Dad was threatened because he refused to support a local politician and it started to get ugly. He got us new passports with help from someone in Athens."

"So naturally you followed your father and went into the army."

"My parents weren't keen on my plan to quit college, but I didn't give them much choice. They would have preferred me being a doctor or something."

"Have you been in combat?" Jonny asked curiously.

"Not yet. I've had a couple of near misses, but they don't count. In seventy-three, we were alerted for the Arab-Israeli War but that got canceled. Then I was on a six-week African thing, but that wasn't considered a combat zone because there were only twelve of us, and then a couple of years later we almost got the first combat jump into England."

216

"England?"

"Funny story. We got alerted during an exercise we were doing in Europe. Some informant told the Brits that the IRA were going to steal explosives from a military base. Unfortunately the base was one where the US stored nukes, so we jumped in to secure the weapons. Everyone thought it was a test of some sort until they issued live ammo."

"Always a good indicator that something is up."

"That was when the older guys got nervous, so we young 'uns did too."

"What happened?"

"Nothing, it must have been a hoax."

"You got a jump out of it."

"Big deal. I had plenty already and the winds were high but our commander—we called him 'Ming the Merciless'—decided we would jump anyway. Unfortunately, I landed badly and broke my leg but they put it back together."

"A good name, Ming the Merciless."

"He was willing to throw people away to get a promotion. All I got was three months in a cast. What about you? How did you get into stuff like this?" said Stavros.

"I got recruited at Princeton. Some pin-stripe kinda guy talked to me and persuaded me to serve my country. It didn't take much, although I had second thoughts a couple of times during the interviews and testing. The psychiatrist was the worst; actually, I think he was crazy but he had me wondering if I really wanted to be a spook. It has all played out well. I've done two other pretty interesting tours and enjoyed working with the outfit. It pays pretty good too."

"Where did you learn your Persian?"

"My father ended up as part of the American Military Assistance and Advisory Group in Iran during the Shah's regime. He was a civilian supply type and I was an impressionable kid who picked up the lingo. I continued to study it in college. I even had a long-haired dictionary for a while."

"A what?"

"An Iranian girlfriend."

"So have you done any other cool undercover work?"

"You know I'd have to kill you," Jonny said.

"I've heard that one before. But here I am with you, along with a Kurdish mercenary and a nuke in the middle of Iran, and you can't tell me where you've worked? I just might have to kill *you*."

"Tell you what, when we get outta here, I'll fill you in on my resumé. The less you know right now the better."

"Okay, it's a deal. I haven't told you anything real about me anyway."

"And there we are," Jonny said.

They lapsed into silence, peering out the window of the Mercedes into the darkness as Kemal drove the twisting serpent of a highway leading to the northwest and the city of Tabriz.

31

Jelinek stood with Bergmann and Becker off to one side of the tarmac. The rest of Becker's recovery team were sorting out their gear as they rigged up behind the dark green and black camouflaged MC-130.

"Becker, I want you to get in and get out. Don't spend any more time on the ground than you must. We'll be up in the C3 bird on this side of the border and will make sure you have overhead cover tomorrow morning. I just need you to stay in good radio contact."

"Roger, sir. We have everything we need and once we are in, we'll be up on the air and monitoring continuously."

"Let me know when you have our guys and the package and are ready for pick-up. The Otter won't land until we hear from you."

"Got it, sir," Becker said. He was getting a little antsy before the mission as he would have preferred to be going over things with his team, but he knew the colonel wanted to make sure his end was tied up securely.

"Last thing, Becker," the colonel said. He paused until he was sure he had his team sergeant's attention. "We think Ivan knows where the pick-up zone is located. We don't think they are there yet, but if you run into them, when you run into them, do not hesitate to take them down. There are no Rules of Engagement, getting our people and the device out is your only priority. Try not to engage the Iranians but if the Russkies try to stop you… You mustn't let that happen and you know the final option."

"I do, sir, but we're all coming out, no worries."

Bergmann changed the subject before the colonel could go off on one of his tirades against the communists.

"Seems like Team 5 are forever rescuing each other. Now, aren't you glad you weren't on the assault force?"

"Now I am, Sergeant Major. But two weeks ago I would have killed to be on it. Things change quick in this business."

"Well, your mission is the only game in town until we figure out where we go next with the hostages. All eyes are on you now."

"That makes me feel real special. No pressure."

"No pressure, Kim. Now go get your guys together. Launch time is in an hour."

Bergmann watched Becker go back to his men. He steered Jelinek away from joining them. He knew that when officers tried to help their men, the work always seemed to end up getting more complicated.

Jelinek put his hand on his sergeant major's shoulder.

"They're our boys, Jeff."

"They certainly are and they'll do you proud, Stan." The sergeant major knew exactly when he could get away with calling his commander, his confidant, and friend by his first name. It was times like this one.

"I don't worry about that, I just want them all to come back home in one piece."

32

The freeway was almost as modern as those of the United States or Europe. It had to be, as it was a lifeline for the country. The one big exception was that the truckers on it seemed to have no fear of dying. The trucks were indicators of how things worked. Or didn't. The last time Stavros had seen so many trucks with bad suspensions, bent frames and tilting cabs rolling at an angle down the road was in Africa. He never could figure out how the tires lasted more than a few clicks when they ran twenty degrees off the straight line. That may have explained why so many trucks were stopped on the side of the road or lying on their sides in a ditch. The only ones that were in decent shape were the few that were registered anywhere west of Turkey. Despite all the breakdowns, commerce was still moving on the Silk Road as it had been for thousands of years, although at a slightly faster pace.

Jonny's Mercedes was a "Q-ship" on the highway: a seemingly run-down, tired vehicle, it blended in and deceived the casual observer. On the inside it was a different matter, the suspension and power train were in superb condition, and the fact that the driver and passengers were well armed wouldn't hurt their odds of survival.

At least the weather was cooperating. It was cool at nighttime running along the southern edges of the mountain range, climbing in altitude a bit as they headed west toward Tabriz, several hundred kilometers away. Then after that, they needed to cover around 75 clicks more to get to the pick-up point—maybe eight hours if things went smoothly. But first, there was a small matter of some pest control issues to be dealt with.

Jonny was watching the mirrors as they moved forward while Kemal concentrated on what was in front. Stavros tried to do both.

"I have an idea. Let's pull off somewhere and when the Peugeot follows us, we take off again slowly. That will confirm they're behind us."

"What if they don't stop?" said Kemal.

"They will have to wait somewhere ahead to pick us up again."

"It may also tell them that we know they are there."

"Maybe, but if you get out and fiddle with something, they'll think we're just taking a break. We don't have much to lose."

"I just hate to throw away any advantage we have."

"I think I have a solution for that."

***

Mischa and Arkady saw the Mercedes at the small fuel stop just before they got to the exit road. Mischa slowed the car, "Do we follow?"

"Yes, stop before the edge of the parking area. They shouldn't see us."

The Mercedes hadn't stopped at the pumps, it was parked on the edge of the road just beyond with the passenger door opened. They saw Jonny came round the front of the truck with a long wooden club in hand. When he got to the wheel well he smacked the tire with the club to hear the hollow echo of a well-inflated tire. He walked to the rear tire and smacked it as well before he returned to the cab and tossed the club under his seat. Before he climbed into the cab, he unzipped his field jacket and shook it off, throwing it onto the seat and giving the Russians a good thirty seconds to look at him. Then he put his foot on the metal step and grabbed the handhold before he pulled himself upward and back inside. As soon as the door closed, the truck rolled forward.

"Checking tire pressure?" The wooden club was a technique Mischa had never seen.

"Maybe. Maybe they're having problems with the steering. The truck is a piece of junk."

"Wait until they are back on the freeway and follow them. Don't turn on the headlights yet."

Mischa did as the smarter of the two suggested and rolled off slowly, making sure he wasn't squashed by the big trucks that couldn't see them or didn't care for French cars.

***

"Got them," Kemal said. "They came in to the stop and then followed us out without using their lights. They turned them on behind a truck so we wouldn't notice."

"But we did. Now what, maestro?"

Stavros had assumed control of the operation. "Phase two is another stop for fuel in about 100 clicks. Preferably a large open area with overnight parking, Kemal."

"Are you planning a rest stop?"

"Not for us. Maybe for Rasputin and Boris."

"If they are Rasputin and Boris, who does that makes us?"

Kemal had no clue what the two Americans were talking about.

One hundred and ten kilometers further on, they found the type of truck stop they were looking for, more a communal parking lot than a formal station like those in Europe. There was a cinder-block building that served as the office for whoever owned the place and four big metal tanks on stilts that held the fuel, all of them diesel. Good petrol was hard to find on the highway. There was one other big freight truck topping off its tanks, which naturally blocked all the positions. It moved out after five minutes and Kemal pulled up to the filler hoses.

"Don't get out, Kemal. Switch places with me and I'll fill it up. We don't want them to see there are three of us," Stavros said.

"It won't take much. We started out full and the tanks hold 600 liters," Jonny said.

"I'll pretend to fill it."

Stavros climbed out of the driver's side of the cab and walked around the front, his footsteps crunching into the loose gravel. The attendant sat in his cheap folding chair. Bad attitude was written all over his face and he stared at Stavros with a look that said, "Don't expect me to actually pump your fuel." He did get up and saunter over to the filler to reset the gauge on the pump and then returned to what he probably thought was his rightful place in the world: his throne. Stavros took the filler and shoved it in the tank all the while watching if the man was even paying attention. When it was clear he wasn't, Stavros left the nozzle in the tank, stuck his hands in his pockets and wandered away a bit to study first the fuel tanks, then the mountains, and last, the parking lot. This last bit he did quickly, scanning the vehicles to locate the sedans among the trucks, which was fairly easy. In a matter of seconds, he located the offending Peugeot and marked it on the sketch map he was building in his mind.

A moment later, he heard the automatic shut-off on the nozzle click. He glanced at the attendant to see if he had noticed. He hadn't. Stavros went to the front of the truck and looked at the large flat parking area that stretched out before him. It was barely lit by light posts along the two paths that dissected the park. He could see about thirty trucks sitting in the dim light, trucks that had been put to bed by drivers who had no specific time limits pushing them to hurry on that night.

Stavros heard the passenger door squeak open, followed by the crunch of gravel, and felt a presence beside him.

"Nice night," said Jonny. "Did you see our friends?"

"They're parked about 75 meters behind us. Looks like they're waiting."

"Got a plan?"

"Yes, you drive the truck over there to the end of the second line of trucks and park where it's dark. Then you get out and walk back to the shop. Kemal stays in the truck ready for any visitors."

"Where are you during all of this?"

"When you turn the corner by the row of trucks, I am going to roll out and wait for Boris and Rasputin."

"So, I'm the bait?"

"Kinda, but at least you will have protection. I think they want to take us alive if they can."

"I heard that line from a lion tamer once just before he got eaten."

"Occupational hazard. Never be over confident."

Their conversation was interrupted by a somewhat irritated attendant who was wondering why Jonny and Stavros were chatting while the fuel filler had clearly stopped a long time ago. He wanted his money and a clear space to make more cash.

Jonny spoke to the man in soothing tones, cleared the bill with a bit extra to shut him up and climbed into the driver's seat. He turned the key and waited for the glow plug light to go out before he pushed the starter button and listened to the contented diesel ticking over under the engine cover. He hoped the fuel wasn't bad, but thus far the service stations had been reliable. Kemal assured him they still were.

"Everyone ready?" Jonny had his CZ stuffed in his belt, as did Stavros his suppressed High Standard. Receiving the positive answers he was expecting, he dropped the parking brake lever and engaged the transmission to roll forward slowly. Several sets of eyes watched the dark patch behind them. And all the while, Kemal was carefully fingering his Stechkin with anticipation and a familiarity borne of hard-won experience.

***

To their front, Arkady and Mischa saw the fueling station and the office where the Mercedes sat. Beyond that was another structure, even more tenuously built of concrete block and wood braces with a corrugated tin roof. There was a big patio enclosed by a knee-high concrete wall around the entrance. Above it dangled light bulbs strung from wooden poles that tilted in many directions, none of them entirely vertical. Most of the lights worked and covered the area with a warm glow that was somehow inviting from a distance. Closer in to the building the stench would tell a different story, but they couldn't know that yet.

When the Mercedes moved, Mischa again followed at a distance. The van turned to the right past the shop and disappeared for a moment before they could see it proceeding along the parked trucks on the path.

"Go slow. They may be planning to stop."

Mischa took the car around the shop and rolled to a stop. Ahead, their quarry had pulled into one of the last spaces along the path and apparently parked. They waited until the truck's lights went out. A couple of minutes later they saw a figure walk across the path toward them before it cut across to the more direct first track.

"I think that's *karlikovyy*—the dwarf—with the beard. He's the one we really need; the tall one is extra baggage. Now is the time to move before they're back together and locked up in the cab. You find him and follow him back to the truck. I'll go take out the other guy. When the dwarf comes back, we'll ambush him—you behind, me in front—and take him alive."

It was not a precise plan, but Arkady knew it was fairly good and, if executed with surprise and speed, it had a better chance of succeeding than a perfect plan done too late. Especially when they were two against one dwarf.

Mischa found a parking spot and bounded out of the car into the dark.

"Slow down," Arkady whispered after him. He too had gotten out of the car.

A damn hell hound unleashed. I hope he doesn't mess this up.

Arkady shrugged off his jacket and withdrew his suppressed pistol before he pushed the door closed. He looked around to orient himself and to be sure he was not observed before he carefully made his way down the line, weaving between trucks to keep out of sight. He was calculating where his target would be.

The dwarf was driving, so my guy should be in the passenger seat.

He was trying to stay on the dirt instead of the gravel to mask his approach but it was difficult in the dark. It seemed like whoever took care of the place liked to throw shovelfuls of the small stones wherever they weren't needed, or wanted in this case. The crunching sounds assailed his hearing. Peeking between a trailer and its big Scania cab-over tractor, he saw what he wanted, the front end of the Americans' Mercedes. Arkady knew he would be seen if he walked around the front and maybe even the back of the big rig, so he slid under the trailer and paused on the other side looking at the rear view mirrors. It was almost as dark where he was as inside the cab. He discerned no movement, no noise and wondered if the second man had gotten out.

Impossible, I would have seen him.

He slowly stood up from his crouched position and readied his weapon before creeping slowly along the side of the van. He considered his options and he knew couldn't risk trying to open a door that was probably locked. He decided to simply use the step to get close to the window and then shoot the glass out and hopefully hit the man with the first shots. He stepped forward and shifted the pistol to his left hand as he grasped the handhold and quietly put his foot on the step.

"*Vecherniy tovarich. Bros' pistolet.*" Evening comrade, drop the pistol. Stavros had almost exhausted his entire NATO Russian dictionary.

Arkady was at a disadvantage. He knew he was stretched out and off balance and his pistol was in the wrong hand. But he had been well trained for situations such as this and he reacted with lightning speed. He pushed off the step and tucked and rolled on the dirt away from where he had heard the voice. He came up in a crouch with his pistol in both hands pointed at where the voice should have been, but now wasn't. Then he saw the open window above him and started to shift his aim. Two muffled spits came from the truck, along with two from behind the wheels of the Scania. Arkady crumpled to the ground, a loose pile of human detritus in the dark.

Stavros walked up to the Russian and put two more rounds into his head before he picked up the fallen pistol. He looked up at Kemal who had opened the door and was sitting with his legs out the door, smiling. Stavros motioned him down out of the truck. They grabbed the body and drug it forward and dumped it into the brush. Kemal kicked the grass around a bit to hide the body.

"Jonny and the other Russian should be coming back about now. You take up a spot at the front of the truck. That way you can move either direction. I'll be at the back. Don't show yourself until we engage the Russian."

"Engage?"

"Shoot. Don't show yourself until we shoot him."

"Oh, you get to have all the fun."

"You got to shoot the first one. What more do you want?"

Stavros looked about him and saw that the neighborhood was still quiet. No one had been disturbed or no one wanted to be.

One down.

***

Jonny walked into the light of the shop's patio. All around him, he could smell a mixture of burning braziers and burnt meat, diesel and fuel oil, and the disgusting smell of poorly sited squat toilets that were too close to the building and had not been cleaned in a long time.

A haze of smoke drifted across the patio and rolled over the walls. When it enveloped Jonny, his eyes stung and the smell of burning dung and charcoal burnt his nostrils. A few men sat on their haunches by the fires and smoked. A few women sat together with small blanket-wrapped bundles at their sides; what Jonny took to be sleeping children. He decided that the place would have looked the same two hundred years ago except there would have been more camels parked in the lot.

There was a black and white television inside the shop playing some snow-stormy documentary about nothing Jonny could understand. It may have been in Armenian. He looked about the shop and decided the safe thing would be to buy something canned that he could easily toss. A can of sardines sufficed and on the way out he picked up a small cardboard box and stepped back outside. Standing on the patio, he put the can in his coat pocket and balanced the box in front of him like it actually held something which it now did—his pistol.

The walk back to the truck was nerve-wracking, knowing he was being tracked by another human. Despite all his training and assignments in strange and sometimes violent places, he had never been really hunted. Watched, yes. Followed by pick-pockets, yes. Accosted by drunks, hookers, and the occasional panhandler, yes.

Being hunted, now that was a new experience. His advantage was that he knew someone was out there and he could anticipate where he would be confronted. He walked deliberately down the second track and saw the Peugeot parked in the shadow of two big tractor trailers. His head was down, but he was scanning the area around him as best he could. There were no natural look backs that would not telegraph his interest to whoever was behind him.

It was quiet until he felt something fly by his head with a flitting and beating of little wings, and then another. He looked up and saw bats in the sky echo sounding on him as they hunted bugs in the night.

Great, just the night to run into vampires.

He was halfway down the line of trucks when he finally felt a presence, just as he had when he knew "Pavlos" was in his house the previous night. The presence was threatening and totally focused on him. He saw the Mercedes ahead and was tempted to pick up his pace but restrained himself and continued with grim determination. He didn't want to goad an overly nervous hunter into shooting his quarry before it got away. Instead, he fixed his eyes on the rear doors of the van and methodically shuffled forward as he slowly reached into the box to grasp his CZ.

This thing will wake the neighbors for sure.

Jonny flipped off the safety.

Then he saw the silhouette of a man in the darkness to his front.

Stavros stepped around from the side of van and faced Jonny, his pistol leveled waist high. Jonny walked on, not entirely comfortable until he could see that it was Stavros. Then he slowed and stopped about 5 meters from the van. Stavros was standing in the dark when Jonny heard the footfalls behind him.

The Russian was 3 meters from him with a pistol held at the waist.

"Hello American. You are to come with us now," Mischa said in badly accented English. He was smiling the same monkey grin he had shown the *Rezident* the other day, happy to have finally cornered his prey.

About then, Stavros realized the fault in his plan. His position was in direct line with the Russian and Jonny was in the middle. It was Jonny who might get shot in the first exchange of fire.

Stavros stepped to the right as he walked forward a couple of paces. There was just enough light for the Russian to realize the man in the shadows wasn't Arkady, but his weapon wasn't ready. Stavros raised his pistol and said, "Drop." He set himself solidly, waiting for Jonny to clear his line of fire. Jonny was quick. He stepped to the right, away from Stavros and spun around, flinging the box at the Russian's face as he pulled his CZ out and went into a wrestler's crouch low to the ground, pointing his pistol at the Russian's midsection. Mischa tried to shift his sights to the new target but the cardboard box and the two 9 x 18mm rounds that slammed into his temple threw off his aim and thought process. The pistol dropped from his right hand as the left flew to his head in an involuntary reaction. No one knew what he was thinking at that moment, but it was irrelevant. He stumbled and teetered for a moment and then fell to the ground in a heap.

Kemal was faster than anyone else. Smoke curled up from the muzzle of his pistol.

They clustered around and looked down at the body.

"Which one is this?" Jonny asked.

"This is Boris, Rasputin's taller and deader. Good decision to move, Kemal," said Stavros.

"I couldn't see from way back there. I thought I would be more useful out here."

"You were," said Jonny.

Kemal nudged the short Russian's body with his boot. It rolled over to lie completely face down, a rather unceremonious position. After they dumped the body alongside his comrade, Jonny searched their pockets and pulled out wallets and documents.

The trio climbed back into their truck.

"Soviet diplomatic passports and not much cash. Some shopping lists in Russian that I can't read. I think this will go back to Langley for analysis."

Stavros compared the pistol he had picked up from the Russian with Kemal's suppressed version.

"I like yours better," he said.

"I do too. No trade."

"Think anyone saw us?" Jonny said.

"It is possible, but most people would not say anything. They would hide their heads. How do you say?" Kemal asked.

"Like ostriches."

"Yes, they would hide like ostriches. They don't want to make trouble."

"I hope so, Jonny. Do you have any other registration plates for the truck?"

"I do, Bulgarian tags with all the papers. We can change them down the road a bit."

"We need to call in our position too," said Stavros.

"Let's roll, then."

"With our carpets 'We take the Golden Road to Samarkand.' That's James Flecker," said Stavros.

"I know, but Samarkand is in the other direction," Jonny said. He was stroking his beard and looking to the west.

33

The MC-130 Combat Talon sat at the end of the runway waiting for clearance. The green light would come from the National Command Authority after much hand-wringing in the White House and head-shaking at the Pentagon. It was a simple rescue mission, not an assault on a sovereign nation, although the Iranians might have disagreed with the finer points of that judgement.

Finally, the word was passed and the airplane began to roll, a conventional takeoff, no hot-dogging by the pilot. He knew the mission ahead needed no bravado, only professionalism. The 130 lifted off and headed west. It would drop into its radar-following, nap of the earth flight mode very soon. About 30 kilometers from the airfield, it descended to around 300 feet and then turned back to the east. The air force controllers watched it disappear from their screens. They knew the plan, no radio calls were exchanged. The low-altitude flight would mask its approach from the Iranian, as well as the Soviet air defense radars. It would also try the equilibriums of the men who would leave their one-way ride in a couple of hours. Some called it hedge hopping, Becker remembered that Stavros called it "Mister Toad's Wild Ride" in honor of a childhood visit to Anaheim's Disneyland. It was a "D" ticket ride of stomach-churning swerves, jerks, and sudden direction changes that led to his being sick for the rest of the day. It had been almost as violent as being on board this airplane, the saving grace being that the crew were just as likely to get sick as the passengers.

They would be jumping at relatively low altitude, but not 300 feet like most combat jumps. There was no reason to risk the danger of a few seconds saved as no one would be shooting at them. Probably. Hopefully. They assumed the Russians would not be on the ground to greet them.

It was evening when they lifted off and with the short counter-surveillance run the pilot was doing, it would be early morning when they got close to the drop zone. Administratively, this event would be logged as a night combat equipment jump on a piece of paper called a DA Form 1307 that would be classified "Top Secret" and get stuffed into the dark recesses of a Class V safe never to be seen again. That is, if and when they returned. Becker didn't care. Just the thought of having participated in a mission like this was enough for him. Most civilians would never comprehend what it was all about anyway. He looked about him in the eerie low green light at his teammates, who were either in conversation with their neighbor or leaning back with eyes closed in the orange webbed seats. The air force crewmen were standing at the rear of the plane, poking at things on the fuselage or toggling switches as they talked with the pilots up front on the intercom. It was just another day at work, only tonight they were going to earn their hazardous duty pay.

Before long, Becker also tuned out the monotonous drone of the aircraft engines and was well braced for the aircraft's maneuvering. He went over the contact plan for meeting Stavros and his Agency fellow-traveler—that was the easy part—and the action plan for contact with any Iranians or, worst case, the Russians. That would be a work in progress because he had no good idea of what the terrain looked like on the ground other than some aerial photos that were difficult to interpret. Last, he went over the pick-up procedures and hoped the Otter would show up on call. He didn't relish a long cross-country trek through the mountains to get back to Turkey. Every man on the team knew how the operation was supposed to go down, who to talk to, and what the code words were. There was no compartmentation on the team; each man was prepared to take over if need be. That was the best way he could prepare his men for what was ahead—to give them all the tools to succeed.

The loadmaster walked up to Becker and leaned in close. "Thirty minutes out," he said.

There would be no radio contact with the ground; no one was there. They would have to rely on the air force's navigation abilities and hope they identified the correct drop zone. It was a clear night and he hoped to at least see the dirt airstrip that was supposed be there. Reportedly, it had previously been used to funnel supplies into some local group but no real details had been provided. The Agency was always reluctant to share details of its operations with anyone not cleared by Langley, which was just about everyone.

Becker stood and hooked his static line to the anchor cable before checking the open doors of the aircraft for anything that might cause a snag. The loadmaster stood behind him holding on to Becker's harness straps. Satisfied, Becker faced forward and waited until the loadmaster gave him another signal. Becker turned to his team and got their attention.

"Twenty minutes," he yelled, giving the hand signal with all his fingers flashed twice.

Everyone rustled about checking tie-downs, pockets, clips and harnesses.

The plane was still acting like a roller coaster as it wound its way through the valleys and under the still snow-capped peaks of the mountains alongside and beneath them. Six minutes out, Becker stood his charges up and began the hook-up and final inspection routine. He then turned to the open door to look for anything he could recognize. His teammates were standing close together in two files holding their static line in one hand, the other hand on the back of the man in front of them. Their eyes were fixed on him waiting for the next command. The air force loadmaster and his assistant stood behind Becker watching the jumpers closely. They were especially careful to ensure no equipment got too close to the doors where it could be sucked out along with anything and everyone attached to it.

The plane was flying on the plotted approach azimuth when Becker spotted what was probably their destination in the moon-light. He turned to Kaiser, the first man in the stick, and barked out, "Stand in the door!"

With jumpers positioned in the doors on either side, Becker resumed his perch to watch the approach. The green light came on as the air force's best-guess navigation computer reckoned they were at the leading edge of the drop zone. Becker stood up from his crouch and gave the order to jump, "Go!" Becker smacked Kaiser on the butt to give him the physical encouragement needed to leave a perfectly good aircraft in flight and he was gone, jumping briskly into the wind howling past at 110 knots. The rest of the team shuffled out the doors. Becker checked the opposite door to make sure everyone was indeed gone and gave the loadmaster a thumbs up as he handed him the last static line and stepped out into the darkness. Less than ten seconds and everyone was out and under canopy at 800 feet above the ground.

With the drone of the 130 gone, there was only darkness and the sound of the wind. The horizon was difficult to orient on so everyone prepared for the landing by looking down to determine wind drift and speed by how fast the shadows were moving. About 100 feet above the ground, rucksacks were freed on a drop line to swing about 15 feet below each man. The equipment would hit first and remove most of the danger of trying to land with too much weight.

Oscillating slowly back and forth, each jumper felt rather than saw the ground rush up in the darkness and did his best to execute a proper landing. Then it was totally quiet.

Becker got to his feet and shed his parachute harness. He did a quick security check and count of the team before he stuffed the parachute into a kit bag. Everyone was on the ground in one piece, no injuries. He was somewhat astonished given that the field was strewn with rocks and debris. They would cache the chutes anywhere they could. Becker doubted that the locals would report the equipment if it was found, the silk was too valuable and everything was unmarked.

They were nine. Nine men sitting on unfamiliar ground across the frontier in enemy territory waiting for two of their comrades to show up so they could take them home. A simple task. The only problem was that some people didn't want it to happen.

The spot Becker occupied was the collection point and one by one the men came in. Through the green lenses of his night vision goggles, Kim could see they were close to the landing strip. At this level, it was harder to see than in the air. It was flat but so overgrown with weeds that it appeared almost the same as the surrounding fields.

The first thing to do was to get to its edge. Becker chose what he assessed to be the best defensible spot near the end and directed Lindt to take point and move them there. They moved out, Lindt in front, followed by Kaiser. Becker was in the number three position with the rest of the team strung out in a tactical spread behind. It was about a 200-meter march before they stopped again. Once in their perimeter, Kaiser suggested setting up a picket, a forward observation element, near the opposite end. Becker agreed. Kaiser tapped "Poncho" Ponchelli to go with him and they traipsed off with a hand-held radio to keep in touch. Now both ends of the LZ were secure and here they would wait out the cold spring night.

34

The high-pitched, whining Klimov TV3-117 turbines of the two *Krokodil* spooled up quickly. Then the rotors began to turn slowly, increasing their speed until the helicopters were ready to lift off. The sinister-looking birds, camouflaged in sand-predominant and green paint schemes, were waiting for their loads.

Pankeshev had split his force into two eight-man sticks, one for each aircraft. He would ride in the first bird occupying the third crewman's seat. He wanted to be in position to identify the target as they came in to claim their prize.

The Mi-24A was ideal for the team's mission. It could carry an infantry squad in its rear compartment and was protected from ground fire with armor plating. These birds were also fitted with two 57mm UB-32 rocket pods on the winglets that projected from the fuselage sides. Each pod carried thirty-two rockets, which made for a total of 128 between the two aircraft. They were loaded for bear.

Well, almost. Pankeshev was still a bit miffed that the pilot had ordered the removal of the Afanasev A-12.7mm heavy machine gun to save fuel. *At least we still have the rockets.*

Nevertheless, he doubted that they would require their heavy artillery. They weren't hunting anything dangerous, just a couple of Americans in a civilian truck who might have a couple of submachine guns between them. Not what he'd call big game.

There was a small possibility they might have to engage the Iranian defense forces, but their intel people told them it was unlikely. The *Krokodil* would cross the border at low altitude and hug the ground for the entire mission. It was doubtful that any radar would pick them up.

A sheep herder might see us.

His Alpha soldiers were relatively lightly armed. Each carried a Kalashnikov AK-74 with plenty of ammunition—six spare magazines of thirty rounds each—a Makarov pistol, plus a couple of hand grenades. It was enough to deal with the expected situation. He wanted to get in and be out as fast as possible. He was looking forward to an easy, successful mission and maybe a bit of a vacation when they returned to base. After Kabul, his team had earned some time off and this op would be the icing on the cake. He felt his father's knife in his pocket and had some thoughts about what to do with the Americans, but that option had already been removed for him. His instructions were to bring them out. Their knowledge was needed for the investigation of the prize and how it functioned.

The technicians who had briefed them on the weapon did not seem to know much about it. All they could say was it weighed around 60 to 80 pounds and they thought it looked like a small metal drum. They had no idea how it worked, what kind of firing system it had, or what its explosive yield might be. They provided several hypotheses but Pankeshev told his men to forget about them as they were just theories. Only when they saw the prize would they know anything. The only thing they were sure of was that it was probably not a good idea to be nearby if the thing went off.

***

Earlier that day, through the window of his team's billets, Pankeshev had seen one of the intelligence officers and General Petr Nikolayev come out of the orderly room and walk toward their building. He decided to meet them instead of waiting for whatever news they might bring.

"Good morning, Comrade Captain," said Nikolayev. "We have bad news and we have good news."

Nikolayev glanced at the lieutenant who looked much like a puppy dog waiting to please his master.

The lieutenant picked up on his cue. "The good news is that the signals detachment intercepted a transmission from inside Iran. It was in code so they couldn't read it, but it was on the frequency that we have been monitoring for the Americans. It was pinpointed just east of Tabriz, about 200 kilometers from the coordinates we received for the pick-up site."

"Coordinates? When and how did you get those?"

Nikolayev took over.

"We received a list of sites from an American source and only now have we been able to determine which one of the locations they would use. It was process of elimination." He smiled inwardly at what he had just said. Several people had indeed been eliminated in the process, an abnormally ignorant American spy and an underperforming Directorate S officer. No great loss considering the gains to be won.

"That means we need to launch immediately," said Pankeshev.

"Exactly, Captain. The crews have been alerted and the helicopters will be able to launch in fifteen minutes. You are ready, I assume?"

"We have been standing by for this moment for long enough, Comrade General. We are ready. But what is the bad news?"

"We have lost contact with our Service 'A' team inside Iran. It's all up to you now."

"It won't matter, now that we know where the Americans will be."

"Go to it then, Captain, and good hunting."

***

240

Praporshchik Voronin took his element to the second helo. As a warrant officer he was the second-most senior man in the unit. Pankeshev had recommended his recent promotion following his actions at the palace. He deserved the leadership position, Pankeshev thought.

Now Voronin looked the part. Although Alpha was highly trained and loosely structured, the men followed Russian army traditions with regard to rank. A private was just that, a private, the bottom of the heap. A sergeant was a little bit more, to be respected but not really feared. If you beat him in a fistfight, you could always take his job. However, a *Praporshchik* was to be reckoned with, especially one the commander supported. Voronin was also known for physically adjusting a soldier's attitude if the measure was called for, although in Alpha that was rarely necessary. Ninety percent of the troops actually wanted to be in the unit; the motivations of the other ten percent were harder to discern.

Seven men loaded onto Voronin's bird before he turned to Pankeshev and saluted across the tarmac separating the two helicopters. He climbed up the ladder and followed his section inside. Only then did Pankeshev climb into the first bird. He confirmed everyone was ready before he entered the passageway to access the cockpit. He climbed into the fold-down seat behind the pilots and clapped a set of headphones onto his head. He clicked the headset's push to talk switch.

"Commo check," Pankeshev said.

"I have you loud and clear, Captain. Are we ready to go?" the pilot said.

"Ready to launch, Captain."

Under the bullet-resistant canopy, the pilot signaled to the ground crewman outside that he was about to lift off. The crewman, wearing what were once blue-gray coveralls now covered in a muddle of dirt, oil, and grease-stains, gave a thumbs up and backed away from the bird. The pilot dispensed with asking the tower for permission to take off; this flight was the only one scheduled and there was no need to alert any unauthorized eavesdroppers to their departure. All buttoned up, the pitch of the *Krokodil's* engines changed as the blades began to grab air and the load lightened on the landing gear. The Mi-24A rolled forward, its exhaust throwing sinuous striations of heat haze down an already hot runway behind it. The pilot handled the cyclic and collective deftly and the helo lifted off. Moving forward and climbing, ever faster along the flight line, the helo's nose dipped like a carnivore on the attack as it rose rapidly from the airfield. The second bird followed close behind. The maintenance crew watched the two helicopters disappear south into the dusty, smoke-streaked sky. Waiting until they became far-away specks, the men turned and walked back to the hangar for tea and a smoke.

In the air, the two *Krokodil* flew toward the frontier at a leisurely 280 kilometers per hour, 55km/h below their maximum speed. There was no need to overtax the engines yet.

"Is number two behind us?"

"Yes, I can see them," said the pilot. "We're on radio silence for the duration, but he's flying on our starboard side and slightly behind."

Pankeshev craned his neck until he could just see out the canopy and confirmed for himself. He didn't want to find out too late that the pilot of the second bird had turned back. Content that his people were still with him, Pankeshev settled back for the ride. They had to make one intermediate stop to gas up at a Forward Area Refueling Point before they crossed the frontier and then it would be game on.

35

They had left Tabriz behind a couple of hours before. First they left the highway and circumnavigated the big city by the back roads. Kemal knew his way, pointing out each village they passed as one that an uncle or cousin or old friend lived in.

"I thought you were from the east."

"I was born in the west, then I went to England. After school I went to the east. I have relatives all over, even some in Dearborn. These days, we Kurds are nomads. We have to be."

"Have to be?"

"Yes, we're not well loved by the other peoples of the region. They want us to lose our Kurdishness and be like them. Or leave. But we won't leave or change, we'll fight."

"Tribalism," said Jonny.

"Yes, I see it everywhere, even in England, although they try to pretend it's not there."

"We have it in America too."

"Yes, my cousin told me about it. Like I said, it's everywhere."

***

The van plunged deeper into the countryside until they reached another even smaller road. The dawn was coming fast and they

243

could see the road twist and turn into the valley and higher into the foothills. Aside from one small checkpoint that Kemal had talked his way through, it had been a smooth journey, but time was getting short.

"Let's go. Our friends will be coming soon and we mustn't make them wait."

Kemal drove on and the road got smaller until it disappeared behind a hill.

"A good place for an ambush," Jonny said, thinking aloud.

Stavros agreed. Kemal knew it was.

The men standing in the road knew it was as well. Oncoming cars or trucks would not see them until it was too late to turn around. And besides, there was no place to turn around. Rising ground on the right, a small stream on the left. A perfect place for an ambush. Kemal drove on unperturbed.

"Kemal?"

"No worries, my friend."

Kemal stopped at the log that had been placed across the road. Jonny and Stavros stared at the men carrying Kalashnikovs and Mauser bolt-action rifles, an eclectic mix of rebel weaponry.

One of the men came up to the driver's side window and spoke to Kemal in a language neither of the Americans recognized. Kemal answered him and turned to Jonny.

"They are *Peshmerga*. We're in their territory. What should I tell them?"

"Tell them you are helping some friends escape the government. Tell them whatever will make them happy."

Kemal turned back to the window and spoke at length to the man.

"He wants to know if we need any help. He knows my uncle."

"I should have known. Tell him, thank you but we won't stay long in his territory, we'll be leaving very soon."

"You have forgotten, this place is also my homeland." It seemed as if Kemal's smile lit up the cab when he said that. He was proud to be back.

Once he explained the situation, the men pulled the log from the road and waved the truck on. Several men on the hillside raised their rifles to the sky in salute as they passed.

Jonny and Stavros finally felt they had arrived in a good place.

Several kilometers on the road straightened out and they drove onto what seemed to be a wide, flat valley with low hills on either side. Kemal stopped the truck.

"The landing strip must be over there, there's no more road to get there."

"That's probably why they chose this spot. It's hard to get to unless you're on foot."

"What do you want me to do?" Kemal said.

"Park. We will walk from here." Stavros said. "Do you want to come with us?"

"Where do you go from here?"

"Probably an American base in Turkey and then home."

"No. Turkey would not be good for me. I will stay with my people, but what do I do with the truck?"

"It's yours," said Jonny. "Take the truck. Sell the carpets and keep the Kalashnikov for your fight."

Kemal pushed the hidden button on the ceiling and watched the radio descend slowly. Then he pushed the shelf back closed.

"And maybe I can tell you what is happening from time to time."

They all climbed out of the cab and pulled their rucksacks out of the compartment along with a dark green canvas container that looked like it held a small barrel.

"Not fun to hump but at least it's padded."

"A W54, 59 pounds, I've had heavier rucksacks," Stavros said.

"Okay, you carry it."

"No problem." Stavros stooped over to pick it up, but Jonny stopped him.

"It's my responsibility. I'll carry it."

Stavros took an azimuth off two of the hilltops that were now visible in the morning light. He had memorized the key features from the E&E report to make sure he knew where they needed to be. He stared off into the distance.

"It should be about two clicks of humping through the brush. Not too hard, it's pretty flat, but we need to go. Our reception committee may be there already."

Jonny lifted the device in its H912 harness up and onto his back as Stavros slipped into his own rucksack. Then he picked up Jonny's and arranged it so that it rode on his chest. With the radios, his load was nearly as heavy as the trash can alone.

"I'm counterbalanced." He faced his comrades. "Go with God, Kemal."

Kemal shook his hand and touched his breast. Stavros turned to the azimuth he had chosen and plunged into the grass.

Jonny embraced Kemal and handed him a pouch he had pulled from his rucksack.

"Something to keep you going."

Inside the pouch was around ten thousand US dollars from his contingency fund that he would report as operational expenses once he got home.

"Keep safe and thank you, my brother. I'll be back… We will be back," he said.

It was Jonny's turn to go and he shrugged his shoulders to make sure the device was well placed and then cradled the AK in his arms. Neither man chose to see the other's eyes and then Jonny turned abruptly and walked off. Following his partner's path through the grass, he shambled ahead without the least indication that he was fazed by the weight he was carrying.

Kemal stood by the truck and watched as the two men got smaller and then climbed back into the cab. He knew a village nearby.

36

Earlier that day, the crew of Lieutenant Colonel Strunk's aircraft had been a little perplexed by his comment that, "We're going duck hunting, boys."

Colonel Alphonse Strunk was the commander and pilot of "Fury Five," an AC-130H "Spectre," an airplane that was armed with two 20mm Vulcan mini-guns, a 40mm Bofors cannon, and a 105mm howitzer. It was the worst nightmare that any enemy infantryman could imagine. Strunk's nickname was "Fonse," but most everyone on the crew called him "Sir."

Fonse was the name he had picked up in his younger days on the prairie of Nebraska. That's where he grew up and when he wasn't baling hay or doing chores on the farm he was hunting. He loved to hunt pheasant, quail, and occasionally duck or goose. He understood how to shoot the birds, although he hadn't when he first started out.

His father was a farmer and not too interested in bird hunting, but he let other folks hunt on his farm. One day a group of men came and asked permission to shoot and Farmer Strunk said go ahead. The young Alphonse asked to go along and everyone was okay with that. One man in the group said he'd look out for the boy. That man was Mister George. Mister George was a cattle broker—the middleman between the farmer or rancher and the meat packer—and he knew

Alphonse's dad well. He also knew pheasant hunting from his days on his own family's farm.

The three men and young Alphonse went out and walked the edges of the fields and along the watercourses. Mister George and his friends knocked down several pheasant with their 12-gauge shotguns before he asked young Alphonse to lead the next part of the walk with his little Savage 20-gauge. Before long, a pheasant flushed in a blur of wings and squawks and Alfonse pulled the trigger. He missed.

"I don't understand it," Alphonse said. "I had him dead to rights."

"That because you aimed at the bird." It was a statement.

"How else am I gonna hit him?"

"If you aim at the bird your shot is gonna go where he was, not where he will be."

"I don't understand."

Mister George drew a diagram on the ground and showed Alphonse how to find the bird with the front sight and then lead ahead of it along its flight path to take the shot. Now Mister George wasn't an engineer, but there was one thing he understood and that was the geometry of shooting upland game and waterfowl. So Alphonse learned and before long he was knocking them down as well.

Strunk wanted to "old school" his quarry today.

"I've been wanting to try this theory out for quite a while. We're going duck hunting with the 105."

"What? How?" Everyone wanted to know. The crew had questions, like "Why the howitzer? Why not just hose them down with our two 20mm? It would be a lot easier."

"Exactly, but too easy. We need a challenge. And this is how we'll do it: we set the fuzes for time delay so they'll air burst next to the birds and then I'll position us to fire on them from above as we follow."

"Pardon my candor, sir, but you're crazy," said his co-pilot, Captain David Moore.

"Perhaps, but just pay attention, rookie. You might learn something."

So, when his crew crowded around, he explained the same thing Mister George had taught him to his crew who didn't know much about shooting ducks. They understood how to kill things on the ground with their airplane's highly accurate weapons but not so much things that were moving through the air at a high rate of speed, which was what their targets would be doing today. That was normally the domain of fighter pilots and even they had computers to tell them where to shoot.

Strunk went on: "Fire control. We're going to need four 105mm MTSQ fused rounds for this run. Set them all for three-second delay. We'll fly 1,500 meters above them, lead them 300 meters and we should nail them. If it doesn't work, we go to the back-up and use your mini-guns."

Captain Moore, being a glutton for punishment, dared ask, "How did you come up with those figures?"

"Simple, David, a 105mm round has a velocity of around 490 meters per second. We need to avoid shooting ourselves down, so a 1,500-meter standoff should protect us. The round will travel that distance in three seconds. An MI-24 will fly 300 meters in that time, hence our lead."

The crew stared at Strunk, unsure if they were listening to a madman or a genius, but he was in charge after all.

Now they were orbiting on the western side of the Turkish border, lurking like a very mean junk-yard dog waiting to be unleashed. They were in contact with another aircraft, an HC-130N, call sign "Red King," that was the command and control bird for the E&E mission they were covering.

Their mission orders were to protect the Americans on the ground at all costs and, for the first time since Vietnam, Strunk was happy to again be hunting communists.

***

On board "Red King," the C2 bird, Colonel Jelinek and Sergeant Major Bergmann sat with their backs to a console listening to Major General Jack Muller expound upon his theories of unconventional warfare and the Philadelphia Eagles at the same time. There wasn't much to do on board the aircraft except to monitor the situation, pass messages, and make decisions that might impact the lives of every man on the ground. That critical point had not yet been reached, but would soon.

Master Sergeant Becker's team had made contact shortly after they had assembled on the drop zone but they were now quiet. They wouldn't come up on the air until Stavros and the Agency man showed up or if there was a problem. The variable that was most concerning was the arrival time of the package. The Agency had reported that contact had been made with their man several hours before and they placed the truck still east of Tabriz. Staff Sergeant Stavros had made contact at almost the same time and reported no issues—actually, he said that several problems had been resolved but he would detail those later—and they should arrive at Escape and Evasion Point TIBET in around four hours. Around four hours… which was approaching quickly, subject to whatever gremlin or ghost decided to interfere with the process. Without real-time communication it was impossible to be more specific.

The HC-130 had been in the air two and a half hours already. They had plenty of loiter time and no real choice but to wait. And then one of the console operators hit his intercom button and gave the first indication things were about to get interesting, as things generally did in military operations.

"We have two low-flying aircraft, moving south across the Soviet frontier into Iranian airspace. They're traveling at around 150 knots, which would indicate they are probable helicopters."

"Can we get a visual?" said General Muller.

"No, we would have to be much closer."

"How far from are they from TIBET?"

"At this speed, around forty minutes."

Muller looked at Jelinek and said, "Game on. We already have authority to engage."

Then he turned to the air force colonel manning the watch.

"Colonel, release the gunship and vector them in. Tell them to confirm what these things are. I want an exact description. They do not, I repeat, do not have permission to engage until I give it to them. Understood?"

"Yes, sir."

The colonel relayed the information over the secure radio system to Fury Five.

The C2 crew waited in silence as Fury Five turned southeast and chased the phantoms. It was a long fifteen minutes before the radio crackled with Strunk's voice.

"Red King, this is Fury Five. We are bird-dogging two MI-24 Hinds flying south. They're military but I cannot identify their nationality."

"Fury Five, this is Red King. Understand you have two MI-24 helicopters, is that correct?"

"Red King, roger, two MI-24s."

The colonel turned to Muller. "No one but the Soviets have MI-24s in this region."

Muller's expression said everything. He alone could decide. The US government-issue ballpoint pen in his hand began to send Morse code as he clicked it rapidly.

"Okay, Colonel. I'll take it now. Make sure you're recording this," he said. "Fury Five, this is Red King Sierra, do you copy?"

"Roger, Red King Sierra. Lima Charlie."

"Fury Five, Red King Sierra. You are ordered to eliminate any threat those aircraft pose to our forces. Do you copy?"

"Roger, Red King Sierra. We are to eliminate any threat. Stand by."

Muller looked at the colonel without the intercom button pressed. "Eliminate the threat, there's some wiggle room in there," he said.

***

The AC-130 was about 5,000 meters above and slightly behind the two helicopters and flying slow. There was a good 500 meters' space between the two helos.

Strunk keyed his intercom with Captain Moore.

"We'll go for the trailing bird first so we don't spook the lead. Those things can surely outmaneuver us at this speed and they can fight back."

"I'll keep my eye on the number one while you're occupied with shooting."

Strunk engaged the intercom again. "Fire Control, lock and load, let me know when the system is good to go."

"Roger, sir. Stand by." A moment passed. "Number One Gun is locked and loaded and the system is green. You have control."

Strunk confirmed that the fire control system was fully armed on his panel and then turned to the heads-up display on his left side. He'd be relying on information from the fire control officer and on Moore to keep the aircraft on course while he tracked the target, but he would pull the trigger.

Only a couple seconds were required to bring the plane down into firing position. Strunk found the Russian bird on the HUD and then shifted his aiming point forward. The lines and crosses began to align and Strunk called out, "Stand by, I have the target." A second or two passed, tense seconds, and Strunk triggered the gun. A dull thump and a small vibration was the only indicator the howitzer had fired, it was so well dampened.

Below, there was a flash.

"What happened?" Moore said.

Strunk stared down into the space below. "Fire Control, what do you see?"

"Ahhhh… I see one helo still flying and secondary explosions behind us. You got one!"

"Yes!" Strunk punched the air. "I knew it would work. Let's go for number two."

There was a red light on his panel.

"Fire Control, what's up? I have a 'no-go' light on my panel."

"Bad news, the fire control computer went down. I'm trying to diagnose it now."

"Damn it. Get it fixed. We only have around ten minutes to get them in the air before they reach our people."

"We're working on it, sir."

Strunk reported to the C2 bird and, from the other side of the frontier, Red King knew there was little they could do to affect the outcome. There was no back-up because, as the Pentagon had told them, one gunship in the air was all that the White House had authorized.

"Roger, Fury Five. Let us know when you're back up and operational."

***

The lead pilot of the *Krokodil* caught the glare of a fireball in his cockpit mirror. He slowed perceptibly and swung the helicopter to starboard in an effort to see what happened.

"Mother of God," he said.

"What is it?"

"'Red Eagle 2' has exploded."

A flaming ball of wreckage hit the ground and flared into a huge, jet-fueled pyre of wreckage.

"How?" Pankeshev said.

253

"No idea. There was a flash and then they were gone."

Krokodil "Red Eagle 1" circled the crash site at altitude.

"They're all gone," the pilot repeated.

"Someone must have dropped a grenade or something. There are no enemy aircraft or missiles anywhere near us," the co-pilot said.

Pankeshev immediately went through his options. Without the second squad, he was down to eight men plus himself. He was already missing his steadfast Voronin, but could they continue anyway? *There's still only two Americans.*

"We continue the mission, Captain. We can't stop now."

37

At the southern end of the airstrip, Becker was beginning to get anxious. The sky was turning blue from its nighttime black and a red-tinged dawn was beginning to show in the east. It would have been a nice day except that it *was* day and they were inside Iran. He was sweeping the northeastern quadrant in front of him with his binoculars because that's where he expected Stavros and the Agency man to appear. The sky appeared to portend a bright day ahead, but the ground in front of him was still dark green, shaded as it was by the surrounding hills.

Finally, he saw dust rising from a road just below the edge of the plateau, and then the boxy shape of a big van as it emerged from the small valley.

I know we just got here but it's about time we left.

Becker watched as the van stopped and saw three figures emerge and begin to pull things out of the back. He wished they had been able to come up with a plan so he could contact them by radio, but now all he could do was to mentally will them to move quickly. He wondered who the third man was.

He could see there was a good-bye ritual going on and decided the man must be a friend. He recognized Stavros getting his gear ready. He saw the second man shoulder what he recognized as the device onto his back. First Stavros, then the second man turned and stepped into the green by the road and made their way in his direction.

Naturally, Stavros would lead...

A lengthening compass arrow of trampled grass followed them as they trudged toward the strip. The last man finally returned to the truck and after a moment it disappeared down the road.

Only two to worry about then.

There was a crackle of static on his hand-held.

"Boss, this is Outpost. Are you monitoring the command freq?"

"Not at the moment, why?"

"You should, Red King says we have visitors headed our way."

"Hostiles?"

"Apparently. It's a Hind. There were two but Spectre took one of them out before it broke."

"Spectre's broke? So we have no air cover?"

"Roger, for the time being at least. They're working to get back into the game."

"Got it. Any estimate on the Hind's ETA?"

"Any moment, they said."

"Good copy. Stay where you are until things sort out. Can you see our package?"

"Affirm, we have them in sight. We'll stay in position until you call us in."

"Do that. I'm going to talk with Red King now."

"Roger, Outpost. We're standing by."

Becker looked to the north, but saw nothing. He knew he would hear their approach before long; his ears were good and the rhythmic bass beat of a helicopter's blades had a way of telegraphing its presence long before you could actually see it.

He turned to his other teammates who were all expectantly waiting to hear Kaiser's half of the conversation.

"Two things: we're on our own for the moment and we have a Hind coming to visit. That means there is probably a squad-sized element of what I would guess to be special purpose troops who want to take our package from us. The OP will stay where it is for now. Let's break into our two cells. We'll remain here. Fred, you take yours and move over to that copse of trees in the middle. Try to take the Hind down if you can get the angle on it as it comes in. Make sure you're up on the radio."

Lindt took Jake Novak and scurried off at a trot toward the trees.

The remaining three rearranged their positions as best they could, not knowing what quite what to expect from the Soviets. Becker was still standing watching Stavros and his companion busting through the brush about 800 meters away. That was when his ear drums started to pick up the thumping of the Russian bird's rotors. He scanned the sky with his binos and spotted a black dot on the horizon. It was getting larger by the second. He shifted his gaze to Stavros, 700 meters away he guessed. He couldn't yell that far, but he hoped Stavros was listening to the environment.

***

Across the field, Stavros was indeed listening. He stopped and looked up toward the approaching sound, saw the dot, and then looked toward the airstrip. He saw a figure waving its arms. *Home base.*

Jonny reached his side, out of breath.

"You keep up a grueling pace, my boy."

"That was only 1,500 meters and we need to move faster," Stavros said.

Jonny caught his glance and looked but didn't see. His wasn't able to focus that far out in his condition.

"We have guests coming and they're not friendly."

"What do you see?"

Stavros pointed, "It's a Hind, about 5 clicks out. I've heard them before in East Germany; they don't sound like our helos. We need to get to our people quick."

Stavros took off at a quick trot and Jonny, reinvigorated by the oncoming danger, took off after him, head down, determined to stay on his heels.

∗

Captain Pankeshev looked around him as soon as the pilot alerted him to their imminent arrival over the airstrip. He first gave his men the signal to stand by and then looked out the canopy to orient himself.

"Do you see a truck or any people ahead?"

"Nothing yet, we're too far to see people. I can see the outline of the airstrip. We're still a couple of minutes out."

He peered out the canopy at what he could see of the airstrip ahead, trying to pick out the details. The curve of the canopy made it difficult, everything was distorted near its edges and that was where he was looking.

The vibrations of the helicopter changed perceptibly as the pilot slowed for his approach. The helo was shaking more than Pankeshev liked.

"Where do you want me to set down?"

"Do a circuit of the field first, maybe we'll see something."

The pilot obliged and came in low over the northwestern corner of the airstrip at about 50 feet.

"There!" The co-pilot shouted. Two men appeared at the edge of the runway. They looked like they were watching the helicopter approach.

"Set down about 50 meters short of their location."

"Roger."

The nose of the bird dipped as he picked up speed and then immediately lifted as the pilot flared the bird for landing. He was about to say they were on the ground, when a loud booming clang rang through the fuselage.

"Damn it! We're taking fire!"

"Set us down, now!" said Pankeshev.

＊＊＊

Outside, it was getting hot.

Lindt watched the Hind's approach from his spot under the trees and stepped out into the open when it was nearly parallel to him. He shouldered the armed Redeye launcher and gave the briefest of looks to his rear before he shouted, "Clear."

Novak knew better than to be anywhere near the end of the launcher and looked away to protect his eyes.

Lindt squeezed the trigger and watched the missile disappear into a cloud of smoke and flame before he saw it hit the helicopter just behind the engine nacelles and disintegrate.

He looked on in disbelief as the helicopter continued forward.

"What the…?" said Novak.

"We were too damn close," Lindt said. "The fuse didn't arm."

Novak wasn't listening. He was sprinting for a pile of rocks to their front and stopped in a crouch long enough to fire a full thirty-round magazine of ammo from his M-16 before he dropped behind cover. It was a futile gesture: the heavily armored Hind shrugged off the tiny projectiles like an armadillo shrugs off a mosquito.

"Stop," yelled Lindt. "We can't kill that thing with our rifles."

He didn't want the pilot to turn on them and wipe them out with his rockets. The Russian was also too close for his rockets to arm but they would hurt the thin-skinned Americans much more than Lindt's missile had hurt the helo.

The Hind hit the ground hard and bounced once before it set down and stopped. The men inside poured out and went to ground on the far side of the runway looking for the enemy. Pankeshev was the last one out, having had to crawl through the access passage. He landed on the ground and tumbled forward to land in a heap as the Hind picked up speed and lifted off.

The pilot did a fast turn and headed back down the runway before setting down about 800 meters from where he'd been hit. He needed to check for damage.

***

Stavros watched the whole scene unfold about 100 meters away before he realized he had to do something. He saw the missile strike the Hind ineffectually and then the Russians jumping out of it. He grabbed Jonny, pulled the device off his back and pushed him in the direction of the man he had seen.

"Go, get out of here. They can't capture you." He tossed Jonny his smaller rucksack and shed his own.

Jonny agreed with Stavros and was especially glad that he didn't add the word "alive" to his warning, but he still had to do one thing. He grabbed the harness and ripped open the canvas, pulling off the cover plate to expose the control panel. Digging into his breast pocket, he pulled out a notebook and opened it. He quickly consulted a list of numbers and typed a ten-digit code into the device, then tripped the safety switch. A tiny green light-emitting diode blinked once and then glowed constant.

"One hour," was all he said before he turned and sprinted away across the airstrip and toward Becker's position.

Stavros looked back toward the Russians, grabbed the device, and started to run after Jonny. He just hoped they wouldn't shoot. He was doing rather well until the small ditch grabbed his foot. He felt his ankle twist as he went down.

Damn. At least it's my good leg.

***

Pankeshev recovered quickly from the embarrassment of his dirt dive in front of the men. First, he realized they weren't even looking at him but were watching their helicopter take off without them. Second, he heard a sharp metallic ping and he knew bad news was coming in his direction. He had heard that sound often enough in Kabul to know what it was. It was the sound of the spoon flying off a grenade. He looked up to see a trail of almost invisible smoke as a dark green object sailed toward their position and yelled, "Grenade!" as he hit the ground once again.

A flash and a black ring of smoke marked the grenade's explosion. Pankeshev looked around him and saw one of his men, helmet gone, sitting on the ground with a dazed look on his face. Another man attended to him, speaking to him in a loud voice, trying to get a response.

"Is he hit?"

"I don't think so, just in shock."

The rest of his men were in a defensive perimeter, stuck in place. Pankeshev knew he had to get them moving. He looked down the airstrip and saw one of the Americans lying in the grass, attempting to stand. Next to him was a small bundle.

The weapon.

He yelled at his men and pointed, "Move it and capture that man! Do not shoot him."

What remained of his squad rose up as one. With one down, they were eight. They took on a wedge shape as they ran. Two were faster than Pankeshev and stretched out their legs, madly running toward the fallen man. He wasn't aware of the enemy fire until he saw a small puff of dust come off Orlov's camouflage shirt. One bullet, then a second struck him and he wobbled as he ran. Then he fell head first into the grass, then legs over head and down for the count. Pankeshev ran by him, no time to stop now. He had to get to the weapon and the man.

Fifty meters is a long way to run in a firefight, even when fueled by adrenaline. Pankeshev could only think about how much time it was taking. He was aware of the crack of rounds around him and the thunder of seven pairs of boots hitting dirt as he and his men ran and ran.

The American was trying to move. Pankeshev could see the man was hurt. His first man got there; he saw it was Lebedev. The American looked up and then sat back on the ground.

***

As he looked up into barrel of the Kalashnikov pointed at his head, Stavros decided that the AK-74's 5.45mm was indeed a large bullet at close range. He could think of only one other thing—how pissed off Sarah was going to be with him.

He was quickly surrounded by other Russians. They were all about his age, wearing the camouflage of the airborne troops and their signature blue and white striped t-shirt underneath. Stavros found himself wondering why they bothered to wear camouflage when they wore the stupid t-shirts. And then one of the Russians began yelling in English.

"Stop shooting, we have your man. You will kill him."

Pankeshev looked down at the weapon and saw the timer. From the ticking down of the seconds, he assumed he had just over fifty-three minutes to live.

"You, turn it off," he said to the American.

Stavros shrugged. "Sorry, comrade, I can't. I don't have the code."

***

Becker had just shoved Jonny down into the grass with a sharp, "Stay there." He was crouching in the grass watching the Russians running toward where he had last seen Stavros. He fired a burst at them and was about to order a counterassault to save his man when one of the running soldiers went down. He saw smoke and dust rising from where Lindt and Novak were located. The Russians were too close, he couldn't risk engaging them without putting Stavros at risk.

That's when he heard the Russian say, "Stop shooting, we have your man. You will kill him."

Becker cursed.

Jonny was lying close at hand. "I armed the device," he said.

Becker looked at him. "You what?"

"I armed it. There's an hour delay."

"Great, now we have to get it back or run away before it goes off."

"Well, so do they. I don't think they will want to take it with the timer running."

Becker grabbed the hand-held and spoke to the team.

"Everyone cease fire, cease fire, acknowledge."

Kaiser came back, "Roger, we never even got a shot off."

Lindt acknowledged: "Roger. FYI, we have a prisoner."

"What kind of prisoner?"

"Dazed, not wounded. Probably knocked out by our grenade."

"Understood, move him away and get him under cover."

"Roger, boss."

Becker switched radios and called Red King with a short situation report. Luckily the radio operator on the airplane knew better than to ask too many questions. The terseness of Becker's voice may have given him a clue.

"Seems we may have a stand-off, although I don't know if Ivan knows that yet."

"They should when they see the timer. Maybe Pavlos told them," Jonny said.

"Who is Pavlos?"

"Your guy, Pavlos."

"Ah, you mean Paul."

"I guess, Paul, Pavlos, cover names, whatever."

"Who are you anyway?"

"Jonny Panagasos, that's my real name."

***

263

The quiet settled in. Lindt and Novak dragged their stunned Russian back to the pile of rocks while Pankeshev and his squad consolidated their position. Pankeshev looked down the airstrip and could see the pilot looking at the fuselage, then realized he had no way of contacting him. He had forgotten to prepare that one part of the plan, communications. He would have to send a runner to get the damn bird to move when it was time.

But right now, I have to get the timer shut off.

He had an idea.

"Lebedev, if anything happens to me, you're in charge. If this doesn't work, shoot the American, leave the weapon, and get the hell out of here. That thing will go off in…" He looked at the timer. "Forty-two minutes. Understood?"

"Understood, Captain." The rest of the squad nodded and then looked at the American and the weapon. A couple of them squirmed a bit further away on the ground.

Pankeshev stood up slowly and looked in the direction of where he had seen the other American run.

"American, are you there? We must talk." He was glad he had opted to learn English at the academy rather than German.

Becker almost smiled. "You were right, Jonny."

Becker slowly stood up too and saw his opposite number facing him about 30 meters away.

Were we that close?

"I am here, Ivan."

"I am not Ivan. I am Captain Vladimir Aleksandrovich Pankeshev of the Soviet Army."

"Of course you are, Captain, and I am Nathanael Greene of the Vermont National Guard."

"Well, Nathanael Greene, I have captured your man and your weapon."

"And I have you surrounded, Captain."

Pankeshev looked around, saw no one, and said so.

"They are there, Captain. We are good at camouflage."

Pankeshev was still skeptical but he had a more pressing problem.

"Your man has armed the weapon. I have told him he must disarm it but he refuses. You must order him to stop the timer."

"Or what? We all go up in a mushroom cloud?"

"I will shoot him."

"That won't solve your problem. Besides, he doesn't know how to shut it down."

"Who does?"

"I have someone that knows how." Becker looked down and kicked Jonny in the leg, whispering, "You do know, don't you?"

Jonny nodded.

"Then give me the instructions or I will shoot your man."

"And what happens if I give them to you?"

"We will go home with the weapon."

"And my man?"

"We take him with."

"That's not very fair."

"No, but if you try to stop us, he will die."

"Well, how about this. I have one of your men, the one you left by the helicopter. I'll trade him for my man."

"You can have him. The weapon and your man are more important to me."

Becker pondered his next move, but really didn't have any except running away and leaving the Russians to their fate. But the Russians could get further away from the weapon with their helicopter. And he couldn't abandon Stavros. He looked down the airstrip at the helicopter. He couldn't see any movement and the rotors were no longer turning.

Curious.

***

Kaiser had watched the confusion at the other end of the airstrip from 800 meters away. He winced when the missile bounced off the Hind and cursed all inertial arming systems. The same thing had happened to him once in Vietnam with an M79 grenade launcher. He was too close to an NVA soldier he shot with a high-explosive 40mm round. The projectile didn't arm and hit the guy without exploding. Luckily, the NVA guy wasn't armored and the round killed him anyway.

Now, although he was wondering what exactly was happening with Becker down range, Kaiser had a different issue on his plate. He watched as the damned Hind sat down right in front of him and Poncho with its rockets aimed straight at them. From his concealed position in the grass, he could hear the engines wind down and saw the blades slowly stop their rotation. The pilot climbed out of the cockpit and started to wander around the fuselage looking at the results of the failed attack. He didn't notice the two Americans in the weeds.

"He probably doesn't know what hit him."

Poncho had another thought.

"We have been presented a gift, my brother," he said as he crab-walked away and began his stalk. Kaiser followed.

They got away from the two crewmen's line of sight and scurried along through the grass.

"Cover me," said Poncho. He set his M-16 on the ground, pulled a pistol from a belt holster and walked toward the bird.

The pilot had climbed back into the cockpit. Poncho stayed low on the starboard side of the fuselage and slid low around the nose before he stood up straight with his pistol pointed at the pilot.

"Hi there, Ivan. You are my prisoners."

The co-pilot struggled to pull his Tokarev from his harness but was rewarded with a crack on the back of his head.

"I thought I told you to cover me?" Poncho said.

"I am, from the inside." Kaiser said from the passageway behind the pilots. "It's just these two and us."

"Now what do we do with them?" Poncho felt like a dog that had just caught the police car.

"Maybe the boss has a need for them. Let's get them both out and restrained."

The crew understood the universal signs for "get out or you will be shot" readily enough and, with Kaiser keeping watch, Poncho handcuffed the two Russians together.

"I've waited long enough to use these things. Genuine Military Police-issue."

"I don't want to know," said Kaiser.

***

"Just forty minutes left, Nathanael Greene. How far can you run in forty minutes?"

"Far enough, Captain Vladimir."

Squelch broke on Becker's hand-held.

"Boss, this is OP."

"Go ahead."

"We have something for you."

"What is it? No games, I'm kind of occupied right now."

"Understood, but I thought you'd like to know we have the helicopter under our control and the crew is alive."

"That is useful news, thank you. Stand by."

"Captain Vladimir, how did you say you were getting home?"

"The same way we got here." Pankeshev pointed at the helicopter. *Curious. Why are the engines shut down? Pankeshev thought.*

"Well, you might want to consider another way home because we have captured your helicopter and the crew. What about my offer of a trade now? I'll give you your helicopter if you give me my man and the device."

Check, Becker thought.

Shakh i mat, thought Pankeshev. *Damn Americans.*

267

"I'll give you your man, but I keep the weapon."

Jonny whispered to Becker, "Let them have it."

"What? Are you crazy?"

"No, I am totally sane. They'll go for that deal and won't cause any problems. They won't learn anything from the device anyway."

Becker paused.

"My orders are to bring the weapon out," Becker said in a whisper.

"Do it! The weapon is my responsibility and we don't have time to fool around," said Jonny.

"Captain Vladimir, agreed. Send him over."

"No, give me the code for the weapon and then we will walk to the helicopter. You can have your man there."

"I'll give you the code when we get to the helicopter. You better start moving, I think we only have thirty minutes to do this."

"Agreed." Pankeshev rallied his men and started toward the helicopter with Stavros in the middle, limping slightly. One of the Russians carried the device.

Becker radioed Lindt, "Bring your Russian out only after we pass."

"Roger."

A long twelve minutes passed before they were at the helicopter. Becker's team formed a perimeter about 25 meters away from the bird. Kaiser was holding the two Russian crew off to the side with his pistol aimed at the pilot's head.

"Now give me the code," said Pankeshev.

Becker motioned for Lindt to bring his prisoner, still somewhat dazed, forward.

"Jonny, give him the code."

Jonny looked at his notebook and wrote the ten-digit deactivation code down on a page he ripped out and handed it to the Russian before pushing him toward his comrades.

Pankeshev grabbed the note from him when he got close and knelt by the device. He punched in the code and waited.

"There is still a green light," he said.

"Flip the red switch," Jonny yelled back.

He did and the light went out. Pankeshev breathed deep and nodded to his men. Stavros, cut free of the rope he had been bound with, looked the Russians over one more time and walked toward freedom.

"About time you got here," said Jonny.

"I tripped."

"Now, give me my crew," said Pankeshev.

"We could keep them, but a deal is a deal, comrade." Turning to Kaiser he said, "Let them go."

Poncho reluctantly unlocked the handcuffs and sent the two to their helicopter.

"Now our deal is complete, Captain Vladimir Aleksandrovich Pankeshev of the Soviet Army. Go home."

"Gladly, Nathanael Greene."

Pankeshev loaded up the helicopter as the pilots spun up the engines. There would be no warm-up or checks, they were leaving quickly.

Becker backed his people off and spread them out in the grass, waiting for their opponent to quit the field.

The Hind shifted its weight and seemed to stretch its legs as the rotors bit into the air and gave it lift. It hopped into the air and backed off in reverse about 25 meters up in the air.

Pankeshev keyed his mike: "Fire your rockets at them, take the bastards out."

The pilot flipped the arming switch for the missiles and was greeted with two red warning lights.

**

On the ground below, Poncho was showing Kaiser and Becker a tool and two metal connector plugs with several strands of wire sticking out of each.

"You were wondering why a commo man always carries wire cutters? This is one reason: the power cables for the helicopter's rocket pods were not very tidy so I decided to make them neat and pretty. There were some extra parts left over."

Above them, the Hind wheeled and disappeared north, the cursing on board drowned out by the roar of its engines.

38

The Twin Otter was flying relatively low, about 1,500 feet AGL on a northwesterly heading, its turboprops humming. The pilot was waiting for the word from his co-pilot who was scanning the ground ahead with binoculars looking for the landing zone markers. He knew the orange panels were out there—a short radio transmission had confirmed that moments before—and he also knew they weren't lost. That was because he was possibly the best in the business. Ryan James had started out flying with Air America in Southeast Asia and by the mid-seventies he had somewhere north of 25,000 hours behind the stick, flying interesting aircraft in places like Laos and Bolivia, or where the border was disputed, or nations that never fully materialized, like Biafra. They were all high per diem places because one side generally shot at the airplanes belonging to the other.

Pretty amazing for a guy with only one leg.

Ryan had taken a 12.7mm round during an air mission over Cambodia and lost his leg. Once he recovered from his wounds, he just kept flying.

"Whaddaya got for me?" Ryan asked.

He was talking loud over the engine noise. Luckily the ground ahead was pretty flat, with not much vegetation to obscure the approach.

"Hang on! I have the strip about 3 kilometers ahead, 5 degrees to starboard."

"Got it." Among Ryan's other faculties was his seemingly incredible visual acuity. He might not see the markers because the sun was just at the right angle to make the color orange difficult to make out, but he could see the outline of the overgrown landing zone. He also navigated by the seat of his pants.

The plane descended rapidly toward the ground and within moments Ryan saw the brush whip by the wheels and felt the plane set down in the field. He stood on the brakes, reversed props, and brought the plane to a quick stop. He released the brakes and spotted the folks he was to meet at the end of the strip, then rolled further along the LZ to where Becker and his men waited.

Ryan did a quick count, eight men in lizard suits and two guys in civilian clothing. That tallied with his briefing notes. They looked pretty relaxed so he was certain the Hind was no longer a problem. He stopped short of the group by about 25 meters and pivoted the airplane 180 degrees before throttling down.

"Get them on board, Chris. We don't need to dilly-dally here long."

"Roger, boss."

Chris McBride climbed out of his seat and scurried to the rear of the airplane to open the door. He too was an Agency pilot, just younger and several thousand hours short of Ryan's flight time.

He pushed the door open and let down the stairs as the men arrived at the tail of the airplane.

"Come on aboard."

One of the two civilians climbed in, followed by most of the others, each clearing their weapons before they came up the ladder. Two men were still standing outside on the ground, watching the sky to the north.

"Thanks for coming, boss," said Stavros.

"You picked me up the last time. The sergeant major thought it was appropriate to send me. I was happy to come," Becker said.

"It's been an interesting ride. I'll tell you about it when we get to wherever. Where are we going?"

"Batman, Turkey. We'll be met by another aircraft there and then we go home."

Stavros nodded and stood silent for a moment. Finally he spoke. "That'll be good. I have some things to take care of."

"In Berlin? Or back in CONUS?"

Stavros smiled. "I think you know."

He turned to the steps and climbed into the plane. Becker picked up a small rock, stuffed it in his pants pocket, and followed. It was one of his obsessions, he collected rocks from the places he visited.

Chris yelled out, "Good to go, boss."

"Are we clear?"

"Roger, all clear!" Chris pulled up the steps and secured the door.

Ryan cleared his airplane nevertheless, looking from side to side as he readied the controls. He would take off with the wind rather than against it, but it didn't matter much. The Otter's engine revved up and the plane rolled forward. With the light load, the wheels were off the ground after only a few hundred feet.

She's a lovely beast.

Flying cover above them, Red King and Fury Five turned and made for their base in Turkey.

39

As his helicopter descended, Pankeshev was relieved to see 3624th Airbase spread out in front of him. The mission was accomplished although he had lost some good men. He still didn't understand the American, Nathanael Greene.

Why was the American not ready to give up one of his men for the weapon? They are soft. They don't understand the necessity of sacrifice.

The *Krokodil* set down on the tarmac and rolled to a halt in front of the tower where a big black sedan waited. As they unloaded, the car door opened and General Nikolayev got out and strode over to Pankeshev's team. He looked at the device sitting next to them for a moment and patted it a couple of times before looking up.

"Congratulations *Major* Pankeshev, you and your men have done a great service for the Motherland. I will see to it that you all receive awards for this success. Did you bring the Americans with you?"

"No, Comrade General, unfortunately they were unable to travel with us."

Nikolayev smiled. "Too bad, but I understand completely, Major."

No, you don't.

"Of course, you and your men will be given a month off. Everything has been arranged. A plane will take you to Moscow shortly. Now, if you will excuse me, I need to get this thing off to our laboratories for inspection."

Nikolayev motioned to his aide to grab the device as he turned and walked toward the waiting Yak-40 and disappeared up its steps. Pankeshev watched him go.

The General didn't even ask about the men I lost.

40

Becker and Stavros sat together for the first part of the flight, talking with their heads bent toward each other. Occasionally, Becker would look forward toward where Jonny was seated with his eyes closed, his body half enveloped in the web seats.

Stavros finally looked at Jonny as well and then stood and walked forward. He motioned to Lindt to make room and sat down next to his fellow traveler.

"Are you in trouble?" Stavros said.

"Nah, I'm good."

"Because I was kind of wondering what happens when you lose a nuke to the Russians."

"Well, they can't blame me. I tried to get it out."

"You're not worried about it then?"

"Nope, not really, it'll turn out all right."

"How? They aren't going to give it back."

"No, but we are alive and that's all that counts."

"You're a mystery to me, Jonny."

"You worry too much. Like I said, it will turn out all right. What can they do, fire me?"

"They might."

"Nah, I know too much."

***

The Otter began its long descent toward the flat plateau below. The ground was only just turning green in the spring, then summer would come and burn everything into brown and dust. Stavros could see drilling and pumping rigs from one horizon to the other and realized he was looking at a huge operation.

No wonder the Turks want to ensure their control over the Kurdish region. Oil.

Ryan brought their plane in straight to the airfield and taxied toward one end where a C-141 Starlifter was parked, its clam-shell rear cargo doors opened. A group of men waited at the end of the ramp.

This time, Ryan shut the engines down before Chris got up and opened the doors.

"End of the line, gentlemen. Thanks for flying Evergreen Air," he said.

Stavros went to the cockpit and shook Ryan's hand.

"Thanks for coming in to get us."

"That's what we get paid for, son." Ryan was in his early fifties.

Stavros turned and saw Becker behind him.

"My turn," Becker said and went into the cockpit while Stavros walked to the rear of the plane, picking up his rucksack on the way out.

Jonny was waiting for him on the ground.

"I think you should meet my boss," he said. "Tell me your real name."

"Stavros, Paul Stavros."

They turned and walked toward the 141. The parties at the end of the plane had split into two groups. Stavros saw his commander and the sergeant major along with several other people in uniform. Jonny was headed toward the civilians in suits. The three men walked toward them as they approached. He was introduced to John Gambel, the DDO, and Frank Conlin, the chief from Ankara Station. Then Jonny turned to Stavros.

"Paul Stavros, this is Charles Singletary, the chief of Near East, my boss. Chief, this is the guy that got me out."

"Impressive, well done, young man."

Stavros wasn't sure if he was being complemented or just tolerated. *These spy guys do think they're cooler than sliced bread.*

The introductions being made, Stavros broke off as Jonny and his people walked off away from everyone. Stavros could see that the DDO and Near East guy were grilling Jonny. The third man was taking notes. From time to time, one of the suits would glare over toward Stavros.

He decided it was time to be with his own folks.

As usual Bergmann and Jelinek were their jovial selves, happy their boys had returned alive and all was well in the world.

Almost all was well, anyway.

"So you had to give it away?" Jelinek asked Becker.

"We were able to do a prisoner swap and then the Agency guy... Jonny's his name, right?"

Stavros nodded.

"... Jonny said to give it to them," Becker finished.

"Why?"

"He only said that they wouldn't learn anything and since time was running out, I agreed."

"It was his call. The weapon is the Agency's problem and we got those two out, so I think we're covered."

41

The Yak-40 set down on the airstrip some 555 kilometers southeast of Moscow. General Nikolayev supervised the loading of the device onto a truck which followed his car to the Main Nuclear Research Bureau Laboratory. Awaiting him on the steps was a small contingent of administrators, scientists, and security officers who were cleared for the event. Nikolayev and the weapon were quickly swept into the building where a couple of celebratory and self-congratulating speeches and shots of vodka were tossed out and down before the gray wool issue blanket that covered the device was pulled off.

Several men nodded and exchanged rather awed looks at the small size of the powerful weapon. They were looking forward to dissecting it to discover the secrets of its miniaturization.

Nikolayev looked at his watch and spoke to the laboratory's director.

"I must continue my journey. I need to make a report to the chairman this evening."

"Of course, General. I will accompany you back to the airfield. But before you go, let's take a photograph together with the weapon. It's an auspicious day."

Nikolayev walked up to the trolley and patted the olive-green device, then turned to face the camera alongside the director.

This will make a nice picture for my office.
He never saw the flash.

***

Far to the south at the 3624th Airbase, the lieutenant barged into the barracks where newly promoted Major Pankeshev and his men were waiting for their airplane to arrive. Pankeshev looked at the wild-eyed soldier, who was winded by his dash from the headquarters. After a moment to catch his breath, the lieutenant spoke.

"There's been an accident. General Nikolayev has been killed."

Pankeshev didn't know the why, or how, but he did know one thing.

The Americans.

42

The next morning at Rhein-Main Airbase, two groups prepared to go their separate ways. There was a C-130 waiting to haul the *Berliners* home and an extended range Gulfstream II standing by for Jonny and his superiors.

Stavros spoke to Becker and handed him the Stechkin pistol he had picked up off Rasputin.

"Don't worry, I'll take care of your souvenir. Wait here," Becker said.

Becker spoke to Bergmann, then came back and said to Stavros. "Go for it."

Stavros walked over to the Agency group.

"Mr Gambel, can I hitch a ride?"

"Where are you going?"

"Virginia, I have a good friend going to school there."

"Where?"

"The Farm."

"Sure, I think we can make room for you. We might want to talk about your future anyway."

Stavros gave a thumbs up to Becker. "I'll be back in two weeks."

Becker returned the gesture.

***

After he stuffed his civilian rucksack into a compartment, Stavros settled into his seat on the Gulfstream II. Jonny sat down across from him. The suits were close by, quietly waiting for takeoff.

"Hey, one of the air force guys told me something he heard on the BBC this morning."

"What?" said Jonny.

"It seems there was an incident at a Soviet nuclear research facility last night, an explosion of some kind. A place called Penza-19? The main laboratory and some other buildings were destroyed."

Jonny settled back in his seat. The suits were listening.

"That makes sense," said Jonny.

"What's that mean? Do you know anything about it?"

"Maybe."

"Didn't you disable the device?"

"Yeah, sort of."

Jonny looked at the suits who had all closed their eyes and appeared asleep.

"What do you mean, sort of?"

"You see the timer has an 'on' switch and an 'off' switch."

"And you turned it off."

"Mostly, but the timer could have been slightly modified."

"Uh oh."

"See, when we retro-fitted it with a digital timer, there might have been a special mode that was hidden. Depends on which key code you enter."

"A special mode? Explain."

"You know there's the 'on' mode, which gives you a regular detonation and a big bang; about a square mile is obliterated."

"I understand that part."

"And there's an 'off' mode."

"That's clear."

"Well, there's one more mode. It's the 'disable' mode that kinetically disassembles the bomb."

"Kinetically disassembles? It explodes?"

"Yes, a low-order explosion. The explosives fire asymmetrically and that small difference makes sure fission doesn't happen. Only a small bang, but a very radioactive one. It takes out about half a city block, but it will be a very dirty one."

"Shit. How long was the timer set for?"

"Eight hours."

"That would place it somewhere inside the Soviet Union, like Penza-19."

"Something like that."

"And it couldn't have been us. No blowback, so to speak."

"Exactly, they screwed up. The Russians must have had some technical problems at their laboratory."

"That's almost funny."

"You know, play with fire and you get burned."

Stavros sat back in his seat and contemplated the last few days and was about to fall asleep when something came to mind.

"Jonny?"

"Yes?"

"Do you think maybe your folks planned it this way?"

Mr John Gambel, the DDO, opened his eyes and leaned across the aisle toward the two younger men.

"Son, that would make a great movie plot, but you don't think we're actually capable of pulling something like that off, do you?"

43

Outside the General Aviation terminal at Washington Dulles, Jonny and Paul stood near their respective rides.

"What now? I mean, what are you going to do after this?" asked Stavros.

"The boss says they've got a desk in special activities I can have for a year. Planning operations. A break before I go back to the field."

"So they're not going to hang you out to dry?"

"No, appears not. Seems they were happy with our efforts."

"*Our* efforts?"

"Yes, I blamed everything on you. What about you?"

"I'll finish my tour and see what's next. Right now, I need to talk with someone about the future."

"When you're finished with that, call me. I owe you a beer or two and there are some people you need to meet."

Stavros watched as Jonny climbed into the big black car with his colleagues and then turned to the long, wiry, athletic man waiting by the deep red Impala convertible who just happened to be going to the Farm. Nicely dressed in a three-piece suit, he was wearing Ray-Ban G-15 Aviator sunglasses. Even his normally unruly hair was in place.

"You clean up rather well, Hans," said Stavros.

"Paul, in this business you have to be a chameleon. You ready?"

"As I, will ever be. Let's go."

An extract from the next riveting instalment of
The Snake Eater Chronicles, coming in 2022
The Snake Eater Chronicles 3
Direct Legacy

Prologue

September 1980

For perhaps the second time in his life, Stavros felt truly powerless. First, there was a small army of trolls pounding on the inside of his head with pickaxes. His tongue told him that they must have marched in and out of his dry mouth with filthy boots. His gut burned from his stomach to his esophagus and his head felt like a hot metal spike had pierced his brain from over his left eye to behind his right ear. It was the worst hangover he'd ever experienced. He struggled to clear the sticky fog that permeated the deepest recesses of his brain.

Second, he realized he could barely move. He felt the coarse manila rope that restrained his wrists and cursed his cover story—a writer of pacific, social interest articles—otherwise, he would have had a blade hidden in the waist band of his pants. If he'd been wearing pants. Those seemed to have disappeared along with his shirt. Now all he was wearing were his shorts and a tee-shirt. Even his socks were missing. No wonder it was cold.

Tell me again why I volunteered for this shit.

The smell of burning peat was the first characteristic of his surroundings that he sensed. It filled his nostrils with a pungent, thick odor that stung.

It was dark. Even the heavy burlap hood over his head couldn't mask the depth of the blackness that surrounded him. It was hushed and, aside from the acrid warmth of the smoke, it was cold. He began to sense other things, the smell of damp wood and maybe potatoes, and decided he was in some sort of underground cellar.

Day or night? Not a clue.

He rubbed his left wrist on the chair trying to feel his wristwatch. Not that he could read it, but it reassured him. It wasn't there.

From time to time, footsteps shuffled on the floor not far above his head. The sound of wood scraping on wood as someone sat and repositioned a chair. Then a laugh came from somewhere, the low murmur of voices, sounded unintelligible to his ears. Then silence. He didn't like the silence; he couldn't try to figure out what was happening if there was no sound.

Recalling events as best he could, Stavros tried to figure out how he had ended up in this position. The last thing he could remember was drinking a beer in a crowded pub and talking to that pretty dark-haired woman he had only just met. Then nothing.

Whatever she used must have been quick and powerful.

He had been in similar situations over the years but those had all been training—SERE, for Survival, Evasion, Resistance, and Escape, they called it. He'd done the training with everyone but the Marines and doubted they had much more to teach him. It was all quite simple and straight-forward. Survival for learning how to eat bugs, snakes, and make signal fires out of nothing. Evasion for the tricks best used to elude trackers, dogs, and circling helicopters—a breeze for someone who'd been an aspiring teenage criminal. Resistance was a dark subject, learning how not to answer questions directed at you at the end of a stick, or a fist, or while stuffed inside a box two sizes too small, or at the end of three-days with no sleep. Escape was the best: getting away from it all without being recaptured. Of course, their attempts never succeeded because they were expected, and on a schedule, but trying is half the game.

How long has it been? They'll be coming down to question me before long.

He assumed they might be letting him stew first, building up his anxiety, but then he wasn't sure if whoever was holding him had a clue about interrogation techniques or even if they knew he was awake. As it was, he didn't know who or what to expect and that worried him.

I'll find out soon enough.

Before then, he knew he had to remember. *Who am I? Why am I here?*

Slowly, painstakingly, he told himself his story. He remembered the details of a life that he knew but had never actually experienced and went back to schools he never attended. It was all close to his real life, but just different enough.

Mentally, he was free to roam, and it was better that way, to be away from where he was. Physically, it was another matter. Trying to get some slack in the ropes that held him, he squirmed, but as he did the restraints seemed to tighten even more. The walls he couldn't see started to feel like they were closing in. It didn't make sense but in his pitch-black world, the air seemed to press down on his chest and ears. His pulse started to throb, he could feel it in his temples and neck. He was getting hot despite the coolness that surrounded him. He breathed in and couldn't get enough air. Filtered through the coarse cloth made damp by his breath, it was stale and heavy. He inhaled long and deeply several times and tried to straighten up in the hard chair. It was his way of preventing an episode. The episodes almost always happened at night, usually a couple of hours after he lay down. But he could feel one coming on now.

Breathe deep and relax.

He went back five years to Walter Reed Army Hospital, lying in his dark room trying to sleep. Sterile, fluorescent green light spilled in through the open doorway from the hall. He had demanded they leave it that way. With the door shut, the room closed in on him. The pain was immense. A compound tibia and fibula fracture, the result of a bad parachute landing; his leg hurt like nothing he'd experienced before. Surgery followed, metal rods through his leg, an external brace, and more pain. He'd wake up and feel like he couldn't get enough air. At first, he became anxious, then panic followed, last came an overwhelming fear of suffocation. Panic, but not hysteria.

He would sit up and take rapid deep breaths—it was not enough—he had to move and move quickly. Only when he slid out of the bed into his wheelchair and propelled himself down the corridor could he find relief. The ward was laid out in a rectangle with nurses' stations in the center. He would race down the hall, pumping the wheels as hard as he could, rolling past the rooms at Mach One, while the officer nurses and enlisted medics hanging around the counter just watched him fly by at three in the morning. After several nights, they had seen him enough not to wonder.

When he told his doctor what he was feeling, she said, "Why did you wait so long to ask?"

The pain killers precipitated anxiety attacks, she explained. After that, he consciously tapered off, pushing the button on the IV or taking the pills only when the pain got unbearable. Even so, the attacks continued, suddenly, unexpectedly, sometimes in small or crowded spaces. He never talked about them again with anyone. Instead, he tried to manage them by himself through exercise and concentration.

This time, he couldn't move. He had only his mind to try and calm the storm. Breathing deeply and rhythmically, he tried to meditate and concentrated on that neutral moment between inhale and exhale. Nothing else. In, out, in, out. Slowly, slowly, he relaxed and then he slipped into a welcome sleep.

1

August 27, 1979
County Sligo, Republic of Ireland

Shadow V, a 30-foot wooden lobster boat, rocked gently in the sparkling sapphire waters of the harbor as its crew prepared to get underway. Paul, a strapping young teenager, a local villager who maintained the boat, coiled and stowed ropes under the gaze of a tall man with a regal, military bearing—the boat's owner.

The owner, even at the age of 79, looked in charge, appropriately enough, because he was Prince Louis Francis Albert Victor Nicholas of Battenberg, better known as the 1st Viscount Mountbatten of Burma or simply, Earl Mountbatten. His service in World War II brought him his title, although some—Canadians in particular who remembered him from the Dieppe disaster—hated him.

There were four others on board: all relatives of the Earl, expecting a quiet day on the water, maybe some fishing, but mostly just relaxation.

Mountbatten took the wheel in hand as the boat slipped its moorings and turned toward the open water of the bay, out of Mullaghmore Harbour. He steered toward a line of lobster pots and cut back on the throttle, so the boat glided silently up to and alongside the first marker buoy. The boat bobbed in the light swells a bit as it inched forward. John, Mountbatten's son-in-law, leaned over the gunwale, snagged the buoy's anchor rope with a gaff hook and began to pull up the trap.

"Lord, it's heavy! We're going to have some lobster tonight!" He said to no one in particular while continuing to pull in the rope. Paul came over to lend a hand.

A thousand yards away, a man standing by his car on the coastal road watched the scene through his binoculars. He was relatively young, late twenties, with dusty, reddish-brown hair. Except for his eyes, which were coal-dark and expressionless, almost dead one might think. It was an unremarkable face that would be hard to place after a casual encounter.

He looked around to make sure he was still alone and then took a small plastic box from the front seat of the car. Pulling out a long silver antenna, he pointed it toward the boat and waited a moment until he saw the orange flag marker on the lobster pot rope through the binoculars. Then he flipped a red safety switch and pushed a button.

A flash yellow and orange and a geyser of water erupted under the boat, tearing the hull apart, shards of broken oak, teak, and brass fittings shooting skyward. A ball of black smoke billowed outward and upward. By the time the sound of the explosion reached the man several seconds later, he was already in the driver's seat and starting the car. He had to admit, thinking to himself, that the engineer's idea to put the bomb in the lobster pot was brilliant. They avoided the constables guarding the boat and most of the evidence was now on the bottom of the bay.

The 10 pounds of gelignite exploded about five feet under the boat and the resulting shock wave and water plume tore the boat and the people on board to pieces. The dead and wounded floated in the water along with the rest of the flotsam. Other boats in the bay turned their prows toward the blast site to see if they could help.

A solitary circular wave rolled out from the smoking hole in the water. Above, on the bluff overlooking the bay, the man drove south, stopping after 30 minutes on the road. He got out and walked to a public telephone standing next to a shuttered public house.

He dialed a telephone number from memory. When someone on the other end of the line picked up he said, "The package was delivered," and returned the receiver to its hook. Turning back to his car, he pulled a cigarette from a pack. He lit it with a match, waved the flame out, and flicked the stick into the gravel. Taking a long draw, he exhaled slowly and focused on the horizon. He slid back into the driver's seat and continued, stylizing himself as belonging to the band of warriors in the great hall of Valhalla.

But I'm not dead yet.

Acknowledgments

This is a work of fiction and, although parts of it are based in reality, the names, characters, places and incidents are the product of the author's imagination or are used fictitiously. Any resemblance to actual events, locales, or persons, living or dead is entirely coincidental.

I had a lot of help and assistance with this book. Among the people I would like to thank are: Ruth Sheppard, Isobel Fulton, Helen Boyd, Michaela Goff, Daniel Yesilonis, Felicity Goldsack, Alison Griffiths, Megan Yates, and David Farnsworth from Casemate. And to Declan Ingram: thanks for the cover!

My thanks go out to the many who contributed to this tale. Above all: MG, Scotty, Stan, Jeff, Stu, Demetri, Richard, Fred, and Bob, thanks for sharing your memories. I would also like thank the soldiers of the KGB *Spetsnaz* groups whose after-action reports helped me describe the assault on Taj-Bek Palace. My pre-publication readers (including the members of the PRB staff) also deserve my thanks, including Sven, whose sharp eyes helped correct several anachronisms that crept into the text.

Finally, this is for those left behind:

"Greater love hath no man than this, that a man lay down his life for his friends."